TEMPT ME LIKE THIS

~ The Morrisons, Book 2 ~

Drew & Ashley

TEMPT ME LIKE THIS
The Morrisons ~ Drew & Ashley

Visit Bella's website at: http://www.BellaAndre.com
Follow Bella on Twitter at:
http://twitter.com/bellaandre
Join Bella on Facebook at:
http://www.facebook.com/bellaandrefans
Sign up for Bella's newsletter at:
http://eepurl.com/eXj22

As one of the biggest rock stars in the business, Drew Morrison can have anything—and anyone—he wants. Only Ashley Emmit, who has joined his tour to work on a college research project, is completely off-limits. Drew promised her father that, once the tour was over, he would send her home pure and untouched by the rock 'n' roll world. But he has never been so tempted by anyone in his entire life. How is he going to make it through this tour without giving in to the urge to drag her into his arms and kiss her breathless?

Ashley has always lived by the rules. But from the moment she meets Drew, none of those rules make sense anymore. Not only does Drew's music affect her deeply...but she's never wanted to kiss anyone so badly. Not that a magnetic star like Drew would ever feel the same way about a brainiac like her, of course. And even if he did, she knows from painful experience that two people as different as they are simply don't belong together.

But when the attraction between Drew and Ashley burns hotter every moment they're together on the tour bus—and they begin to share their deeply hidden and emotional secrets—will either of them be able to resist temptation? Or could giving in to their feelings lead them straight toward a love they never saw coming...

Note from Bella

When I introduced the Morrisons last year with *KISS ME LIKE THIS* (Sean and Serena's story), I hoped readers who enjoy reading about my Sullivans would also love this new family. But your response during the past year has absolutely floored me! Every day, I am flooded with requests for more books about the Morrisons, and I am thrilled that you're about to read Drew Morrison's love story.

As anyone who has read my books knows, I adore rock-star heroes and heroines. But as I wrote Drew's story, I quickly realized that he was far more than just a sexy rock star. So much more that my heart broke for him *and* grew bigger from page to page. Especially when I realized that Ashley Emmit was exactly the woman he needed in his life—and that she needed him just as much.

I hope you fall as much in love with Drew and Ashley as I have!

Happy reading,
Bella

P.S. I can't wait to write the next book about the Morrisons, which will be called LOVE ME LIKE THIS. If you'd like to hear about my new books as soon as they're released, please sign up for my New Release newsletter: http://www.bellaandre.link/Newsletter

CHAPTER ONE

San Diego, California

Drew Morrison was a rock god.

During the hour and a half that Ashley Emmit had been standing in the middle of the very crowded concert venue in downtown San Diego, she'd heard dozens of people say those exact words. Normally, she would have chalked it up to hyperbole or to collective excitement. But in that moment, there didn't seem to be even a hint of exaggeration in the crowd's claims. Not only were Drew Morrison's songs incredible, but from the moment he'd stepped out onto the stage, Ashley hadn't been able to keep her body from moving...or her heart from racing.

She was a numbers girl. She studied facts and figures. Her teachers had always said she was the very definition of a left-brained person. Sure, she'd always been drawn to music—not playing it, but listening to it.

But even when she was on the verge of being swept away by a certain song, her enjoyment had always been tempered by her practical nature. She'd analyze the song's structure, the chord progression, the rhyming patterns. She'd read dozens of articles about how the brain was hardwired to process music, as well. She didn't just want to enjoy something—she wanted to understand *why* she enjoyed it.

That was why she was at this show. She had one last chance to get into Stanford Business School—and it all rested on figuring out every last detail of the way the music business worked. The graduate program had spawned a truly stunning amount of corporate innovation and had been her dream school since she was a teenager. It still hurt to remember the rejection letter they'd sent her: *Our pool of applicants was truly phenomenal this year, most with exceptional real-world experience in their field of choice. We regret to inform you that we do not have a space for you and wish you all the best in the future.*

She'd known it wouldn't be easy to get in, but where other girls had pretty smiles and knockout figures, the one thing Ashley had always been able to count on was her brain. Somehow, though, her brain had let her down. Big-time. But since it was all she had, after wallowing in a freezerful of ice cream, she'd forced herself to brush off the devastating rejection and refocus.

Ashley had read every book written about the music business. She'd listened to every talk given by the experts. She'd pored over financial spreadsheets from both major and indie labels. But she didn't have an ounce of practical experience. How could she truly understand how to innovate in the music industry when she'd never spent any time with a musician?

Going on tour with Drew Morrison was the crucial piece to her new plan: total immersion so that she could finally understand what was happening on both the business and the artistic sides.

As luck would have it, her father had been one of Drew's undergraduate professors at Stanford, so even though Dad would much prefer she chose a steady and safe profession that had nothing whatsoever to do with the music business, he'd been able to pull some strings to get her a spot on Drew's tour.

Ashley was so nervous about traveling from city to city in tour buses with Drew and the group of strangers who were in his band and crew, that she'd done what she always did when she felt unsure about things—buried herself in books and research. Even though she knew it would do absolutely nothing to help her fit in with the rockers on Drew's crew, it had made her feel a little better to fill up a couple of notebooks with notes and questions, at least.

She was a nerd in the normal world. She'd just have to accept that she'd be a nerd to the millionth degree in the rock and roll world.

Tonight, she'd come to the venue armed with her notebook and tablet, ready to take notes on any- and everything. Only, from the moment Drew strummed the first chord on his guitar and began to sing, instead of all of the mental lists she should have been making or the details she should have been noticing, everything had been lost to the music.

To Drew Morrison's genius.

"Thanks for coming out tonight, everyone." His speaking voice was just as sexy and mesmerizing as his singing voice. The screams from his fans nearly drowned him out as he said, "I wrote a new song a while back that I haven't played for anyone yet." More screams came, truly deafening ones. "But tonight..." He'd been smiling earlier, but suddenly he looked terribly serious. And so sad that Ashley wished she were close enough to wrap her arms around him. "Tonight I finally feel like I need to play it. It's called 'One More Time.'"

The rest of the band left the stage, leaving only Drew and his guitar in the spotlight. Watching him, she felt as if he was steeling himself before the first notes rang out from his guitar and he began to sing the most beautiful—and devastating—song Ashley had ever heard. About loss. About his heart breaking. About pain that ran so deep he wasn't sure he'd ever be able to recover from it.

She wasn't absolutely sure what the song was *really* about, but her father had told her that Drew's mother had passed away from cancer earlier this year. She knew what it was like to lose a mother, but hers hadn't died—her mother had simply boarded a plane to Miami seven years ago after her parents had divorced.

The rest of the songs Drew had played tonight had been fast-driving and often upbeat. But this one held hints of sixties folk music. A little Dylan. A harmony reminiscent of Crosby, Stills and Nash. A lyric that she could easily have imagined Joni Mitchell singing. Ashley had never heard anyone combine their own new sound with the past in such an amazing way.

Drew's song reached deep inside of her, deeper than any other had ever gone. Ashley ached for him, even as she found herself aching for her own losses.

Losses she never liked to look at too closely because they hurt so bad.

Tears were streaming down the cheeks of the girl standing next to Ashley. More than one fan, actually, was losing the battle with her emotions. And as he sang, *"I wish I could see you one more time,"* and the final note rang out and the stage lights abruptly went dark, Ashley reached up and was shocked to feel dampness on her own cheekbones. She sucked in a breath, and then another when that first one didn't quite make it all the way into her lungs, as she quickly wiped away the moisture.

She tried to center herself and steady everything that had just gone so topsy-turvy. She knew from reading all those science journals that a good song could trigger a cascade of involuntary physical and emotional responses. That had to be why she'd reacted so emotionally, right? Plus, she wasn't used to being around so many people who had so few inhibitions.

From the first moment she'd set foot inside the venue, just as she'd thought, she stuck out. Her hair was too neat. Her clothes were too plain. Her shoes were too flat. And her makeup was too—well, nonexistent. The women in Drew's audience were openly sexual, both in the way they dressed and in how they danced. And the truth was that at the same time as she felt out of place, Ashley envied them a little bit for the way they owned their sexuality. As if it were something not only perfectly natural, but also wonderful.

But when the girl next to her sniffled and said, "Isn't he amazing? When I listen to his songs, I feel like I can do anything," Ashley was surprised to realize she didn't feel like a total outsider anymore. Drew's music had brought all of them together. And even if the moment they stepped out onto the sidewalk they reverted back to their normal roles, at least for a couple of hours they'd all shared the exact same urge to dance and sing along and even cry.

The lights suddenly blazed back on in a kaleidoscope of colors that had everyone cheering just as Drew launched into "Wild," his biggest hit to date. And even though she *never* danced in public, she couldn't keep from wiggling her hips, lifting her arms to the beat, and clapping along with everyone else.

Suddenly, Ashley could see it all so clearly—*this* was Drew Morrison's gift. Not only could he write one heck of a chorus, but he was also able to tap into the purest of emotions again and again with every song he wrote. Tears to laughter. Pain to joy. And everyone in the venue was more than happy to be taken on the roller-coaster ride with him. To let him take the wheel as he whirled them up and around, inside and out.

After his encore, however, Ashley forced herself to watch, to listen, to examine the reactions of the audience members, the managers of the venue, the employees running concessions, and to note her impressions in the tablet she took out of her bag. An impressive number of people had walked in wearing T-shirts with his face on them before the show, but pretty much everyone bought one on their way out and put it on. She could only imagine how gleeful Drew's label must be at the way his fandom was growing.

A few minutes after he left the stage, the staff was quickly working to clean up, and she was one of the only people out on the floor. Having previously arranged over email with Drew to meet backstage after the show, she fished her VIP pass out of her purse and showed it to the large man guarding the door.

"Drew is just about done with pictures and autographs," the man said as he gave her a surprisingly nice smile, "but if you hurry, I'm sure he won't leave you hanging."

"Thanks, but I'm not a fan." The man's eyes widened, and as she realized what she'd said, she fumbled to say, "I mean, of course I'm a fan. It's just that I'm here to go on tour with Drew."

"Are you Ashley?"

Surprised that this man knew her name, she said, "That's me."

He grinned even wider as he reached for her hand and gave it several good, hard pumps. "I'm James. It's my job to keep Drew safe."

Resisting the urge to rub her shoulder socket after he let go of her hand, she smiled back at Drew's security guard. "It's lovely to meet you." Of course, as soon as the words were out of her mouth, she had to fight the urge to groan out loud. *Lovely to meet you* made her sound like she was an eighty-year-old grandma rather than a twenty-two-year-old woman.

"I'll let Drew know you're on your way." James pulled out his phone and sent a quick text, probably also letting Drew know he should expect a supernerd backstage. "Welcome to the madness, Ashley."

As she walked down the hall in the direction in which James had pointed her, she mused that Drew's bodyguard really was a lovely man. And though he'd just referred to touring with Drew as madness, the truth was that he'd helped make her feel a whole lot less nervous about being here.

Ever since the night she'd introduced herself to Drew after one of his shows and realized just how ridiculously good-looking he was in person, she'd been more than a little anxious. Going on a rock tour at all was a huge leap away from her normal life, but going with Drew?

It might very well be madness.

Ashley took a deep breath and tried to push her nerves away as she walked through the door at the end of the hall. A group of women were all talking and laughing at once, obviously still on a high from the show. She didn't see Drew at first and thought maybe she was in the wrong place. But then, when the crowd parted to reveal him standing in the opposite corner of the room, she swore it was as though everything slowed down and then went completely still as Drew looked right at her.

His eyes held hers with a look so intense, and so full of heat, that she actually forgot how to breathe for a moment.

Oh God. He was beautiful. So beautiful that it almost hurt to look at him.

The record label didn't need to put makeup on him to make him better-looking in pictures. They didn't need to put him in special clothes or cut his hair a certain way to make him attractive to the masses. All they needed was for him to smile...and the person he was smiling at felt as though she was the center of his entire world. Like he would live and die only for her.

A woman's super-sultry voice saying, "Drew, can you do a really *special* signature for me?" broke Ashley out of her frozen stance by the door.

Drew held Ashley's gaze for another moment before turning to the woman. "Sure," he said, his smile easy now, rather than intense. "Where do you want it?"

Before Ashley knew it, the woman had pulled her tank top up—and off! All the way off, so that she was standing completely topless in the middle of a room full of strangers...and the rock god she was obviously hoping to entice with her bold move.

To Drew's credit, he didn't so much as blink. Not even when the woman moved way too close to him and said, "You can write your name anywhere you want on my body. Absolutely *anywhere*."

Ashley was still busy trying to pick her jaw up off the floor when Drew quickly scrawled his name with a black Sharpie on the side of the woman's ribs, about as far from her breasts as he could get while still writing on her skin the way she clearly wanted him to. And when he picked up the woman's shirt from the floor and handed it to her, saying, "Thanks for coming to my show tonight," Ashley could see that the last thing he wanted was to make the woman feel bad that he was rejecting her advance. Even though he clearly was.

She had never seen someone take off a shirt so fast...or put it back on so slowly. She could only imagine the way she'd be fumbling with the fabric if she tried to pull off a move like that. Not that she ever would, of course. Besides, her father would kill her if he found out she'd ever done *anything* like that.

Charlie Emmit had told her he wanted to come to the show tonight to say hello to Drew. But Ashley had known the real reason her father had wanted to come—to go over a huge list of all the potential dangers he wanted Drew to protect his daughter from.

Ashley and her father were usually of like mind, but this time she'd put her foot down. She wasn't going to allow him to drop her off on tour as though she were a little girl heading to her first day of kindergarten.

Instead, she'd promised him that she was going to be smart and safe, just the way she'd always been.

They were two peas in a pod, both of them rational and practical. So unlike her mother, Camila Emmit, who hated lists and rules. Her mother loved music and poetry, but numbers made her go cross-eyed. For the fifteen years she'd been married to Ashley's dad, her mother had been a blur of colorful flowing skirts, laughter in the house when she was happy, yelling reverberating off the walls when she wasn't, and a smell that Ashley realized as a teenager was pot.

But backstage at Drew's show wasn't the place for memories of her mother. And, clearly, given the way the other women in the room were also now flirting with Drew, this wasn't the place to be thinking of her professor father either.

Thank God she'd been able to convince him not to come. He'd *freak* if he saw all the skin and blatant sexuality of the women who were coming on to Drew with everything they had.

Fortunately, Ashley wasn't attracted to the rock star she'd be touring with for the next few weeks.

More specifically, she only had a teeny, tiny little crush on Drew Morrison. But who wouldn't when he was this gorgeous and talented? Okay, so she might have followed his music since he'd put on the Internet a couple of demos he'd recorded at home when he was sixteen. And, sure, she'd watched dozens of streaming clips of his shows—but those viewings were purely in the name of research and in preparation for going on tour with him.

Wild, sexy rockers could never be her type. Her father and mother's terrible marriage was the perfect example of how steady, straight-edged people could never be a good fit for artistic, free-spirited people. Ashley didn't need to do any further research to know that the highest probability of relationship success had her partnering with a business-minded, practical man.

Which meant she needed to shove her secret crush on Drew Morrison as far down as it could go. *Nothing* could be more mortifying than for Drew to think she was just another groupie who wanted him to write his name on her breasts.

"Ashley." He was giving her that naturally super-sexy smile of his, and her foolish heart automatically kicked up in reaction. "It's good to see you again."

"It's good to see you, too." *Oh God, why does my voice sound like that?* A mix of husky and nervous all at the same time that she'd never heard come from her lips before. She cleared her throat. "I really appreciate you letting me join your tour."

"*She's* going on tour with you?" The woman who had put her boobs on display for everyone looked at Ashley as though she wanted to skin her alive. "Whatever she's doing for you, Drew, I can do it a thousand times better."

Drew put his hand on Ashley's lower back and gently pushed her in the direction of the door, where, like magic, James appeared as though he could sense danger. Quickly, James was inside the room and they were out of it, heading down a long, dark hall.

"Sorry," Ashley said immediately. "I didn't think before speaking."

"I'm the one who needs to apologize. My fans are great, but they can be a bit..." He frowned as he searched for the right word. "Overenthusiastic." He shook his head as if to clear it, before saying, "I'm glad you're here."

She almost said, *You are?* Fortunately, she cut off the words before they could come spilling out. "Thank you. I am, too. I already met James, and he was really nice. I just want you to know that I don't want to cause you or anyone else any trouble, so I'll do my best to fade into the background."

He turned his dark gaze to her, and she actually lost her breath. *Whoosh.* Gone.

"You could never fade into the background, Ashley."

Even though the lack of oxygen to her brain was making it hard for her to think straight, she didn't believe he was messing with her. He didn't seem the cruel type to make fun of nerds, like so many kids at school had growing up. But the idea that he might be attracted to her was so preposterous she simply couldn't process it.

Thankfully, before she had to figure out a way to respond, they were at the tour bus, where she could hopefully escape into whatever tiny little bunk she was assigned, far away from him until the next day, when she'd make sure that all the emotion-triggering chemicals currently affecting her brain from his amazing show were *way* more under control.

He punched in a code on the box at the side of the door, and it slid open. "Welcome to your new home for the summer. Living on a bus is a little weird, but most people get used to it pretty quickly." He gestured for her to climb the stairs. "After you."

"Wow." The word slipped out before she could hold it back, but as she walked up the steps and into the bus, she truly was amazed by how sumptuous the interior was. Leather and glossy wood. A large TV and a really nice-looking kitchen, given the space constraints. She assumed one of the side interior doors led to a bathroom and shower, and the back door to a private bedroom. The living space was entirely blocked off from the driver by a floor-to-ceiling wall. It was beautiful and looked surprisingly comfortable to spend a few weeks in, but she was confused about one thing. "Where is everyone else?"

"The band shares a bus. The rest of the crew shares another. You and I will be the only people on this one."

She whipped around to look at him. "I can't share a bus with you!"

He held up his hands. "I promise to be a perfect gentleman, Ashley. I would never do anything to hurt you."

"Oh my God, I'm not worried about that at all." The words spilled out fast in the heat of her mortification that he thought she might be concerned he would take advantage of her in their shared bus. "I just assumed I was going to be with your crew. You're already letting me join your tour. You don't have to make any other special exceptions for me."

"You want to learn about the music business, right? Your father mentioned you're applying to business school."

"I need real-life experience for Stanford to seriously consider my application." For the time being, she left off the fact that it would be her second application.

"My band and crew are great," he said, "but they're not the ones you want an inside track to, are they?"

Of course they weren't. She needed an inside track to *him*. And yet, how the heck could she play it cool when she'd be this close to him all the time? For all its plush luxury, the bus couldn't be more than eight feet from wall to wall. And Drew wasn't a small man.

But in the tiny pocket of her brain that was still able to think clearly around him, she knew he was right—the whole point of her being here was to learn from him, which meant that sharing his tour bus was the best possible thing that could happen. She couldn't let fear of being this close to a gorgeous rock god get in the way of her goal. She'd never forgive herself if she did.

Desperate to salvage a seriously awkward first few minutes, she forced a big smile. "You're right. It'll be great to be on this bus with you. Really great!"

His lips twitched at the corners at her abrupt change of response, and she could feel herself flushing at how she'd managed to make everything as uncomfortable as possible inside of five minutes.

"Good. You can have the back bedroom, and I'll take the bunk out here."

"You're the one who has to play a show every night. I'll be just fine out here." She put her shoulder bag with her tablet, notebook, and wallet on the lower bunk to claim it.

"You've got more than just that, haven't you?"

"I do, but since I wasn't sure if there'd be anywhere to keep my things during your show, I stored my bags at the airport."

"I should have thought about that ahead of time." It was quite possibly the cutest thing in the world—he actually seemed upset at himself for not thinking about where she should have put her bags.

"Things have been crazy lately, but that's no excuse." He pulled out his phone and sent a text. "We should be rolling in just a few minutes. I'll introduce you to our driver, Max, once we get to the airport." He opened the gleaming, stainless steel fridge. "What can I get you to drink?"

"You probably have a really important after-show ritual that I'm completely screwing up. I can get myself a drink so that you can get to it."

But instead of heading back into his private quarters so that she could figure out how to breathe normally again, he held her gaze with his. Yet again, his eyes were dark and intense—and full of so much barely banked heat that it stunned her. Especially since she couldn't possibly imagine how *she* could have inspired any of that in him.

"Tonight, I have only one important after-show ritual." He paused for a beat before saying, "You."

CHAPTER TWO

Holy hell, she was pretty.

The first time Ashley had come backstage to introduce herself at a previous show, Drew had been knocked over by her beauty. But his memory hadn't done her justice. Hadn't even come close.

Her wavy brunette locks were streaked with sun-kissed strands. Her skin was so soft-looking and creamy that when she flushed every time he looked at or spoke to her, he found he could barely keep his hands off her. He wanted to stroke her cheek with his fingertips, wanted to know if her mouth tasted as good as it looked. Because something told him it *definitely* would. She wasn't tall, wasn't little either, and was just curvy enough to make him drool. In her black jeans and long-sleeved shirt, she managed to be a gorgeous combination of sweet and sexy. Although he wondered if she had any idea at all of just how sexy she was.

None of the girls shoving their breasts in his face before or after the show tonight held a candle to her. Ashley Emmit was simply *perfect.*

But she could never be his. Not one beautiful inch of her.

"Take care of my baby." Drew could hear her father's words as clearly as if the man had been standing in front of him right now. They'd spoken on the phone that morning, and the professor he'd had for statistics at Stanford three years ago couldn't have been clearer. *"Don't let anything happen to her. She's the whole world to me."*

"You have my word," Drew had promised.

With two younger sisters—Olivia was going to start a graduate program in education at Stanford in the fall, while Madison would be going into her freshman year, also at Stanford—Drew knew all about protecting the people he loved. He'd do anything for his family, give up anything for them if it would keep them safe.

"I wouldn't let her go on tour with anyone else, Drew." Dr. Emmit had clearly wanted to hammer his point home. *"Just you. After having had you as one of my students, I know you and trust you."*

So even though Drew was probably going to deplete the bus's cold-water storage tank with the copious number of freezing showers he would need to take, it was why Ashley was traveling on his bus. Normally, he traveled solo so that he could write and record without disturbing anyone else. But not only was he not doing any writing or recording lately, he needed to make sure she stayed safe.

The guys in his band and on his crew were great, but they were still guys who were sure to think she was just as pretty as Drew did...and who hadn't made any vows to his professor. He'd already told them all that she was off-limits, but as soon as they turned in for the night, he'd send a text out to everyone to remind them that if they so much as looked at her wrong, they'd have to answer to him. And there would be no second chances where Ashley was concerned.

As pure as she'd come onto his tour, she was going to leave the same way.

Drew got himself a beer and poured her the glass of wine she finally requested in a near whisper. He was used to making girls nervous. It had happened to him and his brothers ever since they were kids. In first grade, he'd gone up to ask Jennie Leland if he could share her crayons, and her eyes had gotten real big right before she'd dropped the crayons on the floor. She'd pretty much hidden from him for the rest of the school year.

But he didn't want Ashley to feel she needed to hide from him. Even if he needed to keep his hands and mouth—and every other part of himself—from touching her, he still wanted her to get what she needed out of this tour. Not only because he felt he owed it to her father, who had been a great teacher, but also because after only a handful of minutes he already liked her.

He could do this, damn it. He could do his favorite professor a favor, could be a platonic friend to Ashley, and all would end well.

"My brother Grant went to Stanford Business School," he said. "Seems like they give their students one hell of an education."

"They do. And your brother is a legend. Collide is by far the best social network around."

Drew laughed, even though every time she spoke, his heart beat a little faster. Her voice was beautiful, a melody unlike any he'd ever heard. He realized now that he'd heard that melody the first time they'd met, but it had been faint enough then for him to let it fade away.

But tonight? Tonight, he wanted Ashley to keep playing that melody for him over and over again.

"He's got a few brains knocking around in there, for sure. And so, I'm guessing, do you, if you're aiming for the biz school."

She frowned, and he wanted so badly to reach out and smooth away the lines on her forehead and the ones that formed at the edges of her beautiful mouth. "*Aiming* is a good way of putting it." She sighed, and he could see what it cost her to admit, "I applied last year, but they rejected me."

"Isn't it the toughest school to get into in the country? Maybe even the world? Doesn't pretty much everyone get rejected?"

"It is tough to get in." Her chin went up. "But I'm good enough. At least I thought I was, until they rejected my application. That's why I'm here, to get my act together so that they say yes when I apply again."

He stilled, suddenly feeling as though he was looking in a mirror. He knew that expression of disappointment and confusion on Ashley's face as she talked about being rejected by the business school. Just as she'd always thought she was good enough to get into the top-notch program in the country, music had always been the one thing Drew could count on. He'd never thought to lose that certainty, never thought he'd have to reach so far or so hard for lyrics and notes, never thought they'd still be out of reach no matter how hard he tried.

It sucked. Especially with the label breathing down his neck for another hit—and the soundtrack Smith Sullivan and Valentina Landon were waiting for him to deliver for their new movie. But all he'd been able to write was one song: "One More Time." Hell, he hadn't even been able to play it for anyone until tonight—not when it was the most raw, intense song he'd ever written. But he hadn't been able to keep it inside himself for a second longer.

Working to push away his thoughts about his mom, he refocused on Ashley. "I have no doubt that you're good enough. The admissions committee must have screwed up. They'll jump at your application this year."

"They didn't screw up," she said softly. "I didn't have any practical music experience, but I definitely will after watching you on tour." Another flush came. "I didn't mean for that to sound stalkery." She repeated the words *watching you on tour* in a low, creepy voice, making fun of herself.

He couldn't keep from laughing out loud. Couldn't remember the last time he'd *wanted* to laugh out loud. Even with his family, who usually made him laugh until his stomach hurt, things had been strained. Ever since their mom got sick the previous year, none of the Morrisons smiled as much. Just thinking about his mom had his smile falling away.

"I meant to tell you earlier," she said into the silence that fell between them as his mood turned darker, "just how great your show was tonight."

"Thanks." His mom would have loved Ashley. But thinking that only brought him down further, unfortunately.

She studied him then, but not in a bad way. It was more like she was trying to figure out how she could help him feel better. "Were you not happy with the show?"

Jesus, he was acting like a total douche. Saying he wanted to hang out with her tonight, then getting all moody. "No, it wasn't bad."

"Wasn't bad?" She leaned forward over the tabletop between them. "It was *amazing.*"

"Our timing was a little rough on some of the faster songs." He just hadn't been all there, hadn't been able to find that feeling he used to get from the songs. No matter how far he reached, no matter how hard he tried.

"I know it's good that you notice all the details," she said, "because then you can perform your songs even better the next time. But I can guarantee that there wasn't a single person in the audience who noticed any timing problems or fumbling. Probably because we were too busy crying—"

Her eyes went wide the moment the words came out. And maybe he should have let it go, but knowing she had cried during one of his songs—it meant something to him. Something big.

"When?" She didn't answer right away, so he asked again in a gentle voice, "When did you cry, Ashley?"

He'd been naked with plenty of women over the years, but no moment had ever felt as intimate as this one, where they both had all their clothes on and weren't even touching. When he was simply waiting for her answer to a question that seemed incredibly important.

She didn't say anything for a long moment, and just when he thought she might not respond at all, she finally spoke. "During your new song, 'One More Time.' The way you sang about pain, about heartbreak, and feeling like you'd never be whole again...it was just so beautiful."

"I wrote that song the day—" His throat tightened down before he could finish the sentence.

"Drew." Ashley's voice was thick with emotion. "I'm so sorry."

For a moment he thought it might happen, that the tears he hadn't shed would finally fall. But then he felt himself shut down, like a shutter clicking into place one slat at a time.

"I am, too." He looked out the window just as the bus came to a stop. "We're here."

He felt her gaze on his face for several moments before she finally looked away and scooted out from behind the table. He should have been glad that she wasn't witnessing his pain anymore, but strangely, it felt just the opposite. He'd been working to hide his grief from the world for so long that it had almost been a relief to think it might finally spill out—and that, even though he barely knew her, Ashley Emmit might be the one to face the flood with him.

His driver opened the door for them, grinning through the piercings that covered his face. "I'm Max. Hope the ride wasn't too bumpy."

"It's nice to meet you." She shook Max's hand. "And the ride was very smooth, thank you."

Max was clearly instantly enamored with her. So much so that for a moment, Drew thought he might give a thumbs-up to Drew right in front of her. Though Max looked like the quintessential rock 'n' roll driver, and had been one for over twenty years, he wasn't a fan of groupies. He had a great wife and three kids at home, and he never looked too pleased with the women who threw themselves at Drew.

For Ashley's part, Drew was impressed with her utter lack of reaction to Max's piercings. Especially given the way she'd gasped when the woman backstage had pulled off her top and bared her chest for him to sign. Just thinking of it now made him smile again.

"James is caught in traffic, Miss Ashley," Max said, "so I'll head in with you to pick up your luggage."

"It will just take me a few minutes to grab my bags," Ashley said as she headed for the door. "Neither of you needs to come with me. Besides, I don't have that much stuff."

But both Drew and Max got off the bus behind her. "I have sisters," Drew said, "so I know *not that much stuff* means different things to different people. A carry-on would be all Olivia would need for weeks. But Madison..." He shook his head. "She'd need to rent a storage trailer to pull behind the bus."

"It sounds like Olivia has me beat," Ashley said. "But not by much." She pointed to the right. "The lockers are over there."

They had taken only a handful of steps when Drew heard the telltale sound of fan recognition— shocked and excited screams followed by, "Oh my God, it's Drew Morrison!"

Max immediately moved to step in front of them, but in an instant, they were surrounded by girls and women of all ages. "Ashley," was all Drew was able to say to Max before he could no longer be heard

over the excited and quickly growing crowd.
Fortunately, his driver was already on it, covering her
first and foremost.

"You're gorgeous, Drew!"

"I love you!"

"I can't believe it's really you!"

"Ohmygodohmygodohmygod!"

There were tears and requests for selfies and
autographs and a ton of flashes going off all at once. He
hadn't thought to put on a low-brimmed baseball cap
before leaving the bus, had been able to think only
about Ashley. Now, he was cursing himself for not
making at least that small attempt to disguise himself.
He tried not to complain about the fame that had come
along with his success—only his family knew just how
much it sometimes bothered him—but things like
always having to put on a hat and glasses when he went
out in public weren't easy to get used to.

Airport security rushed over and quickly pulled
Drew, Ashley, and Max from the group to take them to
a secure, glassed-in area behind the check-in desks.
"We're going to have to file a report about this
disturbance," the head security officer said in a stern
voice. "You created a very dangerous situation for all of
the passengers in the terminal today."

"But none of this is our fault," Ashley protested.
"We just came in to pick up my bags from the storage
lockers, and when everyone saw Drew, they started
freaking out. He can't help it that he's famous."

"I do know who you are, Mr. Morrison," the
officer said, the frown still furrowing his forehead. "My
daughter has your poster on her wall. Which is exactly
why you should know better than to walk into an airport
unassisted by our security staff."

When Ashley opened her mouth to protest again, Drew put his hand over hers. He felt a tremor run through her at the shock of contact—one that was rocking through his system just as much.

"I apologize for the disruption." And he truly was sorry. It was never his intent to cause a scene in a public place or anywhere else. "We should have called to let you know we were coming in."

"Or you could have let me come alone like I wanted to," Ashley muttered as she deliberately slipped her hand out from beneath his.

The security team looked between the two of them with raised eyebrows while Max practically drew hearts in the air around them with his fingertips.

"While you fill out these forms," the officer said, "we'll get your bags, miss. What lockers are they in?"

"Just number 196, thank you."

While Drew scrawled his name and other requested information on the form, he noted that Ashley filled out hers in an extremely neat hand. Jesus...even that turned him on.

He was *screwed.*

A few minutes later, Ashley had her two small suitcases, and the three of them were escorted out a side door and back to their bus by half a dozen of the security officers. "Thanks again for your help," Drew said to them all.

"Before you go," the head officer said with a slightly ruddy glow to his cheeks, "you wouldn't mind taking a picture with me, would you? My daughter would just love it."

"No problem," Drew said, knowing the airport staff could have come down on them a lot harder for the disturbance he'd caused.

When the other officers all said they'd like the same thing for their kids, Ashley offered, "I can take the pictures for everyone, if you'd like."

One after the other, they handed her their phones, and by the time they were done, Max had come out of the bus with a stack of T-shirts and other concert swag for them all.

"Ready to hit the road to Las Vegas, boss?" Max asked when the three of them were alone again.

Drew looked at his new bus-mate for confirmation. "Ashley?"

"I'm ready to go. I've actually never been there before."

"You're going to love it, Miss Ashley," Max told her. "More bright lights than you've ever seen in one place. It will make your head spin."

She looked a little uncertain about whether she'd actually like it. "Okay, I'll try to prepare myself for all the lights and head-spinning."

"Have a good night, you two," Max said with a wink that couldn't have made his hopes for the two of them more clear before he headed out their door and around to the separate driver's area of the bus. "See you bright and early at five a.m. for our first radio spot."

"You have the nicest staff," she said to Drew after Max had closed the door behind him.

"He likes you, too, Ashley."

Drew took her hand before she could move away, that shock of electricity between them even more intense the second time. They both looked down at their joined hands, then back into each other's eyes.

Damn it, if he was trying to keep his distance, he was doing one hell of a bad job. But he simply couldn't keep from touching her again.

"I'm sorry about what just happened. Actually, about everything you've dealt with tonight, starting with the women backstage."

"It's not your fault you're famous and people love you." Her cheeks flushed at the word *love*—or maybe it was his hand over hers that had her flushing so beautifully. But at least she didn't step away or pull her hand from his. "It must be scary for you when that happens."

No one apart from his family and security staff had ever really understood just how strange it was to be the center of a big group's attention—or adoration. He loved his fans, of course, but he didn't love it when the press of people and voices and requests affected anyone else. He'd been worried about Ashley freaking out, but it turned out she'd only been thinking about how he must be feeling.

"I'm sorry if it was scary for you."

"They didn't want anything to do with me, didn't even notice I was there. I was fine. But they were *all over* you."

He shrugged. "It comes with the territory."

She frowned, and just as she'd leaned over the table earlier that evening to make her point, she moved in closer now to say, "Just because it comes with the territory, doesn't mean it isn't frightening to have everyone want a piece of you."

Did she realize she was close enough for him to kiss her? Or just how badly he was dying to taste her skin? Her eyes were the most extraordinary color, amber with flecks of green and blue, and he couldn't stop staring into them, mesmerized.

"Music is amazing, isn't it?" Her voice had lowered nearly to a whisper now. "The way it reaches down into you and makes you feel so much? Makes us feel like we know the singer, even when we don't."

He'd already felt an intense attraction between them. He liked her, too, of course. But now there was even more connecting them—a strong and immediate bond over the incredible power of music.

Already, Drew was less than a heartbeat from breaking his vow not to kiss her, and swore he could already feel the heat of her lips against his, when the bus suddenly jolted into motion.

Ashley was thrown into his arms, where he caught her and held her tightly, working to memorize every curve, her scent, the silky softness of her hair where it brushed against his chin.

Too soon, she was stumbling back, her eyes wide, her breath coming fast.

"It's late." She was looking everywhere but at him. "Really late. I should get to bed now. And I'm sure you must be exhausted, since you were the one doing all the work tonight on stage."

Her words came out in a breathless rush, tumbling over one another as she moved to put as much space between them as she possibly could on the narrow bus. So even though it was the very last thing in the world he wanted to do, and hating that he was clearly making her feel uncomfortable, Drew made himself nod and say, "If you need anything tonight—"

"I'll be fine!"

She turned away and started unzipping one of her bags. He knew he had to go or risk being the one acting stalkery. But even after he had closed the door to his private quarters at the back of the bus, he could still hear her moving around.

What was she doing now? Was she stripping down to her bra and panties? Was she sliding beneath the covers and thinking of him the way he was thinking of her? Was she as disappointed as he was that they hadn't kissed? And was she still replaying the feel of his arms around her the way he was reliving the feel of her in his arms?

Two hours later, still lying in bed staring at the ceiling, Drew knew two things for sure. There wasn't enough freezing cold water in all the tour buses in the world to cool him down.

And it was going to be hell trying to survive this tour if he wanted to send Ashley home to her father as pure as when she'd arrived...

CHAPTER THREE

Las Vegas, Nevada

Five a.m. came *really* early the next morning. Ashley had always been a fairly early riser, but this was pushing it even for her. Especially since she'd set her alarm for four so that she could shower in the tiny little bus shower stall and make sure her clothes were on straight and her hair was brushed.

She hadn't had the best night's sleep either. How could she, when Drew Morrison was only one thin door away? For a while there last night, she'd sworn she could hear him turning over in the bed, could practically hear him breathing. And that was when it had finally occurred to her—could he hear her, too? Just in case, she lay as still as possible in the bunk, but that only made it harder to fall asleep. Finally, exhaustion had taken its toll, but she couldn't have had more than a handful of hours of rest.

She hadn't brought much with her, just a few pairs of jeans and T-shirts, a denim skirt, and one justin-case summer dress. Looking pretty had never mattered to her before—why would it, when she'd always had her nose buried in a book or computer? But as she went to grab the clothes she'd brought into the shower with her from the counter above the sink, she suddenly found herself wishing she knew something about fashion. Her mother had tried to get her interested in shopping plenty of times over the years, would even bring home clothes for her to try on, but Ashley always felt like an impostor in dresses and heels. It was so much more comfortable to go into her father's office on campus to help him with whatever research project he was working on than to try on the too-colorful clothes her mother favored or let her drag Ashley to a makeup counter.

In any case, it was just as well that she hadn't brought anything special to wear since so many of the girls and women who had been freaking out over Drew yesterday were beautiful. Stunningly so, in some cases. He could have his pick of any of them, so there wasn't even the slightest chance that he'd want her.

Besides, whether or not Drew would ever be attracted to her was utterly irrelevant. She was here to do research for her business school application. Period.

Speaking of putting her clothes on straight, however, as Ashley went to get dressed, she was dismayed to realize she'd brought in her jeans and T-shirt, but had forgotten her bra and panties. It looked like she was actually going to have to walk out of the bathroom naked. Nearly naked, anyway, with only one of the towels hanging on the rack wrapped around her. It was still well before five a.m., though, so she figured if she was quick, odds were pretty much nil that Drew would catch her making a mad dash over the handful of feet between the bathroom and where she'd stashed her bags in the little closet behind her bunk.

The mirror over the sink wasn't quite long enough for her to make sure the towel actually covered her breasts *and* hips, but she was pretty certain it did. She opened the door a crack and peered out, confirming the coast was clear. A moment later, she flung the door open, went racing across the bus to her suitcase...

...and ran straight into Drew.

His chest was so hard it was like running into a brick wall. The air whooshed from her lungs as she started to ricochet back from him.

"Whoa." He put his hands on her shoulders to steady her. "I've got you."

But by then she was also working to steady herself by putting her hands on his chest. Which meant that she wasn't holding on to her towel any longer. A towel that had fallen.

All the way to the ground.

Oh God. I'm naked in Drew Morrison's arms.

She froze, unable to remember how to breathe or think or do anything but stare up at him in shock.

"Are you okay, Ashley?"

Do you want me to kiss you, Ashley?

Wait, no, that wasn't what he'd just said. She scrunched her eyes shut and willed her synapses to start firing again. "I didn't mean to nearly knock you over," she said when her brain, and her lips, finally came unstuck. "I forgot something in my bag, so I thought I'd make a run for it from the bathroom. I didn't think you'd be up yet."

"I couldn't sleep." His deep voice made shivers run up her spine. Or maybe it was the fact that she was still slightly damp...and naked in the middle of his tour bus. Drew's fingers tensed ever so slightly on her shoulders as he added, "Your towel fell. I should let you put it back on." It sounded like he was having trouble catching his breath, even though she was the one who'd been rushing. "I should probably let you put your clothes on, too, shouldn't I?"

She finally chanced a look up at his face and swallowed hard at what she saw in his eyes. Something that looked like *desire*. Which, she quickly told herself, would have likely been any guy's reaction to being barreled into by a naked woman first thing in the morning, wouldn't it?

"That—" Her throat felt hot and scratchy, and she stopped to clear it. The one small movement made her naked curves brush against his muscles...and so much heat exploded inside her body that she nearly forgot what she had been about to say. "That would be great." God, it was so hard to breathe right now. Almost as hard as Drew's chest, where her hands were still splayed. "If you could just close your eyes for a few seconds..."

"Good idea. I'll close my eyes so that you can cover up." But for a few moments he simply continued to stare down into her eyes. Finally, on what sounded like a groan of pain, he closed his eyes and stepped back. "I won't look again until you tell me it's okay."

"Thanks." She picked up the towel first, and after she'd wrapped it much more firmly around herself, she hurried over to her bag and pulled out the first bra and panty set she could find. To get back to the bathroom, however, she needed to scoot past Drew. Only, he was still standing right in the middle of the bus, and there was no way she'd be able to get by without rubbing herself against him. And even though she knew *exactly* how good that would feel...

"Could you move just a few inches to your right, please?"

She sounded both hesitant and uptight. Which was funny, considering she'd just been standing butt naked in a rock star's arms a few seconds ago. At least, it would have been funny if she wasn't presently the most mortified she'd ever been.

A muscle jumped in Drew's jaw as he nodded and shifted slightly to the right. She held her breath as she moved past him. Once she was safely locked in the little bathroom, she called out, "It's safe to open your eyes now."

Unfortunately, it wasn't at all easy to get dressed inside the teeny tiny little bathroom stall. She banged her elbows and head and knees on pretty much every hard surface possible before she was done, probably sounding like she was playing Ping-Pong inside the bathroom. She'd never known humiliation could run so hot or so deep. Not until this morning.

When she finally came out, she knew her cheeks had to be blazing red from the hot and steamy bathroom. And her T-shirt, she realized a few seconds too late, seemed to be sticking to her skin.

She had no idea what to say to Drew at this point. Nothing beyond, "Can we both just forget that ever happened?"

The tension still riding his expression seemed to ease a bit. "Do we have to? 'Cause I'm pretty sure that was straight out of an eighties rock-band video. Poison, maybe?"

His unexpected response had laughter bubbling out of her before she knew it was coming. "Actually, I think it might have been Whitesnake."

He laughed, too, and suddenly her morning didn't feel quite so horrible anymore. Not when his laughter was one of the nicest sounds she'd ever heard. Someday soon, hopefully, she'd be able to forget how embarrassing crashing naked into him had been.

Although she wasn't sure she'd ever be able to forget how good it had felt to be that close, or to have his hands on her bare skin. Every part of her still felt hot and sensitive in the nicest possible way.

"Come and have some breakfast," he said. "I've got coffee brewing, and there's cereal and frozen waffles. Eggs in the fridge, too, but I'm pretty sure that involves pans and stoves."

She laughed again, appreciating that he was clearly going out of his way to make her feel comfortable. "I actually know how to use a pan and a stove, so I can make us both eggs, if you'd like."

He looked at her in awe. Truly, there was no other word for it. "I don't want to embarrass you by getting down on my knees and begging, but one more bowl of Cheerios just might push me over the edge."

Maybe she wouldn't be totally in the way if she could at least make herself useful. Eggs for breakfast was a good start. "Fried? Over easy? Scrambled?"

"All of the above."

She opened the fridge and found eggs, butter, and a bag of bread, and a pan in the cupboard. "How about over easy today with toast and then we can try something different tomorrow?"

"I owe you, Ashley."

"Are you kidding? It's the least I can do when you're letting me join your tour."

"Touring is great, but sometimes it feels like we're just doing the same thing every day and every night on repeat. Having you here is already a change for the better."

She nearly forgot to keep an eye on the eggs, she was so stunned by how nice his comments were, and how good they made her feel. *A change for the better.* Last night when she'd walked into the venue, she'd felt she would never fit into this world, that she was kidding herself to think she could ever really be in the music business. But between Drew's amazing show and the lovely things he'd just said, maybe she wasn't too far off base, after all.

She plated their eggs just as their toast dinged in the mini toaster oven attached to the counter.

"Thanks, this looks great," he said as he picked up his fork. "I've never shared a bus with a woman before. Never thought about how you'd need to lock yourself in the bathroom to get dressed in the morning. Are you sure you won't take the back bedroom?"

"Then I'd just be walking in on you naked out here." The words came out before she realized it. *Ugh.* And just when she'd started to feel so comfortable with him. "What I'm trying to say is that I'm just fine sleeping out here and I'll try to remember to bring my underwear in with me next time."

I'll try to remember to bring my underwear in with me next time? Double ugh.

He stopped with his fork halfway to his mouth. "You forgot your..."

She felt her face go hot again and shoveled some eggs into her mouth so that she would only have to nod.

"Well," he said slowly, his voice sounding a little rougher all of a sudden, "I'll try to make sure you've got on more than a towel before I come out."

She took a sip of coffee to try to wash down her way-too-big bite of eggs. "Great! Thanks!" Every time she got nervous, she sounded like a chirpy bird. Which, she supposed, was better than talking about her underwear.

Drew finally began to eat, and before she knew it, he'd polished off his entire plate. Just as she always did with her father, she pushed her unfinished portion over to him, which he immediately shoveled up.

Finally, he pushed both plates away. "You're a great cook, Ashley. I haven't had eggs that good since—"

His words suddenly fell away, and she knew why, knew that he was thinking of his mother. The night before, he'd gotten so choked up when he'd been talking about writing "One More Time" the day his mother passed away, and Ashley's heart had broken for him. She wanted to reach out to him, wanted to find a way—any way at all—to make him feel better. But before she could say or do anything, there was a knock on the door.

"It's Max." Drew got up to let him in.

"Good morning, you two." Max looked impossibly chipper for such an early hour. "Mmm, eggs. Smells good."

"Sit and I'll make you a plate," Ashley said, already spooning what was left in the pan onto a clean plate.

Max's eyes practically rolled back in his head as he ate. "You are quite a woman, Miss Ashley," he said once he'd swallowed. "Isn't she, Drew?"

"She definitely is."

Ashley hopped up to wash the dishes, hoping neither of them would notice the way she was blushing. But before she could so much as rub a sponge over the first plate, Drew was taking it from her. "You cooked, I'll clean."

"But you have to get ready for—"

"Thank you for the best breakfast I've had in a year." He smiled at her, and her breath caught in her throat at being so close to him again. "Now let go of the plate."

She'd forgotten all about the plate, and that Max was right there watching her get all flustered and drooly over the rock star who was a million miles beyond her.

CHAPTER FOUR

When they stepped out of the tour bus a short while later, Ashley was stunned to realize they were already on the Las Vegas Strip. "I guess I knew it would be lit up even at five in the morning, but it's still kind of a shock. And surprisingly pretty, too." She sounded like a goony tourist, but she couldn't help it. She'd never been particularly into flash or neon, but Las Vegas made it work somehow.

"See that couple?" Drew pointed to a man in a dark suit and a woman in a glittering dress. "They've likely been playing the high-stakes tables all night. And those guys over there?" He pointed to half a dozen college guys looking more than a little worse for wear. "I'm guessing it's someone's twenty-first birthday."

She pointed at a gray-haired woman. "What about her?"

"Card shark."

She laughed, realizing she'd laughed more with Drew already than she had with any of the guys she'd ever dated. "Strangely, something tells me you're probably right." Her first sixty seconds in Vegas were already full of so much color and life and wildness, and she was shocked to realize she loved it. Her mother had frequently needed to "get away" to Las Vegas. Now Ashley thought she might understand why...even as she wished she hadn't always turned down her mother's offers of a spa and show weekend here.

"The station is ready for you to head up now," Max said.

"Is your band already upstairs?" Ashley asked as the three of them headed into a skyscraper situated between over-the-top casinos. She'd interned in enough office buildings to feel totally comfortable in this environment—the gray carpet, the elevators that smelled like they'd just been wiped down with cleanser, the early morning staff clutching their cups of coffee for dear life.

"I usually do a stripped-down version of my songs for radio," Drew replied. "A couple of the guys from the band are already waiting inside for us, and everyone else gets to sleep in."

Drew's bass player and drummer were waiting in the hall just outside the studio. "Sammy, Jonas, this is Ashley Emmit. Remember I told you guys she's going to be joining us to do some research on the music business?"

Just like Max, they had plenty of tattoos and a few piercings. And they both also said it was nice to meet one of Drew's friends. The way they said *friends* seemed a little strange, almost as though they thought she and Drew were actually more than friends. But that was so preposterous, she quickly shook off the thought.

Before she'd come here yesterday, her father had warned her approximately a million times not to let herself be swept up by a rock 'n' roll man, à la Elton John's "Tiny Dancer." But she'd known he didn't have anything to be worried about. There was no way she could be the kind of girl any of these rocker types were interested in.

Just then, however, Drew put his hand on hers to draw her arm out of range of the sharp edge of a bongo drum, and her brain flashed back to what she'd seen in his eyes when he'd been holding her naked and wet in his arms. A heat and a desire that she still couldn't quite believe had been real...even if he seemed to be looking at her in the same way right that instant.

Two disk jockeys ushered them all in, and she grabbed a seat in the very back to stay out of everyone's way. The next half hour was a whirlwind of rapid-fire questions that Drew answered with charm and wit, both from the DJs and from the women who called in, desperate to speak with him for thirty seconds.

Finally, he opened up his guitar case, pulled out an acoustic guitar, and asked, "You guys want to hear a couple of songs?"

Ashley had been taking notes like crazy the whole time. She'd listened to plenty of musicians' interviews on the radio, but she'd never realized just how much work they were putting into it. From a casual listener's perspective, it might be the first time you'd ever hear them tell their story about how they got started, or what they were planning for their show that night in town. But for them, she suddenly realized, it was the same thing on repeat every day. How many times had Drew given these answers? And yet, he didn't sound the least bit tired or bored.

She could tell by the power of his songs that Drew hadn't gotten into the music business for fame like many other musicians likely had. Instead, fame and endless rounds of promotion were probably just things he had to deal with in order to pursue his chosen career.

Already, she felt that she had a hundred times more insight into just how much record labels needed to support their musicians. First, they could—

Drew's voice rang out through the microphone hanging from the ceiling, and her well-ordered thoughts fled. Every time he started playing and singing, she stopped being the rational person she'd always been, and her emotions, her passions, bubbled up and up and up, until it was taking literally everything she had just to keep from alternately cheering and sobbing, depending on the song.

By the time he finished his final song, she felt wrung out. Utterly depleted by the emotional roller coaster he'd just taken her on with his music, and this was only their first visit of many on the schedule Max had handed her.

And maybe if she hadn't been looking so carefully, she wouldn't have noticed that although Drew continued to give one hundred percent of himself, he looked a little worn out, too. Although, she thought with a frown, *worn out* wasn't really the right word for it. No, the expression on his face was the same one he'd had when he thought there had been some problems with his show the night before. Everything she'd heard him play had been flawless. But obviously, he wasn't entirely happy with it.

Was it simply that he was getting tired of playing the same hit songs over and over? Or was there something else going on with him and his music?

Of course, not only did she not know him well enough to ask such prying questions, but for the next three hours there wasn't so much as one private moment between them. Not when she was pretty sure he'd visited every radio station in Nevada.

"Is it always like this? So busy?"

"If it's going well, it is." But he was frowning as he looked at her. "If you're feeling tired..."

"I'm great." And she was, because she could listen to Drew's songs a million times and never get tired of them. In fact, the more she heard them, the deeper they went. So deep that she felt more exposed and raw than she ever had before, from nothing more than being in the same room with Drew and his band while they played some of the most amazing songs she'd ever heard. But she didn't want to sound like a drooling, crazy fangirl, so she simply said, "I'm sure I'll get used to sleeping on the bus soon. Besides, all I'm doing is taking notes."

He looked down at her notebook and iPad. "Any chance you're going to let me see them?"

Instinctively, she clutched her tablet and notebook to her chest. Most of her notes were either details of the interviews and radio stations, or brainstorming about how things could be improved for Drew and his band. But a few notes had slipped in along the way about how sexy he was as he sang, and how he drove his fans wild by joking with them over the phone lines when they called in. All in the name of science, of course, but she knew he might not see it that way. Instead, he might think she had a crush on him...and then things would get even weirder on the bus than she'd already managed to make them.

"It's okay, you don't have to let me see anything." His hand on her arm froze her in place. "I wouldn't let anyone look through my unfinished lyrics either."

Just then, her phone buzzed with the ring tone she'd given her father. "It's my dad."

"Why don't you take it while we get set up for our last radio spot? James will stay out here with you."

"I'll be okay in the hall by myself."

But James simply said, "I'll just be down at the end of the hall so you can talk in private," then moved to a spot where she could have privacy but still be in his line of sight.

Drew nodded a silent thanks to his bodyguard, then turned back to her. "Say hi to the professor for me."

It wasn't until Drew disappeared behind the radio station's door that she realized she hadn't taken a full breath all morning. Not since the moment she'd gone flying into Drew's chest...and then immediately dropped her towel. Finally, there was some space between them. A thicker wall than the paper-thin one on the bus.

Her father's call had gone to voice mail, so she quickly redialed him.

"Ashley, how are you, honey?"

"I'm great." She had left her father a message the previous night to let him know she'd gotten to the venue okay, but she'd known he wouldn't feel any calmer about her being gone until he actually spoke to her.

"How's Drew?"

"Really busy doing radio interviews right now. I had no idea his job was this hard."

"Hard?" Her father laughed. "How can partying with groupies be hard?"

"Maybe it's like that for some people," she said carefully, even though there had been plenty of out-of-control groupies yesterday, "but Drew is a consummate professional. And he's really nice, too."

"How nice?"

"Dad." She knew how much he loved her, but he could be a little overprotective sometimes. "He's a perfect gentleman, as you already know firsthand."

"Actually, as I recall, he seemed to have plenty of girls hanging off his arms when he was taking my classes."

She was sure her father was telling the truth. And yet, since she would never be one of Drew's girls, it didn't matter, did it?

"I know you think I'm worrying too much about you," her father continued, "but I just can't stand the thought of anything bad happening to you while you're on tour with Drew."

"I love you, too, Dad." She smiled as she spoke. "And nothing bad is going to happen to me. I'm smart and careful, just the way you taught me to be." She deliberately tried not to think about the way Drew had been holding her naked body tightly to his this morning on the bus, just in case her father had suddenly developed X-ray vision.

"You're the smartest person I know, honey, but you've also inherited your mother's looks." She didn't bother to disagree with him, even though they both knew she'd never be stunningly beautiful like her exotic-looking mother. "And I know how guys think," her father added. "You shouldn't trust a word out of their mouths."

She couldn't figure out why her father thought she was such a target for men all of a sudden. But she knew better than to debate the issue with him when he was one of the overseeing professors of the campus debate team, so she simply said, "I have to get going now, but I'll tell Drew you said hello."

Since she didn't want to accidentally walk into the studio in the middle of one of Drew's performances, after hanging up she quickly checked her email and then walked over to where James had been pretending he wasn't listening to her conversation.

Doing her research well meant not only learning what Drew did on tour, but also learning from his crew. She'd only just realized how important a bodyguard was. "How long have you been with Drew?"

"Two years. I worked for a real piece of work right before him. Can't name any names, but let's just say I'd be happy never to hear the song 'Love Robot' again."

Her eyes widened before she could stop them. James had been Cal Sextin's bodyguard? She'd never been a huge fan of his music, but he was a big star with a string of hits that stretched back at least a decade.

"When I couldn't take it anymore, I asked around, and Nicola Sullivan—you probably know her by her stage name, Nico—who I'd done some work for here and there, gave me a reference for Drew. I owe her."

"Wow, it sounds like you've worked with tons of famous people. How long have you been a bodyguard?"

"Twenty-five years."

"I'm sure you must have a ton of incredible stories."

"I sure do."

She was riveted, despite knowing she'd moved way beyond research and was solely in the personal interest zone. "Tell me one, James. About Drew."

He didn't look particularly surprised by her request. "One night about a year ago, Drew was feeling a little...well...*antsy* is probably the best word for it. Just tired of being on the bus and under pressure, you know."

"I'm sure that must happen a lot," she mused aloud. After only one night in the really nice tour bus, she could imagine how small it could come to feel. "Especially when it's hard even to do things like walk into an airport without calling security first."

"I should have been there at the airport with you guys," James said with a frown. "Anyway, we were out in the middle of the Australian Outback, and he decided to get a horse and go riding for the day. I can't ride, so I didn't go with him. And none of the other guys could keep up. When he didn't show up at the hotel five hours later, we knew something was up. No cell reception out there, of course, so we got in a Jeep and headed out into the wild, praying nothing had happened to him. I was picturing broken bones and snakes and rabid red kangaroos gnawing at his flesh."

Even though she knew Drew had obviously gotten back safe and sound, she was still riveted. "What happened, James? Where was he?"

"Turned out he'd been spotted by a couple of teenage girls on their horses doing their chores. They knew exactly who he was, of course."

"Even in the middle of the Outback, he couldn't escape his fame."

"Nope. Although I think there were plenty of other things he was trying to escape that day," James added in a low tone, and Ashley finally realized the timing worked out to be right around when Drew's mother had passed away. "He'd been helping the girls and the rest of their siblings fix fences all day. Fit right in, just like he'd been born and raised working on an Outback ranch. Took some ugly threats to drag him back to town that night so he could play his show. It's the only time he's ever gone on late. And it was also the last time I ever let him out of my sight on a horse."

Just then Drew walked out of the radio station, before she had enough time to put her heart back together from the story she'd just heard. She knew what it was like to want to ride off on a horse into the desert and never come back. She'd felt that way so many times when her parents were splitting up. But riding away hadn't saved her.

Only Drew's music had been able to do that.

CHAPTER FIVE

The expression on Ashley's face when Drew stepped out of the radio station—a cross between heartbreak and hope—hit him square in the chest. He knew that feeling. Hell, sometimes he felt like he'd invented it, loving so hard and hurting so much at exactly the same time.

"Ashley?" He quickly moved to her side and didn't think before putting his hand beneath her chin to tip her beautiful face up to his. "What's wrong?"

She shook her head, so fast that she blurred in front of him for a second. But when she licked her lips, he lost his focus on everything but how much he wanted to kiss her. More than he'd ever wanted *anything*.

"Nothing." She put a smile on her lips that didn't reach her eyes. "James was just telling me some stories for my research."

What kind of stories could they be to make her look the way she had when he'd walked out? But he never got a chance to ask her, because his bodyguard got off the phone and said, "A big crowd has assembled out front. Do you want to go out the back?"

Drew was tempted to escape without being seen, simply because then he could return his focus to Ashley. But early on in his career, he'd promised himself he'd always be there for his fans the way they'd always been there for him. Plus, in his lowest moments, playing for them had given him a reason to get up in the morning.

"Nope, let's go say hello to the fans."

James nodded. "I figured you'd say that, so I've got a local security crew already waiting downstairs."

"Make sure to write down in your notes that James is the best security director in the business," Drew told Ashley.

"I already have," she said with a smile that knocked Drew's heart around in his chest like a pinball.

"Do you want to head out the back? Max could take you down."

"While I'm here, I need to see and experience everything. At least," she added with one of those beautiful blushes that turned her creamy skin rosy and flushed, "everything you're okay with letting me see."

Jesus. If she had any idea of the kind of things he wanted her to experience with him, and that he wanted to show her...

He'd never been caught in this kind of conflict before—at the same time that he wanted to protect Ashley, he also wanted to do precisely the things to her that he should be protecting her from.

His insides were completely twisted up over her, and yet he still couldn't stop the runaway train of remembered visions that his brain kept sending him about how soft her naked skin had been that morning. Or how good she'd smelled. Or how much he'd wanted to pick her up and carry her back to his bed to—

Damn it! He was doing it again. Completely losing focus. Keeping Ashley safe while she was on tour with him was his number one priority. He couldn't let himself forget that.

Still, this was her first time in Vegas. And he couldn't let her leave without experiencing his favorite part of it. Not the bright lights, but the awe-inspiring beauty that most tourists never even knew existed, let alone saw.

"Max," he said as they headed down in the elevator, "after we say hi to the fans, we've got time for a trip to the Valley of Fire before they need me at the venue, right? I'd like to show it to Ashley."

Max nodded. "If we leave right away, we should have plenty of time to get there and back even if the traffic is nasty."

"What's the Valley of Fire?" Ashley asked.

"Only one of the coolest places on the planet. And no sneaking a peek at pictures of it on your phone. It's better if the first time you see it, it's the real thing."

The words *the real thing* seemed to hang in the air between them, even with James and Max in the elevator with them.

"I won't look online," she said in a solemn voice, one that made it even harder not to kiss her.

A few seconds later the elevator doors opened, and the screams of his fans brought him back to reality. At least, they should have. But just as he'd been so wrapped up in Ashley that he'd forgotten to call for security at the airport, he wasn't at the top of his meet-the-fans game today either. Because while the Las Vegas security team did their best to keep everyone orderly, when a bra went flying, Drew wasn't able to react fast enough to grab it out of the air before it landed on top of Ashley's head.

She stopped dead in her tracks, and through the din of screams from the girls outside, he heard her say as if to herself, "Somehow, I don't think this is meant for me." She took it off her head and reached out to hand it to him, her lips twitching. "A gift for you."

He laughed out loud, even more thankful that she was with him. "Thanks." He wanted to be alone with her on the bus again, wanted to hear her let her own laughter free. But first he needed to get his act together for the next half hour and hang out with the fans who had made the effort to come see him this morning.

He turned to the crowd. "Thanks for coming to say hi."

The entire time he was signing autographs and taking selfies, he was aware of Ashley standing nearby making notes on her tablet. And just knowing she was there made him feel good.

* * *

Ninety minutes later, they had pulled off the freeway and were heading straight for the Valley of Fire. They were sitting in the front section of the bus beside Max so that Ashley wouldn't miss the moment when the national park came into view. James was there with them, too, and Drew was charmed by the honest interest Ashley had in both men's lives. He could tell she wasn't just asking about their wives and kids as research, but because she liked hearing them talk about the people they loved. Some musicians stayed separate from their crew, preferring to keep things as impersonal as possible, but Drew had always enjoyed getting to know everyone. One of his favorite things about touring, in fact, was how much it felt like family after a week of living in each other's pockets. If he couldn't see his real family, then at least he didn't have to feel totally alone.

Ashley was laughing at something James had just said when she suddenly stopped. "Oh my God, look at that!" She pointed at the bright red and orange rock formations rising from the middle of the otherwise flat and barren desert. She turned to Drew with a huge, awestruck smile. "They're like flames rising from the ground."

"Amazing, right?"

She nodded, grinning even wider as she said, "Valley of Fire. What a perfect name for this magical place."

As they got closer to the park, more and more of the incredible rock formations came into view. Drew had been here a good half-dozen times, but it never ceased to blow him away.

Soon, they were pulling into the visitor's center parking lot. Fortunately, Ashley was wearing Converse sneakers instead of heels or sandals, and she immediately hopped out of the bus so that she could see one of the rocks up close.

Drew turned to James and Max. He dug them both, but sometimes he wished he could drive himself around in a car like a normal person. "You guys don't mind waiting here, do you?"

Max nodded, grinning like the true romantic he was. "Sure, no problem for me."

But James was frowning. "Last time I let you loose in a desert, you almost didn't come back." That had been a rough day, one Drew had no intention of repeating. James did his staring-you-down thing for a few moments before he finally grabbed one of the black baseball caps on the dash and shoved it at Drew. "Don't take this or your sunglasses off. And if you run into any other hikers, keep your head down."

At first these precautions had felt like overkill. But more and more, Drew was glad to know that James was there to make sure they got in and out of crazy situations safely. And now that Ashley was with him, making sure nothing got out of hand was even more important.

Baseball cap on, he headed for Ashley. She was running her hand over the red rock, but turned as she heard him approach. Her smile was radiant, and he nearly stumbled at how deeply her pleasure affected him. He wanted nothing more in that moment than to keep giving her pleasure. Any and every way he possibly could.

Down, boy.

"I can't believe we're practically the only ones here. The Vegas Strip is pretty cool, but this—" She waved her hand at what was surely one of the wonders of the world. "Thank you for blowing my mind, Drew."

He put his hand beside hers on the rock. It was warm, but not nearly as warm as her skin had been that morning when she'd barreled into his arms. He wanted to tell her she'd blown his mind from the first moment he'd set eyes on her. But with her father's *take care of my baby* ringing in his ears, Drew simply said, "You're welcome. Ready to explore?"

She nodded, but as they were heading off toward one of the trails, she stopped and looked back. "Aren't James and Max going to come with us?"

"Not this time." In order to distract her from asking why not, he said, "I was ten the first time we came here, all eight of us piled into a beat-up old RV my parents had bought secondhand."

"It must have been such a grand adventure."

"It always was whenever we took that thing out. We fought sometimes, but we played more. And we always knew our mom was going to show us something really cool. Like this sand, for instance." He bent down to scoop up a handful of the red powder, then let it slowly blow out from between his fingers. "Not just because of the amazing color, but also because of how fine it is. I remember coming home after our first trip here and all of us were dumping red sand out of our tennis shoes for days."

"What else did your mom show you?"

He liked that she wasn't afraid to ask him questions about his mother. It was pretty much impossible for him to talk with any of his siblings about his mom, when they were all still too deep in the pain of losing her. And as for his father, Michael? Any hint of Lisa Morrison in a conversation and he went to pieces. Drew hadn't realized just how much he wanted to talk to someone about his mom until this moment.

Not just someone. *Ashley.*

"We traveled all over the country in that RV. We went to the Grand Canyon. We saw the world's biggest redwoods in Humboldt County. We explored the canyons in Carlsbad. And each of us put a foot and a hand in the four corners where Utah, Colorado, Arizona, and New Mexico meet. In fact, right outside of the Four Corners Monument is where my mom bought me my first guitar—from a guy selling a bunch of random stuff on the side of the highway." He smiled, remembering that day. He'd been tired of being stuck inside with his little sisters hanging all over him and his brothers knocking around on him. And his mother had known exactly what he needed to feel better. "It only had five strings and one broke pretty quickly, but it was still the greatest gift anyone has ever given me."

"What happened to that guitar? Do you still have it?"

"I wish." He shook his head. "My brother Justin dropped it out of a tree a few years later."

"Why would he do that?"

"I had it coming," Drew admitted. "I'd narced on him at school for doing something wrong that had been my idea in the first place. He was just dumb enough to go along with me. Anyway, I ended up buying my first real guitar after that, a Martin that I mowed approximately a million lawns to afford. I still have that guitar. I actually played it—"

"On your last album." She bit her lip when he looked at her in surprise. "I kind of have a thing about liner notes. I read them so many times that I end up memorizing them."

"I do the same thing." Now she was the one looking at him in surprise. "You want to find out more about what inspired the artist, right? And it feels like there must be clues in the liner notes."

"It's good to know I'm not the only person crazy enough to think that."

"It's why I always buy the physical album in addition to the digital. I know I can read the liner notes online, but I like being able to flip through the pages."

"No wonder your liner notes are so great. I loved the way you basically put together a big photo album for the last release. Each picture really felt like the song it went with." She shook her head. "I know that must sound weird—to say that a picture can feel like a song."

"If you ask me, *everything* can feel like a song." Especially this moment, when it was just the two of them surrounded by red rocks and brilliantly colored sand and the bright blue sky. "One of the biggest questions I've gotten since putting out that album is why I put all those random pictures in the liner notes. The label wanted it to be just pictures of me, and they weren't particularly happy when I came in with pictures they couldn't understand. I ended up bending on some of them, and some other things on the album, too, which still really bugs me whenever I look at it or listen to it." He stopped, realizing that it sounded like he was complaining about all his good fortune. "Chief Records has done great things for me, but sometimes it feels like they just want me to paint with primary colors."

"If that's what they're trying to get you to do, they're wrong." He'd never heard her sound so firm. So strong. "You should paint with whatever colors you want to use and *never* let anyone tell you otherwise. If you want to use only primaries, awesome. If you want to create brand-new colors that no one has ever seen before, then you should do it. No matter what anyone else says."

He'd never told anyone what his mother had said in the letter she'd written to him before she died, not even his siblings or his father. The letter she'd left for him to read that he kept with him always. It had already been a huge step for him to play "One More Time" last night, but now he found himself telling Ashley, "My mom wrote all of us a letter to read. After." He suddenly couldn't talk and walk at the same time. "It's in my pocket."

Ashley didn't say anything, simply stood with him beneath the blazing sun and waited for him to say what he needed to.

"I wasn't the easiest kid. I liked causing trouble more than any of my brothers or sisters. My teachers always said it was because I wanted to be in the spotlight."

Ashley laughed softly. "No wonder you're so comfortable in it."

He couldn't believe how easy she made everything for him. Even this. "I probably would have ended up in really bad trouble at some point if it hadn't been for my mom buying me that guitar. Music saved me from myself. I always wonder how she knew it was what I needed."

"She loved you, Drew." Her hand slipped into his, and he realized he'd never needed another person's touch more. "That's how she knew."

Ashley's hand felt like his only lifeline as he finally reached into his pocket. He unfolded the letter with one hand so that he wouldn't have to let go of hers, then handed it to her.

She hesitated for a moment before finally taking it from him. When she looked down and began to read, he heard her breath hitch in her throat. "Oh, Drew."

"Read it out loud." When she looked up at him in obvious surprise, he added, "Please, Ashley."

He would never hear his mother's voice again, but at least he could hear her words in the beautiful melody of Ashley's voice.

She took a deep breath before beginning. *"My dearest Drew. Do you have any idea just how much joy you've brought me? Right from the moment you were born, I knew how special you were. You were always moving. Always making noise. Joyful noise that was musical right from the start. And even when you were being naughty and I knew I should be telling you off, it would be nearly impossible for me to keep from laughing right along with you. I still remember the first time you sang. You were barely a year old and there was a James Taylor song on the radio. "Fire and Rain." You had only just started to talk, but by the final chorus, I swear you had learned the lyrics. We sang together, even though I was off-key, and you were always so perfectly in tune with the song in your heart. And it just seems right, somehow, that those first lyrics you ever sang to me would come back around again for us now. Because I loved every single sunny day we shared together. And if it seems sometimes like there are too many lonely days, honey? Just know that I'm always here watching you make the beautiful music you were put here to make. Because when nothing else makes—"*

Tears had been streaming down Ashley's cheeks the entire time she'd been reading, but she'd been able to keep going. Until she couldn't anymore.

So Drew filled in the words she was too emotional to finish reading aloud. *"When nothing else makes the pain go away, all I have to do is put on one of your songs and it works every time. Every single time."*

Ashley sniffled and looked back down at the letter as if she knew that he needed her to say the final five words aloud, needed to hear the beautiful melody of her voice dancing with them. *"I love you, Drew. Always."*

She didn't reach up to wipe away her tears, simply handed him the letter so that he could carefully fold it up and put it into his pocket.

"She wouldn't let me leave my tour to come home." The desert was so quiet that in the spaces between his words, he swore he could hear their hearts beating. "Every time I tried, she sent me back after a few days. She said people needed to hear my music."

"And she knew you needed to be playing it for them, too, didn't she? That you wouldn't be whole without it."

He looked into her beautiful eyes—eyes that saw so deeply it stunned him. "My brother Grant finally called and told me to get on a plane. I had only a few weeks with her at the end. She was asleep most of the time, but whenever she was awake, she'd ask me to play. I'd never been into folk music, like I didn't think it was cool enough. But in those three weeks I learned all her favorites—Dylan, CSN, Joni Mitchell, Leonard Cohen. And James Taylor, of course. 'Fire and Rain' was always her number one favorite, even when she was lying in the hospital and knew she was never going to leave it."

"She must have loved you playing all of her favorite songs for her."

"She did." And he had, too, even if he hadn't been able to play any of those songs since. "Her throat was too dry to sing along, but when she had the energy, she'd mouth the words and even tap her fingers to the beat."

He hadn't talked this much about his mom for...he didn't actually know how long it had been. Since even before she died. And maybe it wasn't fair to lay all of this on Ashley. But he couldn't stop now. He had to get it out.

Finally just get it all out.

"I knew she was going to go soon. We all did. But even though we knew we were saying good-bye, we all broke."

"Drew." Ashley slipped her hand from his and wrapped both of her arms around his waist as she pulled him close.

She wasn't only his lifeline now. She was his strength, too.

"Grant just kept swearing. Dad and Madison couldn't stop crying. Justin kept wanting to hit buttons on the machines all around her, as if science could save her. Olivia went so silent it was scary. Sean looked like he was on the verge of breaking down a wall to get out of there."

"What about you?" She didn't let go of him as she asked the question, just held him so tightly that the words coming from her chest vibrated through his. "What did you do?"

"I nearly slammed my guitar into the ground, but Olivia took it away from me before I could destroy it. I wrote 'One More Time' that day."

"It's the most beautiful song, Drew. She would have loved it."

"I didn't mean to write it," he admitted in a low voice, "but I couldn't stop the words or melody from coming out. And I didn't mean to play it for anyone either. But last night...last night it felt like she was there. Like she really was listen—" The word broke in half as the tears he hadn't been able to cry since his mom died finally broke through the wall of pain he'd built around them. "I miss my mom so much. So damned much, every single day."

Ashley didn't say anything, didn't tell him that one day the pain would go away, didn't make promises about time healing wounds. She simply pressed her face into his chest and held him even tighter—and it was exactly what he needed.

She was exactly what he needed.

CHAPTER SIX

Ashley never wanted to let go of Drew. But as soon as she felt the tension slide from his body, she made herself loosen her hold and step back so that they could continue their hike.

"I've never told anyone that before," he said after a few minutes of silently walking through the sand, side by side.

He'd never know how much it meant to her that he'd felt safe enough to share so much of himself. "I won't tell a soul."

"I know you won't. You would never betray anyone's trust, would never hurt anyone, would you, Ashley?"

"I hope I never do."

When she'd been thinking about going on tour with Drew, she thought she'd only be granted access to him periodically between interviews and shows. She hadn't thought she'd get to spend so much time with him. And the truth was that if she had, she would have been even more nervous. Because when someone had as big a crush as she did—seriously, at this point, she was just going to have to own up to it already—every time he looked at her the way he was right now, she went from zero to a million on the flustered scale.

"Your brothers and sisters all sound really great. I know about Grant's business prowess already, and Sean plays baseball at Stanford, right?"

"He's actually focusing more on photography now. I'm hoping I can convince him to take the pictures for my next album."

"That would be amazing. And if you could convince Grant to open a record label one day, you'd not only get to work on everything with your family, but you could also put whatever pictures you want in your liner notes."

"You know what," he said as his gaze sharpened on her, "Grant would probably run one hell of a label. I always figured the admissions people at the biz school had to know what they were doing, but if they turned you down, I'm not so sure they do."

Ashley couldn't ever remember a man looking at her the way Drew did. As though she was *special*. Feeling flustered by the attention, she quickly said, "You have three other siblings, don't you?"

His lips quirked up slightly at the corners as if he knew exactly what she was doing—redirecting the focus from her back to his family. "Olivia is going to graduate school for education in the fall. She's the most serious one of all of us. Justin is Sean's twin, but they're not much alike. Justin's a science genius and is usually locked away in a lab, also at Stanford. And then there's Madison." He grinned. "She's a bundle of energy. She wants to open a restaurant one day and be a chef and is always giving people something to taste-test. They're all coming for my birthday next week when we get to New Orleans."

"Your family sounds amazing. I can't wait to meet them." She paused for a moment before realizing he hadn't said anything about his father. "How's your dad doing?"

"He's pretty much a shell of himself now. My mom was everything to him—his sun, moon, and stars." He stared out into the desert. "I've often wondered if they were the exception." He looked back into her eyes. "Or is it possible for the rest of us to find a love that strong? That pure?"

When he looked at her like that—with such dark, deep intensity—she forgot how to think, how to speak. How to do anything but *feel.* And in the end, all she was able to say was, "I don't know."

But, oh, how a secret part of her wished that there were a love like that waiting out there for all of them...even though her experience with her own parents had left her with a deep core of cynicism.

"Do you have any siblings?" he asked.

"No, it's just me."

"That's what I thought after seeing the pictures in your father's office. He sure loves you."

"I know, but I wish he'd get rid of those pictures."

"Why? You were a cute kid."

"A cute kid with the world's biggest glasses and braces. And that perm." She had to laugh at herself. "It seemed like a good idea at the time. Needless to say, it wasn't."

"You're really close to your dad, aren't you?"

"We always spent a ton of time together, even when I was really little. I remember doing puzzles with him and reading together."

"What about your mom?"

Compared to what he'd been through, her situation should have felt like nothing now. But she still tensed up simply from knowing she was going to talk about her mom. "We don't have much in common. She didn't have much in common with my dad either. They split up when I was fifteen."

"That's rough."

"It was better that way."

"Why?"

"Because they are so different. You know my dad—he's all about lists and plans and seeing things in black and white. But my mom..." She shook her head. "She hates lists and plans. And her world is all color, all the time. My dad once said that if anyone should have known that the odds of their being able to make it work were next to nothing, it should have been a statistics professor." She'd meant for it to come out sounding like a joke, but it just wasn't possible for her to find any humor in the situation, even all these years later.

"Did they love each other?"

She'd never known a man who spoke as easily about love as Drew did. Then again, she could see how growing up surrounded by so much of it in his great family would have made a really strong impact. Strong enough that he was asking her the really hard questions.

"While you were wondering if anyone else could have the kind of love your parents shared," she finally replied, "I was wondering how my parents could have gotten together in the first place—and why they stayed together for so long." She'd never spoken to anyone else about what went on in her house, but just as Drew had shared so much with her, now she felt the same urge to share herself with him. "They fought all the time, but they even did that differently. My mom fought loud and passionate and hot. My father fought with silences and freezes."

"And you were stuck in the middle of it all."

She looked up at him in surprise. "How did you know that?"

"Because you love them both. And you're also made up of both parts, the passionate and colorful *and* the cool and analytical."

"I'm not like both of them," she said automatically. "I'm just the cool, analytical part like my dad."

"That's not true. I've seen tons of passion from you already."

"When?" It wasn't until the word was out of her mouth that she realized their conversation had just gone *way* off track.

But before she could tell him he didn't need to answer her, he stopped and said, "When we were talking about the power of music. When you were standing up to the security guards at the airport. And out here just now, when we were talking about, well, everything."

Hardly able to believe what he was saying about her—not only that he thought she was full of passion, but also that he had *examples*—she stumbled over a bump in the sand and would have gone to her knees if he hadn't caught her in his arms for the second time in one day.

"I'm not..." The feel of his hands on her bare skin where her shirt was riding up slightly over the waistband of her jeans had her breath going and her sentence faltering. "I'm not normally so clumsy. I promise you won't always have to catch me."

"I like catching you."

His simple words stole her breath...and made her heart pound at what felt like a million miles an hour. Rather desperately, she tried to remind herself how charming he was with his fans. And that if one of them had fallen in front of him, he would have reached out to catch her, too. But just then, with his arms still around her, it was hard to pay attention to those reminders. Hard to do anything but wish he would be overcome with the same attraction that was all but devastating her—and kiss her.

Oh God, she was losing it.

Dreaming of Drew's kisses was a one-way trip to crying herself to sleep at night on the bus if he took some other girl into the back room. Which was why she made herself step back out of his arms...even though she was quickly realizing that it was her absolute favorite place to be.

* * *

All Drew wanted to do in that moment was kiss Ashley.

He was mesmerized not only by her gorgeous mouth, but also by every one of her expressions, from surprised to pleased, from empathy to frustration. And a second ago he could have sworn that she wanted that kiss as badly as he did. But instead of taking it, she'd pulled back.

Damn it, he knew she was right. He'd promised her father he'd keep his hands off her.

Knowing the best first step in trying to cool off would be to head back to the bus, he said, "It's pretty hot out here." *Hot* was a ridiculous understatement for the temperature, just as *desire* didn't even come close to what Drew had felt from the first moment he'd set eyes on Ashley. "Do you want to turn back?"

"Actually, I love the heat." She held out her arms and lifted her face to the sun as if to soak in more of it. She was so beautiful, the most beautiful woman he'd ever seen. "And I've always loved watching the flames dance in a fire, too. I never thought I'd get to see them made out of rock, though. Thank you for bringing me here, Drew. It's been the most wonderful surprise."

"Heat. Flames. *Ash.*" She opened her eyes and looked at him as he said, "It all fits you. Fits you perfectly."

She licked her lips, and he couldn't stop his gaze from dropping again to the damp flesh. Her breathing hitched in her chest, and the very thin thread still holding his self-control together snapped. But when he was halfway to reaching for her to drag her against him so that he could devour her mouth, he looked into her eyes...and saw the panic in them.

Damn it, the last thing he wanted to do was scare her. Especially after he'd promised her last night that he would be a perfect gentleman. Stealing a kiss from her today wasn't just breaking his promise to her father—it was breaking his promise to *her.*

"Maybe," he made himself say, "we should head back before James starts freaking out."

* * *

For the rest of the day, Drew continually reminded himself that he needed to rein in his attraction to Ashley. But every time she laughed—or so much as looked him in the eye—he had a harder and harder time remembering why. She drew him in as no other woman ever had. Not only physically, but also because she got him and his music on a really deep level.

By the time he strode on stage that night, he was more than ready to burn off his pent-up energy. They went five songs over, not just because the crowd was great, but also because he knew what awaited him when he got offstage was another night alone on his bus with Ashley. Trying to stay away. Trying not to kiss. Not to touch. Not to devour every beautiful inch of her.

But even if it was nearly killing him to keep his hands off her, he couldn't have put her in with his crew. She was too fresh, too gentle. He didn't want to risk anyone taking that away from her.

And when he played "One More Time" for the second time, he didn't just play it for his mom. He played it for Ashley, too.

"Great job tonight, guys," he told his band before he headed off to the meet-and-greet room.

James handed him a towel as they walked down the long backstage hallway. "You seemed closer to your old self out there tonight. Got something you're trying to work out of your system?"

Drew could guess his bodyguard knew damn well exactly who he was trying to work out of his system. But it was clearly a rhetorical question, because James followed it up with the piece of information that Drew needed most.

"Ashley is already in the meet-and-greet room with Max."

"Thanks for keeping watch over her." He'd already made it perfectly clear, more than once, to his entire staff that both Drew and her father would kill them all if anything happened to her.

"My pleasure. She's smart, pretty, and has a big heart. I'm glad she's joined us."

They were the same things Drew had been thinking—or, rather, trying not to think about.

Then again, there were a lot of things he was trying not to think about: his mom being gone and his dad being a wreck; the fact that not only could he not write a song worth a damn anymore, but also how he felt like he was faking it more and more every night on stage; how Smith Sullivan was waiting for him to deliver a great soundtrack for his new movie soon and had no idea that Drew had a grand total of zero good songs for it so far; and the meeting he'd be having with the label the following morning, where they were sure to drag out the golden handcuffs again.

Chief Records had sent cardboard cutouts of him to stores with the last album. More and more, he felt like that was what he was becoming—a cardboard cutout of himself. A guy playing the role of *Drew Morrison* for the crowds, for the press. Even with his family and friends.

Only with Ashley in the desert today had he felt a little bit like himself again. At the very least, he'd finally been honest about some of the pain of losing his mom. But even then, he'd made sure not to go too far by admitting that ever since the moment his mom had become so sick that they knew she was never going to recover, his songwriting had left him as if it had never been there in the first place.

He hadn't told her that even the way he *heard* music now seemed to have changed—that what used to move him no longer did, and that now it was almost like he was hearing entirely different tonal patterns in his head.

And he hadn't admitted that sometimes he just felt like getting on a horse like he had in Australia and going walkabout...only this time he wouldn't come back and get on another stage, wouldn't play the same songs everyone wanted to hear, because he couldn't. Because he didn't feel like the same guy anymore.

Because he wasn't even sure who the hell he *was* anymore.

"Drew." He felt James's hand on his arm. "You okay?"

No.

But he stuffed the silent answer down as quickly as it had bubbled up. "I'm good." He'd been raised never to lie, but over and over during the past year that was exactly what he'd been doing. Again and again until it should have gotten easier just to keep telling those lies. Instead, though, it had only gotten harder.

Ashley, he thought as he quickened his pace down the hall. He wanted to see her. He *needed* to see her. Today she'd made everything matter again, at least for a little while. Just knowing she'd be there in the meet-and-greet room made his heart beat a little faster.

As soon as he pushed through the doors, he sought her out. The screams of the fans he was about to meet barely pierced through as he scanned the room and found her standing in the corner with Max. He smiled at her, and she looked surprised for a moment before smiling back. And mouthing, *You were great tonight.*

The answering grin on his face was a real one. And it felt good. So good that when he turned to his fans, he barely felt like he was faking being *Drew Morrison.*

CHAPTER SEVEN

During the meet-and-greet, Ashley watched and learned and took notes on her tablet. Drew had never met anyone so focused on her purpose, and it only served to make her more attractive.

Clearly, he wasn't the only one who thought so, because the venue manager wouldn't stop interrupting her. Every time Drew looked in her direction, the guy was trying to get her attention. With a drink. Or a joke. Couldn't he see that she was working? And why the hell wasn't Max or James squashing the guy like a bug?

If she had looked at all irritated, Drew would have been over there in a millisecond with the guy pinned against the wall begging for mercy. But she wasn't frowning. On the contrary, she was actually smiling a little, even laughing softly at one point.

Jealousy ate at Drew, taking big chunks of him in its jaws and grinding him into pieces. More distracted than ever, he barely stopped one of his more mature fans from yanking off her shirt in front of an eight-year-old girl. In fact, the woman already had her top more than halfway off when Ashley grabbed the little girl's attention by asking if she wanted to put on a concert T-shirt and take a selfie with him.

Drew gestured for James to come deal with the woman, who had no business exposing herself in front of a kid, then turned and gave his full attention to the little girl. Afterward, he went to thank Ashley, but she was back in her corner where the venue manager had clearly been waiting for her so that he could hit on her some more.

Finally, he finished meeting his last VIP fan and headed over to her. Just in time to hear the guy say, "This has been a lot of fun, Ashley. Any chance I can get your number for the next time you're in town?"

Before she could reply, Drew said, "You ready to head to the bus, Ash?"

Her surprised gaze shifted to Drew. He'd called her Ash out in the desert when he'd been talking about all the fire she had inside and how well it fit her. But tonight he'd deliberately said it in the most possessive way possible.

The venue manager put up his hands and took a step away from her. "Sorry, man. I didn't realize she was taken." In a really polite tone, he added, "Great show tonight, Drew. It will be our pleasure to have you back soon." And then he was gone.

Ashley was frowning as she walked out of the room with Drew. A couple of minutes later they were back on the bus, James had wished them both a good night, and Drew had given Max the all-clear to head for Los Angeles.

"Taken? Did he actually think that you and I are..." Ashley shook her head as if the final word was too preposterous to even say aloud. "Together?"

"I'm pretty sure he did." Drew knew he should probably feel a little guilty for helping the guy's assumption along, but he didn't. Not in the least. Not when that guy wasn't good enough to touch even one hair on her head.

"Wait...does *everyone* think that you and I are together?"

"Maybe the guys at the airport did. And I fielded some questions at the radio stations about you." And there had been more than a little speculation online that must have been put up there by the fans he'd met that morning. But he didn't think Ashley needed to know about what people posted on the Internet. Hell, none of them did. "But the guys in the band and the crew know you aren't." Even so, he would place bets on the fact that most of them didn't really believe Drew wasn't going to sleep with her soon. Probably because only a total idiot would keep his distance from a woman like her.

"I suppose there aren't a lot of researchers sharing tour buses with musicians, are there?"

"No, there aren't."

He knew he should stop there. Should call it a night. Should turn and walk away and lock himself in his bedroom. Should put enough space between them that he could remember why he needed to make sure they never became anything more than friends.

But he couldn't do it, couldn't lie to her anymore the way he'd been lying to everyone else.

"They're not totally wrong, Ash. Not about how much I want to kiss you."

If she'd looked surprised by the realization that people thought they were together, now she looked as though someone had just told her the earth had been scientifically proven to be flat.

"Excuse me?"

It was the last response he would ever have expected. And yet, at the same time, it was exactly the right one. Because Ashley wasn't like anyone else. And just because he'd told her he wanted to kiss her, didn't mean she'd jump into his arms like all the women at his show tonight would have.

Instead, she'd do what he already understood was her way of dealing with everything she wanted to understand better—she'd try to dissect and analyze what was actually going on.

Only, he didn't want to let her dissect anything at all when it came to them. He wanted her to *feel* it, to be as overwhelmed by it as he was already.

"I want to kiss you." He knew he should be putting more space between them, rather than closing it by taking a step closer, but where Ashley was concerned, his rational brain was always a step behind. "I've wanted to kiss you from the first moment we met. And I've wanted to kiss you dozens of times in the past twenty-four hours. I know I'm probably totally freaking you out, and I swear I'm not trying to scare you away. I'm trying like hell to keep my promise to be a complete gentleman with you. I just can't lie to you about what I'm feeling."

She didn't say anything for several long seconds until, finally, she said, "I don't want you to feel like you have to lie. Not to me."

"I can't. I won't."

He watched a play of thoughts cross her face, thoughts that shifted from the surprise she'd initially felt, to processing, and then, finally, to a point where it seemed that she was warring with herself.

"I want to be honest with you, too, but I don't..." She paused, licked her lips, and he had to shove his hands deep into his pockets to keep from reaching for her. "I don't have much experience with this kind of thing." Finally, she lifted her gaze to his and held it. "I've been wanting to kiss you, too."

If she were any other woman, he would have been kissing her already. He would have known how sweet she tasted. Would have finally gotten to hear— and drink in—her sweet gasps of pleasure.

Instead, it nearly killed him to say, "But we can't."

At the *exact* same moment that she said, "But we can't."

Perhaps their words echoing off each other's should have broken the tension between them, but it didn't. Not even close. Not when they both obviously still wanted the kiss just as much.

"My father—"

"—would kill me if I so much as touched one hair on your head."

"It's not you," she said, as if she needed him to know that it wasn't personal. "It's what you do. He doesn't think this is a very stable business. And he thinks that—" Her face flushed, and she didn't finish her sentence.

But he could easily finish it for her. "He thinks all musicians sleep around."

When she nodded, he realized he already needed to face the first test of *always honest*. A first test he wasn't particularly proud of.

"I wasn't the worst," he said slowly, "but I wasn't the best either. Not at first." Not when he'd been young and stupid enough to want to take advantage of the fact that there were no limits. That absolutely everything he wanted could be his without having to try for it. "But I didn't act that way for long." Not when waking up next to one stranger after another had come up empty so quickly. And not when his parents had raised him better than that. They'd clearly known that he was sowing some wild oats, and they'd never come down on him for it, but he'd known they hadn't been thrilled.

"You don't have to explain things to me."

But he did. Because he wanted her to respect him the way he respected her. "I want to. No lies, remember?"

She nodded. "No lies." She took a deep breath, one that he knew was going to precede an admission of her own. "First of all, the truth is that my father isn't the only one who assumed there was a stereotype of what a rock star's life is like. How they think and act. But even though I haven't known you that long, I don't think you fit the stereotype at all. And also..." She scrunched up her face as if she really didn't want to tell him anything more. "I was a huge fan of yours. In high school. Way back to when you put out your first demo. And I—" She was really flushing now, her eyes squeezing shut for a second before she said, "I've had a crush on you for just as long."

When she opened her eyes, she was looking at him in that wary way he'd noticed she often looked at things. As if she didn't yet know enough about them, hadn't done enough analysis, to be totally sure that she could trust them to turn out okay.

Neither of them said anything for a while. They both just stared at each other as attraction pulsed hotter and higher than ever. She was clasping her hands so tightly in front of her that her knuckles were white as she finally said, "This isn't going to be easy, is it?"

"No." There was no other answer, no way to get around the truth. "It isn't."

She bit her lip. "Maybe I shouldn't stay."

"No." The single word came out borderline panicked. "I need you to stay. Not just because I want you. But because I feel like I can talk to you. Really talk in a way I haven't been able to in a long time."

"I feel the same way with you."

"Good." Relief was washing over him in a major way. "Then you'll stay."

"This has been the best twenty-four hours of my life. I don't want to go. But..." She bit her lip again, and he nearly lost it at the sight of the soft, wet flesh moving between her teeth. Flesh he wanted against his mouth, between *his* teeth. "Maybe I should move to one of the other buses."

"No." It seemed to be the only thing he could say to her tonight. The only thing he could say to *himself.* "The guy tonight at the venue who asked you out—he's only the tip of the iceberg. I know it isn't fair when we can't be together, but I can't stand the thought of you with anyone else."

"I don't want anyone else, Drew."

That nearly did it, nearly snapped the final thread of his self-control. "I don't either."

She started moving toward him, her hands coming apart to reach for him, and he knew that if she touched him, he wouldn't stop her. Wouldn't stop himself. Even if it meant that both of them would break their promise to her father.

But then, at the last second, she stopped. Inhaled a shaky breath. And said, "I had an idea about the VIP room. If it's okay to share it with you."

She was right to change the subject. To talk about the business she'd come here to learn rather than the fact that they wanted to jump each other. Nonetheless, the thought of moving away from her was physically painful. But he had to do it. And he also had to shift his focus away from kissing her beautiful lips to the intelligent idea he was certain was going to come out of them.

"Of course I want to hear your idea. Tell me what it is."

"That first night when the woman took off her shirt, even though it was pretty shocking, I just figured that was how things were after your shows. But then, tonight, when that little girl was there with her mom...honestly, it totally freaked me out that she'd see another woman behaving like that."

"It wasn't how things used to be after my shows. Lately, things have been getting more and more out of hand." And he'd been letting them go, because he'd been distracted. As if he were watching everything happen from a distance, even while trying to fight his way back to the front lines. Trying and failing. "We really need to screen people before they get into the VIP room."

But how were they going to do that? Make his fans all fill out a questionnaire? *Are you planning to*

*strip off your clothes so that Drew can sign a naked
body part? If so, please step into line B.*

As though she could read his mind, she said, "I
don't know how you could do that, exactly. Especially
because I'm not even sure most of those women are
planning to do anything. They just see you and get
excited." She flushed as though she understood that
excitement, and he loved seeing it despite knowing
neither of them could do anything about it. "But maybe
you could just divide your VIP area so that there's a
special area for kids. Anyone under eighteen can go in
one section so you know for sure they won't see
anything they shouldn't."

"That's a really good idea." Then, only adults
would be ambushed by naked breasts they hadn't asked
to see. "I should have been quicker tonight. If it hadn't
been for you saving the day, that girl would have gotten
an eyeful."

"I'm still trying to get over the eyeful I got that
first night," she said with a laugh.

"Me, too," he agreed, not expecting her to stop
laughing after he said it.

"You didn't like seeing the woman's boobs
either?"

"No." Again with his word of the night. "I
mean, I'm a red-blooded guy and all, but I'm not averse
to a little foreplay," he said teasingly.

Her skin flushed at the word *foreplay*, and just
that quickly, the air in the bus heated up again, sparkles
of electricity bouncing back and forth between them.

Talk about foreplay. Ever since she'd joined his
tour, the attraction had been building up like crazy. If
they were to kiss now, it would be explosive. And he
wouldn't be able to stop with just a kiss. He'd need to

have all of her. Again and again and again, until he'd memorized the taste of her soft skin, the swell of each beautiful curve, the sounds of her pleasure as she gasped her bliss into his ear and begged for more.

"I feel like such a sexist jerk for thinking it wouldn't bother you, too," she said, breaking him out of his desperate imaginings. "You don't know those women. I was just making dumb assumptions based on the fact that you're a guy. No matter what my dad says, clearly all men *aren't* pigs." He could see her brain moving, working, reconfiguring her thoughts into a new pattern. "James, or one of the local security staff he's brought in for the night, could lay down the rules to the adult VIP room after your show. Clothes on. Hands off. And there could be zero tolerance for people going too far. They can say it's a security thing, if you're worried about hurting anyone's feelings. But the fact is that you're too popular now not to have those kinds of rules set up."

He never wanted to upset his fans, but things had been spiraling more and more out of control for a while now. Because he was surrounded by an all-male crew, they'd probably figured he was okay with it, too. It had taken a woman's touch—a brilliant woman's touch—to make a change for the better.

Mom would have loved you, he found himself thinking.

"How about we both talk to James about it tomorrow?" he suggested.

She looked surprised that he would ask her to be a part of the meeting with his head of security, even though it was her idea. "Sure, if you think it's a good idea."

"It's a great idea."

"Thanks. Any other ideas you have, tell me, okay? Like I said, after doing so many shows, we kind of end up on autopilot here. But it doesn't mean we can't do things better."

"Okay, thanks."

"And about the rest of our talk tonight...even though I want to kiss you even *more* now than I did before, I'm going to try really, really hard to keep my promise to your father."

She swallowed hard, her gaze dropping longingly to his mouth for a split second before she looked back into his eyes. "Me, too. Really, really hard."

Sweet Lord, if he didn't get out of there in the next ten seconds, all bets would be off. "Good night, Ash."

"Good night, Drew."

He knew just how this would play out tonight, had already lived through the impossibility of trying to sleep in his bedroom while she moved and breathed and just simply *existed* in the other part of the bus. But tonight, he was surprised to realize things were different.

He still wanted her just as much as he had last night. A hell of a lot more, actually. But tonight, he found himself reaching for his notebook, the one he used to write lyrics in. The one that used to be full of good ideas instead of the crap he'd been scribbling in it for the past year.

He pictured Ashley in the middle of the desert with the sun shining down on her hair and skin, lifting her face to the pleasure of it. He felt the warmth of her arms around him, the sweet pressure of her cheek against his chest. And for the first time in a really long time, he felt as though his heart was actually starting to beat again as he put pen to paper and began to write. None of it was any good, but he figured even *wanting* to write something again had to be a change for the better.

CHAPTER EIGHT

Los Angeles, California

Ashley had been to Los Angeles before. She'd even been in the Chief Records headquarters for an afternoon, during a summer course she'd taken on the music business at the University of Southern California between her junior and senior years of college.

But it was one thing to walk in as a college student dreaming of one day working for the biggest music label in the world...and it was another entirely to walk in with Drew Morrison.

It seemed like every single person in the building came out of offices and cubicles to say hello to him. To fawn over him. To compliment him. To see if he needed a soda or a snack or a bottle of beer or something stronger—anything at all. And by the time they made it to the corner office where Drew had a meeting set up with the head A&R guy who had discovered him and the president of the label, Drew had introduced her to everyone. He'd also made sure to tell them all how smart she was, and how happy he was to have her working with him on his tour.

Working with him? That was stretching things big-time, even if she'd had that one good idea about how to reorganize his meet-and-greet room after they'd been talking about wanting to—and not being able to— kiss each other.

She could still hardly believe the things he'd said to her and that she'd said back to him. The very last thing in the world she'd expected him to say was that he wanted to kiss her. Honestly, she was still stunned by it twelve hours later. Not just that, but that he'd wanted to kiss her from the first moment he'd set eyes on her.

Oh. My. God.

Ashley didn't have much experience with the opposite sex. In high school, between the glasses and the braces—and the fact that she spent nearly all of her free time in the library reading with her headphones on—she hadn't exactly been asked out on a lot of dates. And by *not a lot*, she meant *none*. No dates, no kisses, not even the senior prom.

College had been a little different. The braces had come off, and she'd switched over to contacts during the day, at least. She'd gone out on a few dates, made out with a few guys, even fooled around a little. She was still a virgin, of course, but at least she wasn't totally untouched.

Only, when it came to a man like Drew? She felt as pure as the driven snow.

But even crazier than what they'd said to each other last night was that the more they talked about not being able to kiss, the more desperately she wanted to do it.

Just one kiss.

Just so that she'd know if it was as good as she'd fantasized it would be for the past half-dozen years.

What would that hurt, really? Her father wouldn't need to know about one teeny, tiny little kiss. And it wasn't like she was going to end up dating Drew and become his rock 'n' roll lady.

Besides, if anything, it would just relieve the attraction building up between her and Drew, right? You know, so that both of them could stop turning the kiss into something bigger than it needed to be.

The more she went over it in her head, the more sense it made. They should kiss. Just *once*. Just to get it out of their systems. Just so they could move on and be sensible again. Because surely that's what would happen if they kissed. He'd realize he'd been building things up for no reason, and she'd remember that he was *way* out of her league. As far as a guy could be.

A large man in a dark suit with a booming voice broke her out of her thoughts. "Drew Morrison, live and in the flesh."

"Robert." Drew shook his hand. "It's good to see you."

Drew was as charming and friendly as always, but today he didn't seem quite as full of his easy smiles as usual. This morning, as he'd devoured yet another plate of eggs and toast, he'd simply said, "I've got to go in and see my label. We'll see if we can make you some good connections, okay?"

She'd been so worried about things being awkward between them when they woke up that even though he'd had the look of someone heading in for a dreaded dentist's appointment, she hadn't asked him what was wrong. Now, she wished she'd been able to shake off her own insecurities to check in with him.

In the desert, he'd said a couple of things about how his label hadn't totally understood what he was doing with a few elements of his last album. But was there more than that going on?

"Drew, we're so glad you could stop in today." This second man was as thin as the other man was large. His suit was light gray and tapered down at the ankles so that his pants looked more like leggings than wool slacks. And he was either a lifelong smoker, or he'd spent too much time yelling in loud venues. She made a calculated guess that he was Drew's A&R guy, the Chief Records employee responsible for discovering his talent and bringing him in to sign with the record label.

Drew gave him a one-armed hug. Drawing back, he put his hand in the small of Ashley's back so that she'd move forward into the group, and her entire body immediately heated up, head to toe. "Robert, Ansel, this is Ashley Emmit. She's a friend of mine who's joined the tour to get an insider's view of the music business before she heads off to Stanford Business School."

"The Biz School," Robert said. "Very impressive."

It was on the tip of her tongue to say that she hadn't actually been accepted yet, but before she had a chance to respond, Robert turned back to Drew and said, "Come on into my office and we'll chat."

Inside the large room, there were another half-dozen men who all said hello to Drew, who then introduced her to them the way he had everyone else at the label. She'd put on her one dress, a simple white sundress, for today's meeting, and she could see how much she stuck out amongst the sea of dark suits. In fact, as far as she'd seen, apart from a few administrative staff, all of the employees at the label were male.

Which was funny, considering that well over fifty percent of the people listening to Drew's music were female. Shouldn't at least one person with an X chromosome be weighing in along with all the men?

"Your numbers are through the roof, Drew." The label's president got comfortable in his big leather chair as she and Drew sat on a big leather couch. "We've already talked with Peter to let him know how pleased we are."

Drew's manager, Peter Hemsworth, was president and founder of a high-profile music management company. He managed a dozen top artists and was based out of London, which was why he wasn't here with them today. Drew hadn't said much about Peter to her, just that he liked the guy and appreciated being left alone for the most part rather than micromanaged. Still, she wondered if Peter should at least be on the phone with them during this meeting. After all, Drew wasn't exactly a small-time client.

"We also let him know we're looking forward to finally hearing those new songs you've been promising us. And for you to get back to us with your thoughts on the contract that we sent over a while back for the second album."

"I got Peter's email this morning," Drew said. His words still sounded pretty relaxed, but Ashley had spent enough time with him to notice the way his expression tightened down a bit at the corners of his eyes and mouth.

"The market is primed for a new Drew Morrison album. Social media is going crazy for you. The girls can't get enough. You've done us proud, Drew. Real proud."

Was it weird, she wondered, to hear himself talked about like that? As *Drew Morrison.* But she already knew the answer—it had to be weird.

"Thanks," was all Drew said in response.

"So," Ansel said into the continued silence, "have you brought any songs in for us on a flash drive? Or maybe you'll feel more comfortable playing one of the guitars in my office?"

Instead of answering either Robert or Ansel, Drew looked at Ashley. She wished she knew what he needed from her, because she could see that he was struggling with something. She wanted to reach for his hand, but it seemed so terribly inappropriate inside the office. She gave him a small smile instead. One she hoped he could read as: *Whatever you do, I'm totally behind you.*

After another few seconds, he turned back to the men in suits. "I have one new song I could play for you."

"Great!" Robert clapped his hands as if he were a king on his music business throne about to hear from the jester brought in to entertain him. Ansel's guitar was soon in Drew's hands, and then he began the first few notes of "One More Time."

Ashley had cried buckets both nights he'd played it on stage, and it wouldn't matter that she was surrounded by the music industry executives that she'd always hoped to work with—she knew she wouldn't be able to keep from crying today either. At first Drew kept his gaze trained on the sound hole in his guitar as he played, but when she sniffled just a little too loudly, he looked up...and played the rest of the song looking straight at her. It felt like a concert for one. And it was the most breathtakingly beautiful thing that had ever happened to her.

She honestly forgot all about the other people in the room while he played, but once he got to the end of the song, that final line that absolutely destroyed her every single time—*I wish I could see you one more time*—she was shocked to realize that no one else in the room was crying. Okay, so a couple of the executives' eyes were glassy, but none of them had become a blubbering mess.

Ansel leaned forward. "That song—it's great, Drew. Real moving. But all those hits on your first album—those are what your fans are going to be expecting you to hit them with again. More fun, sexy songs." He held up his hands. "Don't get us wrong, we don't want to stifle your creativity."

She waited for Drew to say something, to defend his musical path, wherever it took him. Instead, he sat silently, a muscle jumping in his jaw. Suddenly, she realized that *this* was why he hadn't been excited about coming here today. He wasn't writing new songs at the pace Chief Records was expecting. And the one new song he had written, the label guys clearly didn't like.

But she did. She *loved* it. And so did his fans. She'd seen it for herself.

The problem was, any response Drew made at this point would only end up sounding defensive—and they'd clearly set up the power structure so that he would be on the wrong foot unless he did anything but kowtow to their demands. Oh sure, Ansel had smiled as he said it, but it was clear that they were still demanding a certain kind of song from Drew.

"Have any of you seen the way his fans react when he plays 'One More Time' live?"

Everyone in the room turned to her in surprise—as though they'd forgotten she was there. Or maybe they were still rolling their eyes at the way she'd sobbed while Drew played. Normally, she would have felt a little embarrassed to be the center of attention, especially when no one had actually asked her to speak up, but she couldn't stand to see them all pile on Drew like this. Even if they were couching the pile-up in compliments about how great he was.

"Drew's hits, they're all amazing, and you're right that people love to dance and sing to them. But they also love being touched by something that goes so deep. There's no one who doesn't understand how painful it is to lose someone you love. And, honestly, it's after they're wiping away their tears that his fans all really come together. It's after 'One More Time' that they vow to be his fans for *life*."

Everyone was looking at her as though she'd sprouted a second head—all but Drew, whose expression she couldn't read—and she knew she needed to try a different tack. Either that or just stop talking, but she figured it was too late now to backtrack. Besides, she didn't *want* to backtrack. She wanted to stand up for Drew's right to be whatever kind of artist he wanted to be!

"During the past two days, since Drew played 'One More Time' for the first time, it is the song everyone is talking about. Literally thousands of people have been posting about it. Clips of the song. Selfies of themselves crying as they listen to it. They're telling their own stories of loss and heartbreak. And they're whipping everyone who hasn't heard the song into a frenzy of anticipation, telling them that seeing Drew play it live will be one of the best experiences of their lives."

"Really?" Finally, Robert looked interested.

"Yes, really." At that point, she'd already stepped so far over the boundary that she didn't hesitate to offer, "I'd be happy to pull together a report on it for you if you'd like."

"Ashley, is it?" When she nodded, he said, "A report would be excellent. In fact, it makes me wonder why my own social media team isn't already doing something similar." He shot a none-too-pleased look at the men in the room.

"We've been busy working on other campaigns," one man said, before quickly adding, "but we will certainly look into this phenomenon Drew's girlfriend has reported seeing."

Her eyebrows went up at *girlfriend*, but she knew right now wasn't the time to correct anyone's assumptions. Not when what mattered most was that Drew should love the music he was making and not feel pressured to paint with primary colors.

"Ashley is right about my fans loving the song. And she's right about a hell of a lot more than that." Drew's voice was low. Firm. As if he dared anyone else from the label to so much as doubt another word out of her mouth. He looked at Robert and Ansel. "I'll look over the contract and let you know my thoughts." Drew stood, then reached out to help Ashley up. "Ready for a bunch more meetings?"

She still couldn't quite read his expression as she nodded. "Meetings are my wheelhouse."

That got a small quirk of the lips out of him, one that she hoped meant he wasn't upset with her for taking over the meeting. Because, truthfully, she couldn't stand the thought of upsetting him.

Especially when all she wanted to do was help.

CHAPTER NINE

Oh man, was Drew not kidding about the meetings. Even Ashley was hitting the wall by the time they met with the Chief Records online team six hours later, despite the sandwiches and bowls of candy and sodas brought in to try to keep everyone from fading.

She was amazed that Drew didn't show one ounce of fatigue. On the contrary, after the difficult first meeting, he took the lead in each subsequent one. He clearly knew exactly what he wanted from each department—how the sales and marketing team should support each overseas market and what the newest online tools were that the social media team should be incorporating into their plans going forward.

She'd admitted to Drew last night that she'd come into the tour with preconceived notions of what a rock star was like. And if she hadn't already realized just how wrong she'd been, today's meetings would have done it. Because while it certainly helped that

Drew had a large team and a powerful record label behind him, the truth was that *he* was leading the charge for his own career, rather than following what other people were telling him to do. Three days with Drew and she'd already learned more than she had from years of reading case studies about the music business.

It was yet one more thing that she hadn't truly understood from all the books she'd read about the music industry—how incredibly difficult it could be to try to strike a balance between art and commerce.

Just as difficult as the balance she was trying to figure out between her growing admiration for and attraction to Drew...and her pragmatic knowledge that, in the long run, the two of them were a terrible match. Because if the thought of sharing one kiss with him was already stretching the boundaries, then the idea of someone like her actually dating Drew Morrison was *beyond* laughable.

People who were as different as they were—the artist versus the pragmatist—were only ever destined to rub each other the wrong way. Sure, there had been attraction and passion between her parents. But that attraction and passion hadn't been nearly enough to sustain their love. In fact, if anything, those emotions had been their downfall. Because if there hadn't been that spark between them in the first place, her parents would never have leapt into such an unsuitable partnership. For fifteen years Charlie and Camila Emmit had lived a roller coaster of either fighting or freezing each other out. And it had been a horrible ride for all of them, Ashley included.

At long last, the final meeting ended, and they stood up to shake everyone's hands again and say good-bye. Ever since they'd stepped out of the president's office that morning, she had been hoping for five minutes alone with Drew so that they could talk about what she'd said in that meeting. Even sixty seconds would have been enough for her to ask him if he was upset with her for sticking her opinions into the mix.

So when the last Chief Records employee had stepped out of the room, she said, "Drew, I just want to make sure that what happened—"

Unfortunately, Ansel walked in and cut her off in midsentence. "I know we're running you ragged today, Drew, but we've got to get you into the studio down the street for several important interviews. Ashley," he said, turning to her, "Robert's assistant would like to get your contact information if you could head back upstairs. You impressed the boss today, something that I can tell you isn't easy to do."

Last week, impressing the president of Chief Records had been Ashley's number one goal. But now? All she wanted was to make sure that she and Drew were still okay.

"You should go ahead and chat with Jeannie." Drew smiled at her, but it didn't quite seem to reach his eyes. "I'll ask Max to come pick you up to take you back to the bus. I know this pace can be crazy if you're not used to it. You should get some rest."

"Okay." She'd been with him all day. Of course he'd want some breathing room. And if he thought she needed some rest, she must look really bad. Likely with big black circles under her eyes.

An incredibly beautiful woman walked into the room just then, and when she crooned Drew's name and wrapped her arms around him as if they were long-lost friends, Ashley quietly slipped out of the room. Maybe closing her eyes and blocking out the world for a few hours wasn't such a bad idea after all.

* * *

Ashley never usually napped, but then again, she wasn't exactly used to waking up at five a.m. every day after going to bed at midnight. After meeting with Robert's assistant, Max had taken her back to the bus, where she'd planned on closing her eyes for only a few seconds before fleshing out her notes from all the meetings today. But the next thing she knew, the clock on the microwave read nine o'clock. Which meant the local opening band was through with their set and Drew would be going on soon.

She sat up so fast that she hit her head on the wood slats of the empty bunk above hers. She was rubbing her head when she finally saw the note he'd left for her. Which meant he'd come onto the bus and seen her drooling facedown into her pillow.

Ashley,
If you want to check out tonight's show after you wake up, just text Max and he'll bring you backstage. It's a big crowd tonight and I'd feel better knowing you're close by.
Drew

It was so tempting to read more into his note than there really was, to tell herself that *I'd feel better knowing you're close by* meant more than simple concern for the safety of anyone on his crew attending a show in a 20,000-person venue.

But she wouldn't let herself do it. Nope, she thought as she scooted out of her bunk, from this moment forward she'd force herself to be all about business. She'd refocus on her plan to get into the Stanford graduate program and stop thinking about kissing Drew.

Of course, that didn't mean she shouldn't change out of her terribly wrinkled dress. And maybe put on a little mascara and lip gloss. After all, just in case anyone she'd met at the label was there tonight, she wanted to keep making a good impression. On them, not Drew. Especially since he was unlikely to get the image of her drooling and snoring out of his mind anytime soon...

Fifteen minutes later, feeling slightly more presentable, she texted Max to let him know she was ready to head over to the venue. Seconds later, he knocked on the door and gave her a big smile when she opened it for him.

"Have a good nap?"

"I can't normally sleep during the day, but I must have really needed that." As they headed through the venue's huge back lot and through a big steel door, she asked, "How do you all do it? The pace is so intense."

"For us guys on the crew, it's no big deal. We can rest when we need it. Drew's the one who's going pretty much twenty-four seven. I've talked to him about slowing down—we all have—but he says he likes to stay busy. Especially since..." Max shook his head. "Nothing's been the same since his mom got sick. That was one great lady. And an amazing mother. You never saw anyone prouder of her children." He paused, and with a frown he said, "Even before that, though, Drew was starting to look a little caged in, if you know what I mean. Speaking of cages, I heard you were fierce in the meetings with the label today."

"Fierce?" She was hardly able to believe that anyone would have used that word to describe her. "I just wanted the people from Chief Records to understand how powerful Drew's new song is and how much his fans love it."

"You're a good one, Miss Ashley. Sounds like he really needed someone in his corner today, even more than he usually does when he's dealing with those label guys. They put on a ton of pressure at the best of times, but at the worst of times?" He scowled. "That kind of pressure can break a man when he's already busting his ass on a tour that's lasted years by now." But then he brightened as he told her, "Drew also wanted you to know that they've separated out the meet-and-greet rooms for after the show, just like you suggested."

Even though she was pleased that they'd run with her idea, the lump in Ashley's throat grew even bigger. Clearly, Max thought Drew was running himself ragged in an effort to have no leftover energy to think about losing his mom. From what she'd seen so far on this tour—and from what Drew had told her—she wondered if Max was right. And what about his belief that Drew was feeling caged in by his label and their expectations about writing more "fun and sexy" songs?

There were so many things she wanted to talk about with Drew. Not just about what had happened in the morning meeting, but also about why he hadn't been writing new songs, apart from "One More Time." In the interviews she'd read over the years, it had always sounded like songwriting was a totally natural part of his life, unlike some other artists who really struggled over creating new music. But was that not true for him anymore? And if so, had it started even before his mom got sick?

Just minutes ago, she'd sworn to be all about business from here on out. And yet, she knew better, didn't she? Because after everything they'd said to each other in the desert, and then in the bus later that night, Ashley felt she knew Drew better than any of those people at the label today. They liked him, of course, and admired him. Not to mention the way several of the women—and men—had been drooling over him. But he hadn't bared his soul to any of them...and they hadn't bared theirs right back.

Her heart was racing like crazy by the time she and Max made it to the side of the stage. She needed to see Drew again, needed just five seconds with him. The crowd was chanting Drew's name when she suddenly heard her own. She turned to see Ansel walking toward her and tried not to betray her disappointment.

"How were the interviews?" she asked him.

"Great. Drew had them all eating out of his hand."

Something about the way the A&R guy spoke about Drew grated. As if he thought Drew had simply been reading from a brilliant script they'd written together.

But then, a moment later, she felt fingers brush lightly over hers. This time, she didn't need to look to her side to know who it was. No one else's touch affected her like this.

Only Drew's.

Ansel was saying something to him about killing it tonight, but Drew was looking only at her while he stroked his thumb across her palm in a way that made her shiver despite the warmth of the crowded area where they were standing.

It was the smallest, quickest caress in the world, one that no one else could have spotted in the darkness behind the thick curtain that separated the backstage area from the bright stage lights. And just as she couldn't help but want to read meaning into the note he'd left her while she was sleeping, now she couldn't stop herself from doing the exact same thing as the skin on her palm continued to tingle even after he walked on stage to begin his set.

* * *

Most nights Drew talked to the audience between songs. Tonight, he had only the words from his songs. Fortunately, his band was adept at following his nonverbal cues by now and kept up with his pace no problem.

He wasn't planning to play "One More Time," honestly just didn't feel like he could bear the weight of it tonight. Especially not after the way the label execs had pretty much given him a polite golf clap after he'd played it in the office today.

But it turned out that telling himself he wouldn't play the song wasn't much different from telling himself not to keep looking over at Ashley in the wings throughout the show. She didn't smile when he looked, didn't give him a thumbs-up either. She simply watched him play with those big, beautiful eyes.

And she *cared.*

She'd shown him again and again just how much emotion, how much passion she was capable of. Which was exactly why he'd had to shut her down halfway through the morning during his meetings at the label. Because just as his new song affected him too deeply, so did she. And when a guy was barely holding himself together...

Before he realized it, his fingers were playing the first chords of "One More Time" and his band was stepping back. The crowd went crazy...but every word he sang, every note was for Ashley.

He left the stage after that song, just walked off with his guitar, and stopped in front of her. There were tears running down her cheeks, and he reached out to brush them away the way he'd so badly wanted to during the meeting that morning. "I've got to head back to the meet-and-greet room. But do you want to get out of here after that? Head down to the beach, just you and me?"

When she nodded, he almost felt like he could breathe again.

He knew Ansel and the rest of the Chief Records employees who had come to the show tonight would be expecting him to party with them, but he couldn't do it. Not tonight. "Max, can you tell the label reps to go ahead without me and that I'll swing by if there's a chance I can make it later? And whatever you do, don't mention anything to them about a beach."

"I wouldn't dream of it," Max said with a smile. "In fact, I'll let them know you've got a busy schedule tomorrow and are probably going to need your rest after the nonstop day you had in their offices."

Drew wanted to take Ashley's hand as they headed down the hall to the meet-and-greet rooms, wanted so much more than just that slight brush of his fingertips against hers before he'd walked on stage. But he knew that one touch wouldn't be enough, just as the earlier one hadn't been. If he held her hand, he'd want to hold all of her.

"Drew," she said in a soft voice, "about what happened this morning at the label—"

"I can't talk about that now."

She flinched, and he cursed aloud. Damn it, he hadn't meant for it to come out so sharply. He just didn't have much control right now. Not on any front. Not when everything inside his head, his heart, felt like it was spinning out.

He stopped walking and reached out to take her hands. "I'm sorry. I'm being an asshole."

"You're not."

"I am." He nearly cursed again. "See, I'm doing it again." He made himself pause to try to get his shit at least a little bit together before saying, "I've just got to make it through the meet and greet. And then we can get out of here, get away from all this, and talk about what happened this morning or anything else you need to talk about."

But even as he said it, he knew *he* was the one who needed to talk. To confess. And to face up to all the things he'd been trying so damned hard to hide from for so long. For longer even than before his mother had become so sick.

"That sounds great."

He should have let go of her hands then. Should have headed into the first meet-and-greet room where everyone was waiting for him. But just as he'd known would happen, he couldn't bring himself to let go of her. "You don't have to do this, Ash."

She didn't ask what he meant. Instead, she answered in a way that told him she didn't need to. "You were there for me when I needed you. Now I want to be here for you."

He wanted to ask what she meant—how had he ever been there for her? She was the one who had held him while he cried over his mother in the desert.

But before he could, James opened the door to the room full of fans, and the young girls inside saw him and started jumping up and down and calling out his name.

CHAPTER TEN

An hour and a half later, Drew paid the taxi driver and stepped out with Ashley's hand in his. They hadn't spoken during the drive, but just being with her was enough. He'd made sure to put on his baseball cap before leaving the venue and had asked the driver to take them to a deserted stretch of beach that his friend Nicola Harding—Nicola Sullivan now—had told him about the last time he'd seen her. She'd scoped out lots of great places to get away while playing shows in big cities. Evidently, he wasn't the only one who needed to get off the bus and away from the crowds from time to time.

"I've always loved the sound of the ocean," Ashley said after taking a deep breath of the sea-salt air. "The way it's never the same beat, never the same rhythm, and yet I can always count on it to make everything better."

"Just like I can count on you." Still holding her hand, he stopped their progress across the sand. "Thank you—not just for what you said in Robert's office this morning, but for noticing the way fans have been reacting to the song in the first place."

"They all really do love it. And maybe one day," she added with a tiny quirk of her lips, "I'll figure out how to listen to it without crying the entire time."

He reached up to brush the thumb of his free hand over her cheek, right where her tears had been after the show. "Is it bad that I'll take any excuse to touch you?"

In the slight ebb of the ocean tide, he heard her breath hitch. "It doesn't feel bad."

Jesus, the urge to kiss her tore at his insides, it was so strong. But that wasn't why they were here. They were here because after this morning, he owed her the truth.

"Everyone says I'm living the dream," he began, then shook his head. "I hate to sound like I'm complaining."

She put her hand on his arm. "That's not what it sounds like."

"I know how lucky I am."

"Yes, you're lucky. But luck wouldn't get you where you are without talent and hard work. I've seen how much you do every day. It's not like you're lounging on the beach between shows." The little smile she gave him was so beautiful as she added, "Well, most of the time, anyway."

Maybe it was her smile, maybe it was the moonlight shining over her like a halo, or maybe it was just that he'd kept it all bottled up too long, but before he could stop himself, he was saying, "This morning, at my label, it was like you saw through the act I've been putting on for everyone. That's why I shut down on you afterward. Because I knew I was finally going to face the truth. I kept trying to tell myself that maybe I wouldn't have to face it if I just pushed you away instead. But you're the last person I ever want to push away."

She held his gaze, as fiercely strong and passionate as she'd been that morning with the executives. "What's the truth, Drew?"

His mom would have asked him that same question, just like that. No pauses. No trying to make it all easier.

"The truth is that I've always loved writing and playing songs. I never had to think about it, never had to try, it was just always there. I knew the sound I wanted to make and I made it. And it was great when I found out other people liked it, too. Liked it enough to come out and see me and download my demos online. When the label wanted to sign me, it was just another thing I didn't have to think about. But maybe I should have." Though she was frowning, she waited for him to continue his thought. He liked that about her, how she knew when to push and when to pause. "It's great most of the time, but sometimes...sometimes it's like being in a cage. A really nice one, with plush leather seating and a built-in coffee maker." He was glad when she smiled at that, and it made it easier to continue. "Back when my mom was alive, she would ask me, 'Are you happy?'"

"Are you?"

"Right now? Here with you?" He stroked her cheek again. "Yes. I'm happy."

When the pad of his thumb brushed over her lower lip, she closed her eyes for a moment, and he could feel the ragged breath she inhaled. But a moment later she was opening her eyes and asking, "What about tonight, on stage? Were you happy then?"

"I tried to be. I wanted to be." He pulled away, hating that he didn't know how to put words to it. "Those songs, my songs—like I said, I never had to think about them. They were just there and they felt right. But now... Now they don't feel totally right anymore."

"Only 'One More Time' does, doesn't it?"

"It shouldn't. It doesn't sound like the rest of my songs. Doesn't sound like anything the label wants. Doesn't sound like anything on the radio right now. Doesn't sound like what I'm sure Smith Sullivan wants me to do for his movie soundtrack. It's why I haven't written anything else." His hands were fisted now at his sides in frustration. In anger at himself for being so screwed up. "I don't know what the hell I'm doing anymore."

"Yes, you do. The one new song you've written is amazing. Yes, you break our hearts, but you're breaking them in the best possible way." She squeezed his hand tightly. "Do you want to know what I hear in your song?"

He was almost afraid to say yes, but he was done hiding out from the truth. At least this one. Because he knew he still needed to fight the incredible temptation to kiss her. "Tell me, Ash. I need to know what you hear."

"I hear the kid whose demos I downloaded from the Internet when I was fifteen. I hear the rock star whose music has taken over the world. And then, blended in perfectly with everything else, I hear the son who learned every folk song on the planet for his mother. Because she loved those songs and he loved her." He felt as though she was looking straight into his soul as she said, "Somewhere along the way, you fell in love with those songs, too, didn't you? With that sound?"

It was one of those rare moments when things suddenly became so clear you wondered why you hadn't seen it before.

"You're right. All those songs—I thought I was just learning them for her. But I wasn't, not after the first couple of days. I was like an addict, searching for the songs they only performed live in concert, the cuts that never made the albums."

"How could anyone walk away from a song like CSNY's 'Suite: Judy Blue Eyes' or Leonard Cohen's 'Hallelujah' and not be moved?" Ashley asked. "Not be changed? What those songs did for you once you started learning them for your mom is what your songs did for me when I was a teenager."

"Before we went into the meet-and-greet room tonight, Ash, you said I was there for you when you needed me. Is that what you meant? That my songs helped you?"

She was silent for a long moment. "I've never talked with anyone about this. And I certainly never thought I'd be talking to *you* about it."

"I don't want our friendship just to go one way. I want to know you. Hell, I'm dying to know more about you." When she still didn't say anything, and he could read the silent *Why?* in her eyes, he told her, "I feel a connection with you. Don't you feel it, too?"

"I do, but..."

"You just told me what you hear in my song. Do you want to know what I see whenever I'm with you?" His question clearly made her nervous, and when she dropped her gaze, he put his hand on her chin and tipped her face back up to his. "Beauty. Incredible beauty. I'm not going to lie and say that wasn't what struck me first. My jaw hit the floor the first time I set eyes on you."

"It did?"

"Of course it did. Every guy who looks at you has the same reaction."

"No," she said in a serious voice. "They don't. I would have noticed if they did."

"Are you sure about that?"

"Of course I'm sure. My mother is the beautiful one. I'm nothing like her, not in looks or personality."

He raised an eyebrow. "Or maybe you just haven't looked in enough mirrors lately. Maybe you're still seeing the cute girl you were and not the gorgeous woman you've become. Don't look so upset about it, Ash. It's not a bad thing to be beautiful."

"But I'm the brain. *Not* the beauty."

"Actually, you're both."

She looked hugely shocked. It wasn't too different from his own shock at realizing that the music he was hearing in his head was no longer just rock, but a blend of rock and folk.

Looked like all the things that had once seemed so black and white to both of them, weren't anymore.

"The first time we met, I was still so busy being knocked over by your beauty that when you started speaking, if my mind hadn't already been blown, it would have been then."

"Wait." Her frown was so deep now that he couldn't stop himself from reaching out to smooth it with his fingers. "How could hearing my voice have blown your mind?"

"Because I heard a melody in your voice that's haunted me ever since. I've tried to play it with my guitar, and on the piano, but I can't replicate the sound. Every time you speak, I hear that melody, Ash."

"You do?"

"Always. That's why I asked you to read my mother's letter. Because I needed to finally hear it put to music. Sometimes," he added with a little grin, "I want to ask you to talk just so that I can hear that melody again."

He was so damned glad when her lips tipped up at the corners. "I could read the phone book for you sometime, if you want."

He laughed, loving being with her. Everything that should have been so hard was just easier with her. And better. So much better. Which was why he needed her to know something else. "And then when I got to know you, I found out you're not just one of the smartest people I've ever met. I also learned that your brains don't come at the expense of your heart. You've got both, Ash, and that's rare."

He knew her well enough after three days to guess at what she was thinking: Could she trust him enough to answer his earlier question about how he'd been there for her when she'd needed him?

Finally, she said, "You already know what a fan of your music I've been since I was a teenager. But the truth is..." She took a deep breath before meeting his gaze. "Your songs saved me, Drew. I don't know what I would have done without them when my parents were splitting up and it felt like I was tearing in two, like no matter what I did or what I chose, I was letting someone down. I couldn't talk to anyone about what was going on, but even though you didn't know me, listening to your songs made me feel like you understood what I was going through. And that maybe everything was going to be okay in the end, if I didn't give up hope. You were my refuge, Drew. You and your music."

"Ash." He had to put his arms around her. Had to hold her. Had to try to make her feel better in any way he could. "I'm sorry they did that to you. Your parents should have known better than to tear at you like that when they were the ones having problems."

"I chose my dad." Her confession was barely louder than a whisper. "Mom wanted me to leave with her when I was fifteen, wanted us to move to Miami and start over. She promised me that it would be fun and exciting. But I'm not like her. I love her, but I've never been like her. I've never been fun and exciting like she is."

He knew he shouldn't interrupt her story, but he needed her to know, "Yes, you are. Beautiful. Passionate. Fun. Exciting. Brainy. Those are all words that fit you perfectly, Ash. Those and so many others that I've yet to discover, but I will."

She didn't say anything for several moments, simply stared at him as if she was trying to process what he'd just told her. "How can you see me so differently than everyone else does?"

"How can you *not* see yourself the way I do?"

It wasn't enough just to hold her. He'd known it wouldn't be, but he couldn't leave her standing there hurting. She'd needed his songs as a teenager, and now she needed *him.*

"Ash, I know we said we wouldn't—"

But he never even got the words out to ask her if they could break the rules, just this once, because the next thing he knew, her hands were on his jaw.

And she was kissing him.

CHAPTER ELEVEN

Drew Morrison's mouth was a miracle.

Ashley had been kissed before, of course, but *she'd* never made the first move. A part of her could still hardly believe that Drew's stubble was scratching against her palms and that his arms were around her waist as she pressed her lips to his.

She'd never expected anyone to say such wonderful things about her. And, honestly, she wasn't sure if she'd ever really believe they were all true. But knowing even one person on the planet felt that way about her had given her a boldness that she'd never known was there. Yet another adjective to add to the others: Beautiful. Passionate. Fun. Exciting. Brainy. Colorful. *Bold.*

He'd said he didn't know who he was anymore, but tonight, Ashley was the one who felt entirely different. All because of the man she was kissing.

For several long moments, their kiss remained sweet. Soft. Gentle. The barest brush of lips.

And then, on a groan—she honestly wasn't sure who broke first—their kiss shifted from gentle and sweet to pure, unfettered passion. She was overflowing with need, with desire, with the urge to give Drew everything she was. And, oh, how perfectly he took what she had to give, his tongue sliding against hers, his teeth nipping at her lower lip.

His hands curved down over her hips, and he lifted her so that she could wrap her legs around him. He growled her name against her mouth as he lowered them both to the sand.

She'd never felt like this before, had never known such heat. Or such hunger. Hunger that seemed to come from a boundless well inside of her that had been deeply hidden for far too long. A well that only Drew knew how to tap into.

He rained kisses across her cheeks, and when she arched her neck, she shivered at the shockingly delicious sensation of his teeth scraping across her sensitive skin. She threaded her hands into his hair as his tongue licked out over her collarbone, and then lower, over the upper swell of her breasts.

Pleasure whiplashed her at the feel of his hands on her hips dragging her against him, and his mouth on her bare skin—and destroyed any rational thoughts that might have tried to invade. All she knew was that she wanted *more.* More of his mouth and hands on her. And her own on him, too.

She didn't think, couldn't process anything apart from how much she wanted him as she pulled at his shirt. But when her hands found his bare stomach, muscles rippling beneath her fingertips, the shock of just how hot, just how hard he was—*everywhere*—momentarily broke the spell. Just long enough for her to realize she was beyond overwhelmed by one kiss that had so quickly spiraled off into more.

All her life she'd worked to be rational and analytical. She'd always believed that thinking things through would keep her safe. But right now, with Drew lying over her on the sand, with his hands on her curves and his mouth on her skin—and with arousal swamping her system—she couldn't figure out how to go back to that analytical, rational place.

And, in that moment at least, it scared her. Scared her enough that she began to pull away.

Drew lifted his head to look down at her. "Ash?"

"I thought it would just be one kiss," she blurted. "Just one quick kiss so that we would stop building the idea of it into this big thing. Just one kiss because we're here at the ocean, beneath the moon, and you understand even more than I already thought you did just from listening to your songs." She shook her head, her lips, her skin, still tingling from his kisses. "But I was wrong. It's so much more than that. And I didn't know."

"I did. I knew better." He looked as though he was warring with himself for a moment before he finally went up on his knees and brought her up, as well, so that they were facing each other on the sand. "I knew I would never be able to stop at one kiss. Even kissing every perfect inch of your body won't be enough. I'll only keep needing more, Ash. So much more."

Her whole life, she'd been sensible. Careful. And her life had been fine. Good, even. There had been laughter. And happiness. But nothing she'd ever felt had been like *this*. Nothing had come anywhere close to the way she felt when Drew was kissing her. Not even listening to his music had taken her this high.

Coming on this tour with him was already a break from her normal life. What if she took the next step? One that suddenly seemed inevitable. Ashley's choices had always been clear to her before: *Get good grades. Be a good daughter. Carve out a place in the corporate world via Stanford Business School.* And one day, she'd always assumed, she'd find someone just like herself to date and eventually marry.

But for the first time ever, she found herself wanting to make a different choice. A choice so wild, so crazy, that a truly rational person would have stepped back from it immediately. Only, maybe Drew was right and she was made up of more shades, more contours, more colors than just the "rational" ones.

"Maybe," she said slowly, "maybe we shouldn't stop." It was so hard to get the words out that she couldn't quite bring herself to look at his face. "When you were kissing me, I finally *felt* beautiful. And passionate." *Really* passionate, as though she'd never be able to get enough of him.

"If I kiss you again," he said in a low voice that caressed her skin just as wonderfully as his mouth had, "I won't be able to stop."

She'd never been so scared—or had such clarity—as when she finally looked him in the eye and said, "Don't stop, Drew. I want this. I want *you.*" She put her hands flat on his broad chest, where his heart was beating hard and fast. As hard and fast as hers. "What if you and I *did* get together while I'm here on tour with you? I mean, we're clearly doing a terrible job of pushing away our attraction to each other. No one needs to know. Just you and me there on the tour bus, having a good time for as long as we're both enjoying ourselves."

He was so close that she could feel the warmth of his breath on her lips, and she was trembling from wanting him so badly. This was it. She and Drew weren't just going to kiss tonight. They were going to make love. It wouldn't matter that it was her first time. She knew he would make it perfect. Because he thought she was beautiful *and* brainy. Passionate and exciting.

"Ashley—" His breath was coming fast, his chest rising and falling beneath her palms. "I can't."

Wait...

What had he just said?

And what was he doing, moving away from her instead of closer? Why was he pacing on the sand and cursing instead of taking off her clothes and kissing every inch of her skin the way he'd just said he wanted to?

She got to her feet, too, her face so hot and tightly drawn that it was as though she'd been slapped instead of told, *I can't.* She'd never been so embarrassed. And had never felt so rejected.

She could feel tears start to come, knew they'd be falling soon, and she didn't want him to see that. Couldn't let him see that. But even though she all but ran down the beach, Drew was fast. Faster than she was. And when she didn't stop after he called her name, he passed her and made her stop with his own body.

"Ash, don't run. Please don't run from me."

She kept her head down, but she knew what was coming. That he'd put his hand beneath her chin and make her look into his eyes. And when he did, the raw desire she still saw on his face shook her. And confused her like nothing else ever had.

"Do you actually think I don't want you? Can't you see that I haven't been able to think about anything but you since you came into my life?" His words stunned her just as much as the look in his eyes did. "Damn it, I want you so badly I can't see straight. Hell, I can barely remember the words to my songs when I'm on stage and I see you dancing, because just watching you move to the music gets me so turned on."

"Then why?" The pain of his rejection made her question fierce. "Is it because I'm not like the other girls? The ones who whip off their shirts so that you can sign their big breasts?"

"I would *never* want you to be like them. Never." He was just as fierce as she. "It's your father. You know that I promised him I wouldn't touch you."

She felt her eyes go big. "I know you said you would make sure nothing bad happened to me. But you actually promised him that you wouldn't touch me?"

"He said he trusted me. He said that's why I'm the only musician he would have let you tour with."

Drew had already made it clear that her safety on his tour was his top priority and that he'd promised her father he'd take care of her. But she hadn't known that *taking care of her* extended to who she kissed. Her body was her own, damn it. And just because she hadn't yet exercised much of her sensuality didn't mean anyone else got a say as to when she finally did.

Her body. Her decision. Funny, it had never seemed so clear before. Then again, she'd never wanted anyone the way she wanted Drew. Had never even come close to making love with anyone else.

"He's not my keeper. He's my father, and I love him, but I'm not a little girl."

"I know you're not, Ash." Drew's eyes were hot, so hot she could feel the heat all along her skin. "Trust me...*I know.*" He closed his eyes as if to try to get a grip. "But that doesn't mean he wants you to be hurt. Or taken advantage of."

"Here. Tonight. What we were doing before you said you couldn't—were you taking advantage of me?"

"No." He almost looked offended that she would even ask. "Of course not."

"Then I don't understand why you feel we have to stop."

He ran a hand over his hair, which only made him look sexier. "I'm trying to respect your father's wishes."

"What about *my* wishes?" Her words were loud over the sound of the surf. "What about what *I* want?"

But she already knew the answer. Drew had made a promise to her father, and he was the kind of person who stood by his promises. She didn't want to hurt her father either, but she'd already chosen him over her mother, had already chosen a steady, measured life over the much more exciting one her mother wanted to give her. And she'd never been tempted by anyone to step outside that comfort zone before.

Only, now that she'd finally met a gorgeous guy who tempted her like crazy—and who, miraculously, was just as tempted—nothing could come of it.

Because her father had made Drew promise to never, ever touch her.

"Ash—"

She put her hand up before he could say anything else. She was too upset now to listen anyway, miles away from the rational person she'd always been before. "I know you're in a bad position. Let's just forget it."

He looked as frustrated as she felt. "I don't know if I can."

She *knew* she wouldn't. But unless she wanted her heart to be even more flattened than it already was tonight, she'd have to take her best shot at forgetting her feelings for Drew. Starting right this second.

She pulled out her cell phone to text Max to ask him to come pick them up.

CHAPTER TWELVE

Phoenix, Arizona

The moment Ashley's lips met Drew's had been the best of his life. There wasn't anything else that had ever come close.

Her mouth had been so soft. So sweet.

Perfect.

By last night, his need for her had already grown to such a fever pitch that before he could stop it from happening, their kiss had gone from gentle to desperate. He couldn't stop tasting, couldn't stop touching, couldn't stop *taking*.

He'd known kissing her, touching her, would be good—but he'd never known hunger like this before. Never known pleasure so raw. So all-encompassing.

And while they'd been kissing, he'd forgotten everything but how good she felt, smelled, tasted. Right and wrong had been lost to him as he'd completely lost sight of his promise to her father to keep her safe. But then, when something had startled her and she'd pulled back to tell him how shocked she was at how deep their attraction really went, Drew's promise to her father had slammed back down on him like a two-by-four crashing into his chest.

Of all the women in the world, she was the one he couldn't have. So he'd forced himself to stop them from taking the next step. From stripping each other's clothes off and making love on the deserted beach. Even though there was nothing—*not one single thing*— he'd wanted more than that.

God, he'd hated seeing the hurt in her eyes, and hadn't wanted to let her think for one second that he was keeping his distance because she wasn't beautiful or desirable. She was. So beautiful, so desirable that being close to her in his bus all night as they'd driven to Phoenix, and then all day as she shadowed his interviews, had been hell. Pure, unadulterated *hell*.

But even worse than knowing he could never kiss Ashley again or hear her incredibly seductive sighs of pleasure as his mouth roamed down over her skin, was the fact that since that moment when she'd told him just to forget it, she'd shut down on him. She was still friendly. And he could see that she still loved his music. But the closeness that they'd been building—the friendship he'd quickly come to count on—had come to a stop.

While they'd waited for Max in the parking lot, her body language had spoken volumes about how she felt—with her shoulders and face turned as far away from him. And when Max had come to pick them up from the beach in the bus, she'd immediately gone into her bunk and closed the curtain to block him out. Drew had wanted to say something, anything, to make things better. To go back to the way they'd been before he completely screwed things up by trying to do the right thing. But he'd been afraid of making things worse, and had told himself that, hopefully, by the following morning things would be better and they could at least go back to being friends again.

But when morning came in Phoenix, though Ashley had still made breakfast for both of them, by the time he'd thrown on clothes to come out and eat with her, the curtain on her bunk was drawn and he'd heard the clicking of her fingertips on her computer keyboard. She hadn't come out until James boarded to grab them for interviews.

James obviously immediately noticed something was off between the two of them, but Drew wasn't going to kiss and tell, and he definitely didn't want James to say anything to Ashley that would make her any more uncomfortable than she already was.

Now he was finally with her again at a TV station in Phoenix. She looked beautiful, but pale, as if she hadn't slept much better than he had. Which was to say, barely at all.

All day long he'd been trying to figure out what to say to her when they were finally together again. *I'm sorry* wasn't right. *I wish I'd never made your father that promise* wouldn't work either.

Drew had never second-guessed himself like this before. On the contrary, his decisions, his path forward, had always been obvious to him. But now, not only was his music tying him up in knots, but so were his feelings for Ashley.

The station was in a historic four-story building downtown. He'd toured through here before and when he saw the interest in Ashley's eyes as they got out of the town car, Drew said, "I heard that the building was built as a love letter from a poor man who had nothing more to his name than his hammer to the wealthy magnate's daughter who was off-limits to him." At this point, he would take any excuse to get Ashley to talk to him again, even if it was just about some building in Phoenix.

For a moment she seemed to forget to keep her distance. "What happened to them? Did they fall in love?" In the moment their eyes met, heat sizzled between them just as much as it had on the beach.

"The night before she was to marry the wealthy fiancé that her father had chosen for her, but that she didn't love, she went to tell the builder she would run away with him. But when she got there, she found him lying on the floor, unconscious from a piece of cement that had hit him on the head."

Too late, Drew realized that he should have kept the sad story of star-crossed lovers to himself, because instead of opening up more, she said, "That's really sad. Sometimes I guess people really aren't meant to be together."

The next time he looked into her eyes, it was as if she'd pulled shutters down over her emotions.

Damn it, for a moment there he'd thought that she might be about to open up to him again. And even though he understood why she was wary—there was no way to sugar-coat the way he'd flat-out rejected the offer she'd made last night—frustration was still eating him up from the inside by the time they stepped into the lobby and the elevator came to take them up to the fourth floor.

James waited for Ashley and Drew to get in before saying, "Looks like a pretty tight fit in there. I'll take the stairs."

Ashley quickly said, "There's plenty of room," but by then the doors had closed, leaving the two of them alone in the small space.

Drew didn't want to make things even worse, but he couldn't stop himself from asking, "Did you sleep okay?"

She didn't quite look at him as she paused for a long moment. "I—"

Before she could say anything more, the elevator suddenly jolted to a stop...and then the lights went out.

"Ash?" He instinctively reached for her hand. Damn, it was dark in here. "Are you okay?"

"I'm okay," she replied, but her voice sounded a little shaky, and she was holding pretty tightly to his hand.

"I'm sure they'll have the elevator up and running again in just a second. I'll text James to let him know we're stuck, just in case they haven't figured it out yet."

"Great." But, again, she didn't sound particularly great.

As he pulled out his phone and sent the text without letting go of her hand, she took out her own and turned on the onboard flashlight. But even with the light on, her breath seemed to be coming a little faster. "I'm not always great in small, enclosed spaces."

"I've got you, Ash," he said in a gentle voice as he drew her closer. "Just close your eyes and we can pretend we're somewhere else." He was glad when she wrapped her arms around him. Nothing had ever felt as good, or as right, as having Ashley in his arms.

"Where?"

"Back in the Valley of Fire."

He stroked her hair, then her back. She smelled amazing, like the lavender and roses in his parents' backyard. And she was his perfect fit absolutely everywhere.

Don't stop, Drew. I want this. I want you.

Oh hell, he needed to stop thinking about what could have happened if his goddamned honor hadn't stopped him from tearing off her clothes last night. But focusing on how much he wanted Ashley wouldn't help her right now, so he tried to take her back to the Valley of Fire in her mind.

"The sun is bright yellow. The sky is blue. And the sand is that incredible red."

She moved closer, her breath warm against his neck. "Ever since that day you showed it to me, I dream of it."

"I dream of *you*." In the small, dark space, the words came before he could yank them back, and he couldn't stop himself from brushing his lips over the top of her head. "Every night."

He was holding her closely enough that he could feel the rise and fall of her chest and hear her soft gasp of awareness at his words. If she had any idea just how sexy his dreams were...

"You can't."

She whispered the words, but every part of him was attuned to every part of her. To her heart beating fast against his, to the heat of her body everywhere she was touching him, to every sound and breath she made.

"Do you, Ash?" He brushed his fingertips across her cheek in the dark, and she turned it into his palm with a soft moan. "Do you dream about me the way I can't stop dreaming about you?"

"Drew, *please.*"

He didn't know if she was whispering his name to ask him to stop...or to beg him to give her another forbidden kiss. Praying she was dying for his mouth on hers as badly as he needed to feel hers beneath his, he cradled her jaw in his hand and began to lower his mouth to hers, beyond desperate for another taste of her.

Sweet Lord, he'd never been looking forward to a kiss so much in all his li—

Ashley was jolted nearly out of his arms as the elevator came back to life and the overhead lights turned on.

Her eyes were huge as she took a step back and pressed herself against the elevator wall in an effort to get as far away from him as she could. And yet again, before he could find any of the right words to say— whatever the hell those could possibly be at this point— they reached the fourth floor and the doors opened.

She was out of the elevator in a flash, and James was clearly concerned as he took in her flushed cheeks. "Ashley, do you need anything? A drink of water? Or maybe just to look out a window for a few seconds?"

"No, thanks, I'm fine."

But anyone could tell that she wasn't. And Drew knew it was entirely his fault.

He wasn't the kind of guy to play mind games with a woman. What's more, Ashley was the very last person he'd ever want to mess around with. Especially considering how great she'd been to talk to about his mom and his music.

The problem was, he'd never felt about anyone the way he felt about her. When she was in his arms, he wanted to hold her forever and never let her go. And every word she spoke played straight to his soul, affecting him more strongly than any song ever had.

James didn't ask Drew how *he* was doing after being stuck in the elevator. On the contrary, his bodyguard scowled at him. *Don't hurt her,* was the clear message in the other man's eyes, right before they stepped into the TV studio.

Drew worked like hell to concentrate on his job and give his fans the best interview he could, but with Ashley only a few feet away behind the cameras, he knew he wasn't coming anywhere close to pulling it off. Because even though he'd vowed that Ashley would leave his tour as pure as she'd come, he still couldn't stop hoping that her answer to his question about whether she dreamed of him was *yes.*

CHAPTER THIRTEEN

Ashley was standing in front of the table on the bus, quickly reading through her email before heading into the venue to watch Drew's show, when she suddenly felt him move behind her.

"Close the computer and turn around, Ash." When she didn't obey his command fast enough, he put his hands over hers and bent his mouth to her ear. "I promise you'll be glad you did."

Together, they closed her laptop, and then he moved his hands to her waist to turn her around to face him.

"I thought you were about to start your show," she said, her voice sounding far huskier than it normally did.

"The opening band went on late." His eyes were dark as midnight. "Which gives me time to make up for what happened in the elevator."

"*You don't have to—*" *Her words fell away as he stroked his hands up her back from her waist to her shoulders.*

"*I do.*" *He brushed her hair over one shoulder, then bent his head to press a kiss to the skin he'd exposed at the side of her neck.* "*You taste so good. Your mouth. Your neck.*" *He licked out against her, and she shuddered at the pleasure of it.* "*I need to taste more of you. I don't care what anyone else thinks about the two of us. Just you.*" *He took her earlobe between his teeth, and she couldn't hold back a moan of pleasure as he lightly scraped over her sensitive flesh.* "*Do you still want me the way you said you did?*"

She couldn't stop herself from saying, "*Yes,*" *and the next thing she knew, he was lifting her up onto the tabletop and moving to stand between her legs. It was pure instinct to throw all caution to the wind and wrap her arms and legs around him as his mouth crashed down on hers.*

While their first kiss out on the beach had been gentle, this kiss was ferocious, as if both of them were desperately trying to get their fill before they were yanked apart again. She threaded her fingers into his hair to bring his mouth even closer, and when his tongue swept out against hers, she gasped at the pleasure of it.

"*The sounds you make when I'm kissing you, touching you,*" *he said in a raw voice against her jaw as he nipped at her. She arched back to give him better access, and he nuzzled in against her neck, his stubble grazing her skin in the sexiest possible way.* "*There's nothing sexier, Ash. Not one goddamned thing.*"

It was warm on the bus, so she'd worn a tank top with her jeans today. Drew clearly appreciated the bare skin as he first ran his big, warm hands over her shoulders, and then bent his head to follow up that caress with a trail of kisses.

"Your skin is so pretty, so soft. I can't wait to see all of it. All of you."

She shivered at the thought of being completely naked in front of Drew. Not only was she a virgin, but the truth was that she hadn't actually gone all that far with any of the guys she'd dated. Clothes had been unbuttoned and unzipped, but her panties and bra had always stayed on...and no one else had ever made her come. Not because she was a prude—she figured she had the same sexual urges as anyone else. But because none of those guys she'd dated had turned her on that much.

Not like this. Not the way just one look, one touch, one kiss from Drew did. Heck, she was nearly all the way there, and she still had all her clothes on.

"Do you want that, Ash? Do you want me to strip you bare? Do you want me to kiss every beautiful inch of your body?"

His eyes were intense as he asked her his sexy questions in a voice made raw with need. The same desire that had been eating her up day by day, hour by hour, second by second, ever since the moment they'd met.

She tried to remember why this was a bad idea, but her brain and body felt fuzzy and thick with wanting. Need that obliterated every rational thought. "Yes," she told him, "I want that. I want all of that. Now."

"Thank God," he said as he put his hands on either side of her face and leaned in for a kiss that she felt in all the places he hadn't yet stripped bare, hadn't

yet touched. "Because I can't wait any longer, Ash. I need you bad. So damned bad I'm going crazy from being with you but not being able to touch or kiss you."

His callused fingers were wonderfully rough on her jaw, and his chest was rock hard where her breasts pressed into him. Slowly, too slowly for the fever pitch he'd roused her to, he slid his hands down from her face and back over her shoulders and arms, until he reached her waist. Her breasts ached for his touch, under her cotton top and bra. But he was teasing her, teasing them both, by coming so close without actually touching her where she needed it most.

Finally, he gripped the hem of her tank and began to pull it up, his fingertips grazing the sensitive skin of her stomach. "Mine," he whispered against her lips as he drew the fabric higher and higher until it was just below the bottom edge of her bra. "I can't wait until you're mine."

"Yours."

It was all she wanted, too. Everything she'd dreamed of for so long. His songs had helped get her through her awful teen years...and now Drew would be the one to take her all the way into adulthood. It felt right, so incredibly right, that he was going to be her first.

The knocking came loud and suddenly, jarring Drew so that he jumped away from her, his hands dropping, his face blurring.

Blurring?

Why was his face blurring?

The knocking came again, louder this time, and she closed her eyes and shook her head.

When she opened them, she wasn't sitting on the table in the bus—she was lying in her bunk with the tank top she'd gone to sleep in bunched up in her hand. That was when she heard footsteps on the other side of the thick, dark curtain that enclosed her bunk, and then the door being opened as male voices drifted into the bus.

Oh God. It had just been a dream.

* * *

Albuquerque, New Mexico

Five minutes later, though Ashley was fully awake, she remained lying in her bunk as still as a statue. She was utterly mortified at the thought that Drew—or anyone else who had come onto the bus with him—might have guessed at the sexy dream she'd been having.

Had she been talking in her sleep?

Or, worse still, had she actually moaned out loud?

She'd never had a dream like that before. Not one that felt so real...or that she so desperately *wished* were real.

But the truth was that embarrassment over talking or moaning in her sleep wasn't the only reason her body felt overheated. Normally, if she were at home in the small studio in her father's backyard in Palo Alto, she would have taken a few minutes to fantasize a little longer beneath the sheets in secret. But she couldn't touch herself on Drew's bus, could she?

For nearly a week now, she'd been riding the edge of desire, and her dream definitely hadn't helped. Not one bit. If anything, she was more frustrated than ever. Especially since it had ended before she got to the really good part...

Unfortunately, she couldn't stay in her bunk forever. Especially since now that she'd looked at her watch, she knew Drew's workday was due to begin soon. She wasn't here to hide out in her bunk twenty-four seven, she was here to learn as much as she possibly could.

So even if she'd never been so confused, or so frustrated before, that didn't mean she could lose sight of her goals. She'd just have to make sure that she didn't spend too much one-on-one time with Drew. Because that's when things always got out of control. Like in the elevator yesterday, when it had been just the two of them in the small, pitch-black space, and all she'd wanted to do was—

No. She couldn't go there again. Couldn't let herself keep fantasizing about a man she couldn't have. She was far too pragmatic for that kind of behavior. At least, she'd always thought she was...

Sitting up carefully so that she didn't hit her head on the bunk above her, she put on her glasses, then did her best to smooth down her hair and clothes. She didn't sleep with a bra on, but since she was going to head straight to the bathroom for a shower and didn't hear voices anymore, she figured Drew must have gone into his back bedroom and the coast was clear.

Deciding it was safe to push back the curtains, she had just stepped out of the bunk when he emerged from behind a cabinet door where he'd been kneeling. "Morning, Ash." She jumped, her hand going to cover her thumping heart as he said, "I thought I'd make us eggs today, but I can't find the—"

When he finally turned all the way to face her, his words fell away. His hot gaze moved from her face to her light blue tank that didn't quite cover her hips, then to the soft leggings she slept in, and then back up to her face. He'd never seen her in glasses, and though it shouldn't matter if he thought she looked extra geeky in them, it did. Simply because everything about Drew mattered to her, whether she wanted it to or not.

But judging by the incredible hunger in his gaze—hunger she knew for a fact that she was echoing right back at him—her glasses didn't turn him off. And every single sexy moment of her dream came back to her as they stared at each other across the bus.

It was just a dream, Ashley. Snap out of it!

But even as she reminded herself that it hadn't been real, her body couldn't help but remember how amazing it had felt to be in his arms on the beach in Los Angeles. All he'd need to do to make the dream real was move toward her, lift her up onto the table, and kiss her. Not even a half-dozen movements, and then she could have everything she wanted.

For a moment, as he continued to stare hungrily at her, she thought he might do exactly that. But then a muscle jumped in his jaw, and he stayed right where he was as he asked, "Did I wake you?"

She opened her mouth to say something short and impersonal. But what came out was, "I was in the middle of a dream."

Oh no, where had those words come from?

As if he couldn't stay away another second, he finally moved closer. But she was stuck right where she was, one hand on the wooden base of her bunk, the other still between her breasts over her racing heart.

"What were you dreaming about?"

She shook her head and pressed her lips together. She couldn't tell him the truth, could she? Couldn't admit to him that he'd been starring in an X-rated dream.

"I dreamed about you again last night," he said in a low voice. "Were you dreaming about me, too?"

The heat in his voice swamped her, made her brain even slower than it already was. Her resolve to keep her ever-increasing feelings secret from him dissolved at the same moment the word, "Yes," slipped from her lips. God, how was she ever going to forget about her feelings for Drew if she kept blurting out things like, *I was dreaming about you.*

"Ash."

The air inside the bus started to crackle with such intense attraction she actually felt the fine hairs rise on her arms. Drew was moving even closer, reaching for her, when his cell phone rang.

"Damn it," he said when he heard the ring tone. "That's my sister Madison."

"You should get it."

Since Ashley couldn't figure out how to keep her mouth shut around him—who knew what she'd be telling him next, probably every single sexy detail of her dream—she made herself dash into the bathroom, turn on the shower, strip, and step in before it was even close to hot.

And as she stood and shivered beneath the icy-cold spray, she hoped it would freeze some sense back into her.

CHAPTER FOURTEEN

Oklahoma City, Oklahoma

Ashley had been dreaming about him.

For the past twenty-four hours, that was the only thing Drew had been able to think about. Along with the fact that when he'd seen her in her pajamas for the first time—all of her curves on incredible display—he'd nearly lost it right then and there in the middle of his bus at seven in the morning.

And the glasses she'd been wearing?

They'd only made her hotter. Especially because he knew just how big the brains were behind those glasses. And how big the heart behind her gorgeous curves.

He'd had to leave the bus for an interview before she got out of the shower yesterday, and after that she'd done her best to stick with his crew. By the time he made it back to the bus after the meet and greet that night, she'd already been back in her bunk with the curtains drawn. And then, by the time he'd come out of his room this morning, she'd been outside talking with Max.

Making absolutely sure that the two of them were never alone.

Today, Drew had arranged his tour promotion schedule so that they could drop by the house Smith Sullivan and Valentina Landon were renting while they filmed their new movie in Oklahoma City.

It had been a dream come true when they'd asked him to work on this film with them—and the rushes he'd seen had been incredible. If only he could write something for the soundtrack that was worth a damn. As it stood right now, not only was he going to have to bow out of the opportunity of a lifetime, he was also going to leave them hanging.

If only he could push past his songwriting block, damn it!

In the backyard, Ashley's voice floated over to him from several feet away. Just like always, the sound was much-needed music to Drew's soul. He had wanted to keep Ashley by his side until he was sure that she wouldn't be overwhelmed by meeting Hollywood royalty, but Valentina and Ashley had immediately hit it off when Smith's fiancée found out that Ashley was working on her application to business school. Smith had scored big-time with Valentina, and from the smile on the guy's face every time he looked at her, it was clear that he knew it.

Drew hated to bring Smith and Valentina down today, but he couldn't live with himself if he didn't come clean about his inability to write a decent song for the soundtrack. He was heading over to them when he noticed one of the party guests who looked like he'd had a little too much to drink was gesturing in a crazy way as he spoke. If he wasn't careful, the guy was going to knock Ashley into the pool.

A couple of people tried to stop him to chat, but Drew was focused on getting to her before disaster could strike. But before he could, the guy with the wild arms knocked Ashley in the shoulder so hard that she started to topple over toward the water.

Drew leapt the final few feet over the cement patio that surrounded the pool and got close enough to catch one of her hands. But there was already too much momentum to her fall, and instead of keeping her out of the pool, they both plunged in with a huge splash.

Not sure if she could swim, he put his arms around her to pull her to the surface. As they came out of the water, her arms naturally moved around his neck.

"Do you know how to swim? Are you okay?"

"I do and I am." She wiped water out of her eyes before she opened them, her hair slicked back from her beautiful face. "Thanks for trying to keep me from falling in. You didn't have to do that."

"Of course I did." Everyone was staring at them, and he figured it wouldn't be long before people started taking pictures with their phones, if they hadn't already. In that moment, however, he couldn't focus on anything but how good it felt to have her in his arms again. Still, even though he couldn't keep holding her forever in the pool, he really hated having to say, "Ready to get out?"

She made a little face. "Actually, I'm pretty sure my dress has gone completely see-through."

Drew fought like hell to keep his arousal under control. But it was already difficult enough when she was wet and soft and so damned perfect in his arms.

Knowing her cute white dress was now translucent? There wasn't enough self-control in the world to fight what that vision did to him.

"Only I could do something like this at a fancy Hollywood party." She closed her eyes in mortification. "And now I can't even get out because it will be like everyone is seeing me naked."

He was about to tell her he'd get out first and grab her a towel to cover up with, when he looked up and realized Valentina was already on it. "Valentina's waiting by the shallow-end steps with a towel. I'll come out of the water behind you so that between the towel and me, no one will see anything they shouldn't."

Ashley nodded, but she didn't let go of him or start swimming. As if she didn't want to let go of him any more than he wanted to let her go. Finally, however, she said, "I guess we should swim over there, shouldn't we?"

Unfortunately, the longer they stayed wrapped around each other in the pool, the more people would talk. And if pictures of the two of them holding each other ever got back to her father? Well, Drew could only imagine how angry he would be, even though there was a reasonable explanation. Especially when something told him Professor Emmit would quickly see through the "reasonable explanation" and straight to Drew's unstoppable attraction to Ashley.

Fortunately, between Drew and Valentina, they were able to get Ashley out of the pool with only the two of them seeing the way the white dress clung to her gorgeous curves. A true gentleman wouldn't look, but Drew's control was already hanging by such a thin thread that he didn't have a prayer of not drinking her in. If Valentina noticed the way he was clearly losing his mind over Ashley, she didn't give anything away, but simply helped wrap Ashley up in the thick beach towel and took her into the house through a side door.

Smith came over with a towel for Drew a couple of seconds later, grinning as he said, "Valentina and I have been too busy to enjoy the pool. Glad someone is."

"Thanks for the towel." Drew ran it over his face and hair. "I was actually just heading your way to see if I could chat with you and Valentina for a few minutes."

"Why don't you change into something of mine while we stick your clothes in the dryer? Then we can talk."

Five minutes later, Drew had on a pair of Smith Sullivan's jeans and a Hawks Baseball T-shirt. Valentina and Ashley hadn't yet emerged, so they were sitting in Smith and Valentina's home office talking about how the team was doing this year.

"I caught your brother's last no-hitter on the TV on the bus," Drew said, "but it's not like being there when Ryan throws a—"

His sentence fell away as Ashley walked into the room...and his jaw dropped. She was wearing another dress, pink instead of white. And sexy in a way that nothing else she'd ever worn had been.

"We were so lucky," Valentina said as she beamed at Ashley. "Tatiana left this dress in the closet after her visit with Ian. It fits you perfectly."

So perfectly, in fact, that the edge Drew was on wore so thin it nearly broke, almost exploding into a million pieces right then and there in front of Smith and Valentina.

* * *

Ashley felt just about as self-conscious in Tatiana Landon's dress as she had in her see-through white dress in the pool. Tatiana was a gorgeous movie star who probably wore outfits like this all the time, but Ashley wasn't used to wearing anything quite so form-fitting. One big breath was all it would take for her breasts to come spilling up and out of the bodice. Plus, since her underwear was currently in the dryer, she wasn't wearing any. And from the way Drew was looking at her with so much heat even the air conditioning couldn't keep her cool, she wondered if he'd developed X-ray vision and could tell that she was completely bare beneath the gorgeous dress.

She'd been nervous about coming to this party, considering Smith Sullivan was one of the biggest movie stars in the world. But in her worst nightmares she couldn't have come up with falling into the pool. Only, the truth was that she couldn't entirely regret what had happened, if only because of the way Drew had pulled her close in the water and held her as though he never wanted to let her go.

Just the way he had in the elevator yesterday. And on the beach. And in the desert in the Valley of Fire.

Every time she'd ever been in his arms was imprinted on her memory like a brand. When this tour was over, she'd be replaying each and every one of those delicious moments over and over in her fantasies.

Fantasies that she knew better than to be having right this second, so she worked to pull herself together as she smiled at Valentina. "Thanks again for finding

me the dress. And"—she turned to include Smith—
"I'm so sorry I made such a spectacle at your party."

"You have nothing to apologize for," Smith said
as he reached out for Valentina's hand so that he could
draw her closer. "We should have fired that grip a week
ago."

"He should know better than to get drunk here,"
Valentina agreed, looking utterly content in Smith's
arms.

They were such a beautiful couple. It clearly
didn't matter to them that Smith was famous and
Valentina wasn't. They were not only equals, they were
also so clearly in love that they were always either
holding hands or Smith's arms were wrapped around
Valentina's waist.

Seeing how good they were together, Ashley
couldn't imagine that Valentina had ever worried about
fitting into Smith's Hollywood world. But given the
crazy business he was in, Ashley figured it was far
more likely that they'd run into at least a few bumps on
the way to true love. If only she knew their story, would
that help her make sense of what she was going through
with Drew?

"I'll go take care of the situation with the grip in
a minute," Smith said to Valentina, "but first, Drew said
he'd like to chat with us about something." He shifted
his gaze to Drew. "I'm assuming it has to do with the
soundtrack?"

Ashley couldn't miss the tension in Drew's face.
No one could when a muscle was jumping in his jaw
and there were deep creases beside his eyes.

She realized it was the way he always looked
when he was talking about the problems he'd been
having with songwriting. *Oh God, the soundtrack.* She

hadn't even thought to ask him if that was giving him problems the way the songs for his next album were. And despite the strain between them since the beach in Los Angeles, her every instinct was to try to figure out a way to protect him.

But at the same time, while Drew had involved her in all of his other meetings so far, today she was here only because she'd fallen into the pool. She very much doubted any of them wanted her to witness this discussion.

"I should leave the three of you alone," she said, already heading for the French doors in her borrowed pink dress.

"Ashley." Drew's deep voice—and his hand over hers—stopped her in her tracks. "Stay. Please."

She looked into his eyes, and when she saw just how much he seemed to need her support, she moved back to sit with him on the couch opposite the one Smith and Valentina were sitting on. She squeezed his hand, a silent message of support that she hoped he'd understand.

She watched as he steeled himself to deliver the bad news, turning to Smith and Valentina and saying in a grave voice, "Working on the soundtrack for your movie is the opportunity of a lifetime. Honestly, when you asked me to do it, I was floored. But even then I should have been upfront with both of you about the problems I was already having." He ran his free hand through his hair, leaving it standing on end. "The rushes are incredible. You deserve a soundtrack just as good. I can't do it justice."

"Of course you will," Valentina said. "We wouldn't have asked you to work with us if we didn't think you would more than do our film justice, Drew."

Valentina's words were as firm as they were soothing. Ashley belatedly remembered that she had managed her sister's acting career for a long time. Clearly, she was good with artists.

But Drew shook his head. "Everything I've tried to write for your film—it's not coming out the way you're expecting."

"How so?" Smith asked.

Ashley couldn't quite read Smith's expression, although he didn't look worried or angry. Instead, it was as though he needed more data before he decided which way to feel. Clearly, neither he nor Valentina were the type to jump to conclusions. Not even when someone they had hired told them flat-out that they weren't up to working with them on a film.

"The songs I've been hearing in my head aren't rock. Not like my last album." Drew looked at Ashley, and even though she'd been trying like crazy to avoid temptation these past few days by keeping her distance, she hoped he knew she was on his side. Always. "There's still a little bit of rock there," Drew continued, "but there's some folk, too. Even some classical." He scowled as he admitted, "Honestly, I don't know what the songs are yet. Just that whenever I try to force them in the direction I know you're looking for, everything stalls out."

Smith looked at Valentina and Ashley got the sense the power couple was having a silent conversation before Smith said, "We trust your vision, Drew."

"Whatever your vision ends up being," Valentina added. "Rock, folk, classical, zydeco—all that matters is the emotion behind it. Style really has nothing to do with it as far as we're concerned."

After a bit of a pause where he looked more than a little gobsmacked by their instant and unconditional support, Drew said, "I appreciate your vote of confidence. But I'm sure you want to sell a lot of soundtracks, and without a guaranteed hit—"

Smith held up a hand. "Ever since Nicola married my brother Marcus and Ford Vincent married my cousin Mia, I've learned a few things about the music business. Mostly that hits may come, and that it's great when they do, but the most important thing of all is that the musicians truly believe in what they're creating." Smith looked at Drew with laser focus. "All we're asking you to do is to put your heart—the whole damned thing—into the music you create for this movie."

"That's all, huh?"

Ashley nearly sighed out loud with relief when Drew's mouth quirked up slightly at his own question. So, she thought, did Smith and Valentina. Clearly, they hadn't wanted to lose Drew.

"Keep writing for the film for another couple of weeks," Valentina suggested. "And then if you're still having trouble, let us know. But we still have a good feeling about what you're going to give us, Drew."

Drew stood up to thank both of them for giving him another chance to get it right. Ashley hoped at least a chunk of the huge weight on Drew's shoulders had just fallen away.

A few moments later, Smith headed outside to deal with the drunken grip while Valentina went to see if their clothes were dry.

When they were alone, Ashley needed him to know, "I think they're right." She didn't want her voice to carry, so she spoke softly, but she hoped Drew could hear the passion behind her words. "I know we talked about it in the desert, and then again on the beach, but Smith and Valentina both just put it perfectly—you need to trust your new musical vision the way you've always instinctively trusted your old one." She hoped it wouldn't hurt him to hear her say, "It's like your mom said in her letter—you've always been perfectly in tune with the music in your heart."

His eyes were dark and intense as he reached for a lock of her damp hair curling over her chest and wound it around one of his fingers. "Thank you for being here, Ash. And for understanding, even when I barely can myself."

She was about to tell him he was being too hard on himself—and knew that confessing how badly she'd missed him these past few days would be only a beat behind that—when James knocked on the French doors.

Poking his head in, he said, "We've got to get moving, or we'll be late to the studio for your next round of TV interviews. In fact, we've got to call in to the first one in five minutes. Hey, nice dress, Ashley."

For a few moments there, she'd hoped that maybe she and Drew could get things back to where they'd been before their night on the beach, when everything had fallen apart. But within minutes of saying good-bye to Smith and Valentina, who told her to please keep the dress, not only were they back on the insanely paced treadmill of Drew's tour as he headed into a glass and steel building to do the first of a half-dozen back-to-back interviews...but her father also chose that moment to call.

Right when she felt as twisted up inside as she ever had.

CHAPTER FIFTEEN

"Honey, how are you?"

She gestured to Max that she was going to head back into the bus before saying, "I'm fine, Dad."

"You don't sound fine." That was the problem with being so close to her father. He was way too attuned to the tone of her voice. "What's wrong? Is Drew—"

"Being the perfect gentleman!" She couldn't stop her irritation from spilling out. "Why are you so worried about him hurting me? You had him in your class, so you should know how great he is." *Great enough that you shouldn't have felt you had to warn him not to come near me.*

"Ashley." Her father was clearly hurt by her outburst. She'd never spoken to him like that before. "Why are you so upset with me for asking a simple question?"

Because you made Drew promise not to touch your precious little girl!

But she couldn't bring herself to say that to her father, not after a lifetime of believing he was right about absolutely everything. And that was part of it, she suddenly realized as her father waited for her to tell him why she was angry with him: Ashley hadn't learned how to fully trust herself, not when she'd always looked to her father for help in making her choices. But if what she'd said to Drew about not being her father's little girl anymore was true, then she couldn't do that anymore, could she?

"I'm sorry, Dad," she said, feeling like a balloon with all the air slowly fizzling out of it. "It's been a long couple of days. I know you just want to make sure that I'm doing okay."

"Are you?" He asked it much more hesitantly this time.

She couldn't lie to her father, so she simply said, "I'm learning so much. In fact," she added, hoping to distract him from asking any other questions about her emotional state, "I just met Smith Sullivan. You know, the big movie star."

"Of course I know who Smith is," her father said with a laugh. "He was also one of my students way back when."

"No way." How many other famous people had her father taught that he'd never mentioned to her?

"How is Smith?"

"He's engaged to this great woman named Valentina, and he's very kind." She almost told her father about falling into Smith's pool, but she had a feeling that would only make him panic again when he seemed to be feeling better about things.

"That's good to hear, honey. I always hope that fame won't lead people astray."

"It definitely hasn't. Not with Smith." She couldn't stop herself from adding, "And not with Drew either. They're both great people."

"So are you, honey. You've always made me so proud."

His gentle, heartfelt words made her wish she *was* a little girl again, if only for a few moments, so that he could stroke her hair and tell her what she should do to make everything feel okay.

But she wasn't a little girl anymore. And she needed to figure things out for herself this time...even if some of the things she couldn't help but want to experience with Drew would surely upset her father a great deal.

And even if she knew better than to think Drew could ever be *the one* for her.

"I've got to go now, but I love you, Dad."

Ashley hung up with so many different emotions and desires and questions careening through her. She had always believed she was the straight and narrow, the clear-cut, just like her father. But Drew had insisted that she was more—that she was as exciting and creative as her mother as well. And when she looked at her reflection in the window across from where she was standing, she suddenly saw a likeness to her mom that she'd never noticed before. That she supposed she'd never *wanted* to notice before.

But then she noticed something that took her even more by surprise: She wasn't just made up of parts of her parents, put together like pieces of a puzzle. Take her eyes, for instance—they were neither brown like her mother's, nor blue like her father's. Instead, they were uniquely hazel. And her hair wasn't a mass of wild curls like her mother's, or pin straight like her father's. Instead, soft waves curled over her shoulders.

And most important, she was starting to see that what she wanted was neither the pure academia that her father loved, nor the total freedom that her mother craved. Because if Ashley had learned anything from being on tour with Drew, it was that carving one's own unique path was the most important thing of all.

Carving a unique path. The spark that had gone out on the beach in Los Angeles suddenly lit up inside of her. She grabbed her computer and tablet and notebook, and before she knew it, the ideas started flowing so fast that she could barely keep up with them. Ideas that were a full one-eighty from what she'd thought she had come to learn from Drew's tour. Because instead of going deeper into the standard major-label music system, every new idea she came up with was centered around a completely independent framework.

One where the musician ran the show, rather than the label.

A part of her was scared that so many things in her life had taken a complete turnabout from the moment she'd set foot on Drew's bus, but the other part of her was so excited and intrigued that she refused to let that fear stop her from fleshing out the new ideas in as much detail as she could. At least where work was concerned, she could make sense of things if she just worked at them hard enough.

Where Drew was concerned, on the other hand?

Well, between saying he couldn't be with her, but then telling her he dreamed of being with her, and a million other conflicting signs...she honestly didn't know what to think, or how to feel. Ashley shook her head and refocused on her computer screen, diving back into the work that felt a million times safer than her emotions.

When her stomach started grumbling, she suddenly realized just how late it was. Late enough that she'd not only missed Drew's show, but he should also be done with the meet and greet.

Where was he?

And what was going to happen when he came back to the bus tonight? Because, honestly, the tension between them—both sexual and emotional—had been ramping up more and more, to the point where she'd actually felt as though she might combust soon.

Just then, her phone buzzed with a text from Drew.

Got a chance to drop into a local recording studio for a few hours tonight.
Sleep well, Ash.

She was thrilled by the news that Drew was obviously feeling inspired enough to head into a recording studio. But at the same time, she already knew she wouldn't get much sleep at all.

Not when everything between them was still as uncertain as ever.

CHAPTER SIXTEEN

Dallas, Texas

The following morning, Drew watched Ashley as she worked on her laptop in the eating nook on the bus, her brow furrowed in deep concentration. Since she didn't seem to realize he was standing there, he just let himself drink in her beauty for a few seconds.

He'd gone into a local recording studio for a few hours the previous night, hoping that being in what used to be his favorite place in the world would help him to push past his stupid songwriting block. But all he'd wanted the entire time was to be back on the bus with Ashley.

Smith and Valentina had been great—a million times more understanding than he deserved. Not only had they given him two more weeks to see what he could come up with, but they'd also told him to write whatever the hell he wanted.

And still, the songs wouldn't come.

Drew didn't know what he was going to do about his music, but he did know one thing for sure: He and Ashley couldn't go on like this. At least, *he* couldn't. They needed to sit down, clear the air, figure out how they could at least be friends again in the wake of their no-touching-each-other rule. Because their connection was too strong just to let it burn out like this.

And if he only kept wanting her more by the second, rather than less?

Well, he was just going to have to work like hell to figure out how to deal with it without losing her as a friend.

Since he didn't want her to look up and see him staring at her like some stalker-perv, he knocked on the door that led from his room at the back of the bus into the common area. "Can I come in?"

She slammed the screen shut on her computer, as if he'd caught her doing something she shouldn't. "Of course you can. It's your bus. You don't have to ask for permission to go where you want."

"Is your work going well?"

"I hope so. I've just been working to get my thoughts down and also trying to make sense of them."

He wanted to ask her if she could do the same for him, to try to make sense of the mess his mind had become. But since nearly all of his thoughts were about her, he couldn't. "Can we talk for a few minutes, Ash?"

"Sure." She didn't sound sure, though, as he slid into the booth across from her. His cell phone buzzed in his pocket, but he ignored it, focused only on Ashley now.

He hated not talking to her. Hated trying to corral his feelings. No matter what else happened between them, he needed her to know one important thing. "I miss you."

Her breath hitched, and she bit down on her lip as she stared across the table at him. Her hazel eyes were so clear and beautiful that he swore he could see all the way down to her very soul as she admitted, "I miss you, too."

Relief washed over him in a huge wave. "I know things got weird after LA, but I don't want to lose your friendship."

"I don't want that either. It's just..."

"Before we kissed, remember I told you that whatever you need to say to me, I don't want you to be scared of saying it?" When she nodded, he reached for her hand. He simply couldn't stop himself from touching her. "Tell me what's going on. Tell me what you're feeling."

Her cheeks were already flushing. "I don't know how to be friends with you without wanting to be more, too. I thought maybe if I kept my distance, it would make the wanting go away."

"But it hasn't." It wasn't a question. It was a statement. Because he felt exactly the same way.

"If anything, I only want you—"

"More," he finished for her.

They stared at each other, his hand still over hers, until, slowly, she turned her hand so that her palm faced his.

It was an electric moment. Just holding hands like this should have been innocent, but amazingly, just the slide of her palm over his felt as powerful as their kiss had been on the beach.

"I was so happy to hear that you were in the recording studio last night. How did it go?"

"It didn't." His gut twisted. "And since you've seen all the shows, I know you've seen the way I'm even screwing up there."

"Your shows have been great," she said, "but I know how much you've been wanting to write again."

"I couldn't write anything worth a damn last night, but I did think a lot about what you said, and what Smith and Valentina said, too. You're right that my influences have changed a ton from when I was a teenager making demos. And I think I'm okay with that. Even if people don't end up liking whatever I finally write as much as they like my old stuff."

"They will."

He smiled at her, her hand warm against his, her fingers long and pretty as they wrapped over his. "You're so sure, aren't you, Ash?"

"Only about you." Her cheeks flushed as she amended her sentence to, "I mean your music."

But he liked thinking that she'd meant it the first way. His mom had always been sure of him, and it had made it easy for him to be certain about things, too. In his pocket, his cell phone continued buzzing with incoming text messages, but he didn't want anything to come between him and Ashley. Not when they were finally talking again. Whoever was trying to reach him could wait.

"What about you?" he asked. "You were so deep in concentration just now. Are you working on your grad school application?"

"I started out trying to put together my thoughts about how major labels could work better with artists and the emerging digital industry for my application, but I keep veering."

"Veering where?"

She looked a little uncertain for a moment, before seeming to come to a decision. "Toward this." She slid her hand from his so that she could open up her computer.

At the same time that he was glad she trusted him enough to show him what she was working on, he hated that they weren't touching anymore. But when he looked at her screen, his eyebrows went up. "You're putting together a business plan for an indie, artist-run label?"

"I've learned so much this week with you, Drew—learned things I never could have from a book or case study or documentary. And the biggest thing of all that I've learned is that you not only know your music and what makes it special better than anyone else ever will, but you also understand your fans better than anyone else does. All I could think of as I sat in those meetings earlier this week at your label, and then during every interview and planning session you have with your crew, is how incredible it would be if *you* were running your own label. And when you said to Smith and Valentina that you were worried about not having a hit for them on the soundtrack and they said they didn't care about hits, only that your heart is behind the music, everything fell into place. What you're doing—it doesn't have to be about hits that radio stations have to approve before playing. You can put out whatever you want on the Internet in whatever format you want. Or you can just play songs live at shows and never play them the same way twice. Your fans love what you do so much that I know they're going to follow you wherever you are and love whatever songs you write. At least, they will as long as *you* love the songs you're writing."

Her eyes were shining with excitement and all of that incredible passion that made him fall even harder for her. He had quickly scanned the charts and documents on her computer, but even though it looked great on paper, he liked listening to her talk about it even more. God, how he loved hearing that melody in her voice that he'd missed so much during the past few days.

Because *she* was the most beautiful melody he'd ever heard.

"Tell me more, Ash."

"I know you wouldn't be able to do it all, not if you wanted to focus on creating and playing great music. You'd need a great staff, but if it were your label, *you* would be in charge of hiring the staff to run it. Just like you brought in all these great players for your tour, and Max and James. You're a great judge of character, and they'd be answering to you, rather than you feeling as though you have to answer to them the way you do with Robert and Ansel."

When she halted suddenly, he could fairly easily guess that she felt she'd just overstepped her bounds. But she hadn't. On the contrary, she had everything exactly right.

"That's just how I feel, Ash. Like I'm locked in a cage, one I've given Chief Records the key to. It's funny, actually—when I was signing with them, they wanted to do a multi-album deal, but even back then I couldn't do it. Not just because my brother Grant advised me that I'd be able to negotiate an even better deal for the second album if the first did well, but mostly because I couldn't stand the thought of wearing handcuffs that tight."

"*You* are the one who made yourself an indie success when you were a teenager," Ash told him. "The label has been lucky to have you for this album, and they'd be crazy lucky to get you for another. But I can't stop thinking about your brilliant entrepreneur brother and wondering if he might have any interest in partnering with you on something new."

"With Grant, anything's possible. Especially if he senses a challenge."

"He sounds a lot like you."

As he stared into Ashley's beautiful eyes, Drew's focus shifted from the music business to the woman he'd been obsessing about ever since he'd first seen her. He'd desired her from the start. But it hadn't taken long for him to *need* her, too. Her smile. Her laughter. Her brilliance. Her support.

And especially the way he felt when she was in his arms—as though he'd finally found the other half of his soul.

"Do you have any idea how much I want to kiss you right now?"

"Yes." The one word was barely more than a whisper. "Because I want to kiss you just as much."

He lightly stroked his fingers over the incredibly soft skin on the inside of her wrist, and the way she trembled at his touch made him crazy. Absolutely crazy for her in a way he'd never been crazy for anyone else.

"Ash, I swear I've been trying to keep from doing this..." But even as he said it, he was moving closer, needing to erase the space between them.

"So have I," she said as she leaned in toward him, too.

"What if we can't stop it, Ash?" He moved another inch closer so that he could see the way her pupils were dilating and her skin was flushing with heat. "What if we *shouldn't* stop it?"

When her tongue flicked out to lick her lips, Drew knew that nothing could stop him from kissing her. He reached out to tangle his hands in her hair, and she made a little humming sound of anticipation that heated him up even more as he lowered his mouth to hers.

He was just about to taste her, could feel her warm breath across his lips, when a loud knock sounded at the door.

"Drew," James called out, "you in there?"

Drew cursed under his breath, and Ashley let out what sounded like an extremely frustrated sigh. And as James let himself onto the bus, she grabbed her computer and slid out of the booth.

"Hey, Ashley," James said, "how's it going?"

"Good," she replied, but Drew could hear the way the four letters trembled slightly on her tongue. As if she was as twisted up over missing out on their kiss as he was.

"I've been texting you for fifteen minutes, Drew. We've got to get to the photo shoot before the photographer the label hired has a coronary."

The very last thing he was in the mood for today was posing for a bunch of pictures, even if the photographer was reputed to be one of the best in the world. But his mother had taught him not to take his career for granted—and not to waste anyone's time either—so he stuffed away his frustration as best he could. He slid out of the booth on the side opposite

Ashley, who was standing by the table holding her laptop in front of her chest like a shield.

"Ready to go?"

For a moment, he worried she was considering going back to keeping her distance the way she had for the past few days. But, thank God, she nodded and gave him a small smile instead.

"Let's go."

* * *

Moment by moment, as Ashley watched Drew during his photo shoot, the heat built inside of her. And when the photographer—a woman who clearly wanted to have Drew for lunch *and* dinner—asked him to take his shirt off, Ashley actually started to worry that someone on set was going to slip on her drool.

The last week had been the biggest tease of her life, and she had finally hit the point of no return. She'd never been a sex-crazed person—at least, she hadn't thought so, not when she'd easily managed to hang on to her virginity for twenty-two years. But today the sound of Drew's laughter and the way his bare abs rippled sent every last hormone into overdrive. Especially after he'd told her how much he missed her, and then had been on the verge of kissing her again.

So when the photographer said, "You're looking *amazing,* Drew," for the millionth time and the woman's assistants chimed in to agree, Ashley knew it was long past time to deal with the heat inside of her in the hopes that she could function at least halfway normally again.

She got up out of her seat, intending to slip away. Everyone but James was taking the day off while

Drew did this shoot, and though there were several people there from Drew's record label, they weren't paying any attention to her. Ashley tried not to run off the set, even had a conversation for a good fifteen minutes with the guy running the craft services table in the next room, but she couldn't remember ever feeling like this before, where she could only think of one thing: *sex with Drew Morrison.*

His hands on her.

His mouth on her.

His body moving over hers. *Into* hers.

Oh God...she was just making it worse, having these thoughts, letting herself spin off into fantasies again before she got back to the bus, where she could lock herself in and finally try to take the edge off her insane need.

Her hand shook as she typed in the code to unlock the bus's door. Jesus, she was panting, too. Crazy. This was crazy. Crazier than she'd ever been before.

With Max on a day off as well while they stayed overnight, the bus was completely empty and silent. Of all the things she'd expected to learn this summer, she'd never imagined that one of them would be how to sneak away to touch herself on a tour bus. But as she locked the bus door behind her, she was too far gone to care.

The curtain was pulled in front of her bunk— she tried to be extra neat in such close quarters. She yanked it back and threw herself on the small bed. She didn't even take the time to kick off her shoes before pulling her skirt up and slipping her hand against her heated, already damp skin.

It wasn't nearly as good as she imagined Drew's touch would be, but it was *so* much better than continuing to suffer with no touch at all, the way she'd been for the past week.

She still remembered how it had felt when he'd kissed her on the beach. The way his tongue had stroked over hers. The way his teeth had scraped her lower lip. The way his hands had gripped her hips to squeeze and pull her closer. So close that she'd easily been able to feel just how much he wanted her.

Ashley closed her eyes, and as she lay back on her pillow, letting her legs fall open even wider, she pretended he was with her in the bunk, kissing her again right now.

Would he say she was beautiful?

Would he take her shirt in his fist and rip it away so that he could kiss her breasts, too?

Or would he just keep kissing her while he slid his hand right where hers was, beneath the cotton, where she was *aching* for him?

She was right there on the edge, but she wasn't ready to stop yet, wasn't ready to go back to having to try so hard to be in control all the time. For a few more minutes, all she wanted was to enjoy the forbidden pleasure of indulging her naughty fantasies about Drew.

CHAPTER SEVENTEEN

Holy hell...was this really happening?

Drew had ducked into his bedroom on the bus to grab his guitar for the next set of photos. He'd needed to get away from all those eyes on him for a few minutes, take a momentary break from all those expectations and people from the label telling him what they thought he wanted to hear. Saying how hot he looked. That he was going to smash sales records with his next album, whenever he finally got around to signing the contract and recording it. Telling him he was a superstar.

But he didn't care about any of that. Didn't need their praise. Didn't, frankly, care what any of them thought about him and his music. Only one set of eyes mattered today. Only one opinion.

Ashley's.

It figured, then, that out of everyone watching the shoot, she would be the only one he hadn't been able to read. Did she hate it? The flash? The props? The fact that the photographer had nearly sprayed his bare chest with oil? All the big-budget, borderline ridiculous things the label had convinced him were expected at this stage of his career?

Already, he'd come to respect Ashley's opinion a thousand times more than those of any of the Chief Records guys in suits. She knew the business as well as any of them—better, probably, because he'd never known anyone to read so much, not even his sister Olivia.

What Ashley innately understood that the guys from the label never would was what was *behind* the music. The heart and soul of a lyric, a melody, a rhythm, that drew ears to it. She could break a song down and analyze each piece, but she could also simply close her eyes and let the magic of it wash over, and through, her.

All through the photo shoot he'd been thinking about the ideas she'd shared with him this morning on the bus. Could he go indie? Could he put together his own company and do things *his* way?

But overarching even those huge career questions had been an even bigger one. Namely, how much longer did he have to wait to kiss Ashley again? All week had been a series of near misses, and frustration was bubbling up inside of him as he grabbed his guitar, opened the bedroom door to head through the living room...

And realized he wasn't alone.

He smelled her before he heard her, the vanilla from the body wash she used in the shower instantly turning him on. He was on the verge of saying her name to let her know he was in the back of the bus when he heard what sounded like a moan.

A moan of pleasure.

A rash of jealous thoughts hit him first. Was she with someone else? Had she brought a guy back to the bus while he was doing his photo shoot?

Thoughts of anyone else touching her, kissing her, hearing her gasps of pleasure skewered him one after the other until he realized he couldn't actually hear anyone else.

Only Ashley and the sweet little sounds she was making from her bunk.

Sounds that were so damned good, he had to move closer, had to find out if one of his biggest fantasies could actually be coming true.

Night after night, as he'd gone back into his bedroom alone to try to take the edge off his need for her, he'd wondered if she was doing the same thing. But to be lucky enough to stumble onto the bus just as she was touching herself?

Jesus.

Just then, she gave another little moan, and Drew couldn't stop himself not only from moving closer…but also from putting his hand over his rock-hard erection.

He could hear her breathing now, the way it was speeding up as she came closer and closer to her climax. Somewhere in the back of his mind, Drew knew he should stay in the shadows, that he should let her finish getting off without realizing she had an audience. But he couldn't think straight anymore. Couldn't think beyond the desperate need to *see* Ashley when she took herself over the edge.

When he finally got close enough to see into her bunk, he couldn't believe his eyes. Not when the most erotic vision in the world lay only feet away.

She was lying on top of the sheets. Her skirt was up around her waist, and her hand was inside her panties. Her other hand had found its way up her blouse where he was almost positive she was playing with her breasts. Her hair had come part of the way out of the clip she wore to hold it back, and her skin was flushed with heat and arousal. Her mouth was wet, as if she'd been licking it while she lifted her hips up into her hand in what had to be the sexiest rhythm he'd ever heard.

"Ashley."

He didn't realize he'd said her name aloud until it was too late. Her eyes flew open, and her hand immediately came out from between her legs. Of course, that only made him hotter, hungrier, when he saw how wet her fingers were.

"Don't stop," he found himself saying. "I swear I didn't know you were here. I didn't plan this. But, please, don't stop."

He watched as embarrassment shifted to indecision on her face. But beneath both was the arousal she hadn't been able to bank. Not when she was obviously so close, hovering on the edge of what he suspected was going to be one hell of an orgasm.

Thank God, it didn't take long for desire to win. "I won't stop," she whispered, "but only if...only if you touch yourself, too."

He couldn't get his pants undone and his hand around himself fast enough. "I'm already nearly there, Ashley." He throbbed hard into his hand as she let him watch hers disappear again beneath the thin white fabric. "God, you're sexy."

Her lids came halfway down as she began to touch herself again. But she didn't take her eyes from him as she said, "So are you."

It took every ounce of control he possessed not to leap into the bunk with her and replace her hand with his own. Or better yet, his mouth.

He wasn't going to last. Wasn't going to even make it until she came. But then, a beat before he lost it, he watched as her hips lifted up off the bed, her eyes closed, and she whispered his name in a broken voice.

Not wanting to miss one second, Drew stilled his hand over himself and watched with wonder as she gave herself over to what looked to be one seriously hot and powerful orgasm. And when she finally opened her eyes and looked straight into his, her hands now unmoving inside her clothes on bare, damp skin, even though he was standing fully clothed in the middle of his tour bus on a Wednesday afternoon, Drew came harder than he could ever remember coming before in his life.

* * *

It took way too long for Ashley's heart to stop racing and for the fog in her head to clear.

Oh God.

What had she done?

Of course, given that her body was still tingling in the most delicious way, she knew darn well what she'd just done. She'd not only locked herself in the tour bus to touch herself and then kept going once she realized Drew was there watching her...but then had actually been bold enough to ask him to touch himself, too!

She felt so out of her element. Beyond mortified. She couldn't stop her hands from shaking as she shifted on the bunk to pull her skirt down. Of course, that was when she also finally realized that somewhere in the madness that had taken over she'd pulled her top open, too.

At this point, there wasn't anything left to say to him but, "I'm really embarrassed right now."

"Don't be," he said, his clothes already put back together. He grinned at her. "It could have happened to anyone."

His easy, teasing response caught her off guard, so much so that she actually forgot to be embarrassed. "Really? Other people have come onto your tour bus to—" Ah, there was the mortification flooding back in. Seriously, if the earth could just open up to swallow her whole...

She licked her lips nervously, and his gaze fell heavily to them before he grinned even wider and said, "No. You're the first."

How was it that she was on the verge of grinning back at him after what had just happened?

But she already knew the answer: Drew owned his sexuality so well that he seemed to assume she would own hers, too.

Now *that* was quite a thought, one she'd been circling more and more during the time she'd been with him. Why did she always feel like she needed to run from something that she knew was perfectly natural? And what would happen if she simply embraced it instead?

But she still couldn't forget the hurt from Drew's rejection on the beach, when she'd asked him to be with her. As the remembered pain whiplashed her so hard that she swore she could feel the sting of it, she said, "You probably need to get back to the set, or they're going to think something happened to you."

"Something *did* happen to me. Something *amazing.*"

She wanted to believe that what had happened meant as much to him as it had to her, but it was scary to let herself go there. So scary that she knew she couldn't be anything but honest. "I can't do this again, Drew. It hurt so much when you told me you didn't want to be with me out on the beach. But now..." She bit her lip. "Now it would crush me to hear you say it."

"Ash." He reached for her hand and tugged her closer. "That night, it nearly killed me to walk away from you. And now—" His phone rang with James's special ring tone. "Damn it, can't I just have five minutes alone with you?"

"As soon as James sees me, he's going to know. They all will."

She might admire those women in the audience every night who owned their sexuality, but who was she kidding? She wasn't one of them. Slipping her hand from Drew's, she turned to look for the shoe that had fallen off the side of the bunk.

"Ash." Drew's voice was so full of warmth that she had to turn back to face him. "What just happened was beautiful. The most beautiful thing I've ever been a part of." She felt herself flush all over again as he continued. "I have to get back to the shoot now, but we need to talk tonight. As soon as I can get away from everything."

She took a deep breath, trying to get her brain to work right in the aftermath of her shockingly good orgasm. But she already knew he was right, even without her synapses firing. There was no way to hide from what was happening between them anymore. Not now that they'd both just watched each other break apart into a million perfect pieces.

And when James called *her* phone, she knew Drew's bodyguard was about to storm onto the bus to lay into his rock-star boss for skipping out in the middle of his photo shoot. "Okay, we'll talk tonight. You need to go, though. This shoot must be costing a fortune."

"Do you want to come back with me to the set?"

For a moment she was tempted to hide out on the bus. But that's just what it would be—hiding. And, suddenly, she was sick of hiding. Sick of sitting on the sidelines of life. No, she wasn't yet ready to propose a fling again the way she had in Los Angeles, no matter how many sweet and sexy things he'd said to her since then. But just because she was still trying to figure things out, didn't mean she wanted to figure them out in the shadows. Not when it seemed she'd been doing that her entire life.

"I like having you there," he added when she didn't answer quickly enough. "But I know you're probably bored senseless."

"I wasn't bored." Which was an understatement, given the fact that she'd been riveted by every flex of his abs, the slight sheen of sweat that had begun to cover his tanned skin under the hot lights, and how funny and clever he was as he joked with the photographer's staff. "I like being there, too."

He reached for her hand, and it felt more electric than ever. "And then after, we'll talk. Tonight."

She couldn't look away from his beautiful eyes as she echoed, "Tonight."

CHAPTER EIGHTEEN

Ashley was on pins and needles as *We'll talk tonight* played over and over in her head like a song on repeat. She didn't want to make the mistake of getting her hopes up again and letting anticipation take over, but every time she thought about what had happened on the bus that afternoon...

"You're a trouper, Ashley." James took the seat next to her. "Hanging out all day while Drew makes pretty faces for the camera."

"I hate having my picture taken. He makes it look so easy, though."

"Some things come easy to him, other things come easy to you, like whatever you're doing on your computer all the time. I think that's why you and Drew fit so good together—you round each other out just right."

She was so stunned by his comment that she couldn't stop herself from echoing back to him, "You think we're good together?"

"Sure do," he said with a nod. "I've worked for plenty of guys like Drew who make it big real young.

It's natural for them to want to sow some wild oats. But as soon as you came into the picture—" He grinned at her. "Let's just say I've got a feeling about the two of you."

Ashley was floored by everything James was saying, that he had *a feeling* about her and Drew. He couldn't possibly know about what had happened on the bus that afternoon, but her face still flamed with heat as she asked, "Has he sown a lot of wild oats?"

Obviously sensing that he was about to enter a minefield—one that he'd accidentally just set up—James held up his hands. "No more than any other guy in his position. And I'm sure he's done with all that now."

She shouldn't be bothered by finding out about all the women Drew had been with, but hearing the words aloud still made her feel as if she'd been punched in the gut. It didn't help that a group of the most beautiful women she'd ever seen walked into the room just then.

"Who are they?" she asked James.

"The label decided to bring in some models for a few of the shots."

Models who quickly began to drape themselves all over Drew, even before the photographer encouraged them to do just that. Ashley couldn't stand to watch—but she couldn't look away either.

Mine, she thought, even if all they'd shared so far was a week in a bus together and a few stolen moments of pleasure. *He's mine, not yours.*

"The label is throwing a party tonight," James told her. "Might be a little fancy. You still have that pink dress from Valentina and Smith's party?"

She knew what James was telling her, that maybe she should think about trying a little harder than her usual black and white outfits for once. "Valentina emailed and said Tatiana wants me to keep it. I think it's a fancy designer dress and probably costs a fortune, but she wouldn't let me give it back." Ashley had never thought she'd be getting fashion advice from a bodyguard, but given that pretty much everyone understood fashion better than she did, maybe it wasn't all that surprising. "Do you think I should wear it tonight to the party?"

Just as the photographer encouraged the most stunning model of the group to pucker up and pretend she was kissing Drew, James said, "Yes. You should definitely wear that pink dress tonight."

* * *

Ashley was even more nervous tonight than she'd been the night she'd joined the tour. Back then she hadn't even dreamed of kissing Drew, of him holding her in his arms, of him whispering words like *God, you're sexy* to her as desire took them both over. She hadn't given much thought to her clothes, her hair, or the fact that she wore mascara and lipstick only on special occasions.

She was wearing makeup tonight, along with her new pink dress. She didn't have any heels, which was just as well, considering that even in her flats she felt more than a little wobbly from sheer nerves. The last thing she needed was to fall on her face in front of the photographer and the people from the record label and the models.

It was funny, she thought as she headed into the hotel to join the party, the only person she wasn't worried about falling on her face in front of was Drew. Partly because she'd already done plenty of embarrassing things in front of him. But mostly because she knew that whatever happened, he'd just give her one of his gorgeous, teasing smiles and make her laugh about it.

No question, he'd been raised well. In two days, she'd get to meet his father and siblings when they came to New Orleans for his birthday. She'd find out if all the Morrisons were as great as Drew. She had a feeling they would be. She really hoped that the gift she'd been working on since he'd mentioned his birthday in the Valley of Fire would be ready in time.

The valet at the front door took a long look at her cleavage as he held the door open for her. She wasn't used to that kind of attention—wasn't quite comfortable with it either, to be honest—but told herself it was a good sign that she might not be totally overshadowed by all the models.

Laughter bubbled out of her at the absurd thought. *Of course* she would be overshadowed by the models. They were all tall and glossy and perfect, whereas she was just…her.

But he seems to like "just you," a voice inside her head reminded her. *And I thought you were sick of hiding?*

As she walked inside, she made herself hold her shoulders back rather than rounding them forward to hide her chest in the form-fitting dress. Insecurity didn't become anyone, so even though she'd been hit with it big-time as soon as the beautiful women had joined Drew's photo shoot, she wasn't going to let it take over.

Not tonight.

Laughter and music were spilling out of the ballroom as two gorgeous women who looked to be her age walked out in sky-high heels and teeny-tiny shimmering dresses. They hadn't been in the photo shoot, although they were certainly pretty enough to have made the cut. They didn't even spare her a glance as they walked by, arm in arm, laughing.

The insecurity she was so bound and determined to push away tried to rear its ugly head again, but she'd made it through Smith and Valentina's party in one piece, even with falling into the pool, hadn't she? So what if there were dozens of gorgeous women here tonight? All that mattered was that she and Drew had formed a connection. Even James had commented on how well they seemed to fit together.

No, it didn't make the least bit of sense that a star like Drew would fall for someone normal like her. And Ashley had always worked hard to make sure things added up, both in math class and in life. But maybe everything in life didn't always have to make perfect sense.

Could some things just be pure, sweet joy and pleasure?

The room was packed, but thankfully James spotted her within seconds. She figured Drew had asked his bodyguard to keep a special eye out for her the way he usually did. "You look great, Ashley." She smiled at him, really glad to see a friendly face. "I'll get you a drink. What's your poison?"

James was drinking a beer, but she'd never been much for alcohol. Besides, she didn't want to feel at all fuzzy once she and Drew finally got a chance to talk. "Sparkling water would be great, thank you."

"You're a good girl," he said approvingly, almost like a father would to his daughter. "I'll be right back."

Ashley knew she was a good girl and had never worried about that before. No one wanted the CEO of a company to be wild, after all. But she didn't think she wanted to be that good girl anymore. At least, not tonight. Not when she was finally realizing just how much joy and pleasure there was to discover in Drew's arms.

She tried to be casual as she leaned against the wall and waited for James to bring her drink, but it wasn't easy when she felt so far out of her element. She'd rarely been to parties even in college, though she'd gone to plenty of clubs in San Francisco to watch up-and-coming bands of all styles.

So far on this tour, she'd done plenty of things outside her comfort zone...especially this afternoon on the bus. But where that had been more enjoyable than anything she'd ever imagined, maybe coming to this party had been a mistake. Then again, if she wanted to work in the music business, wouldn't she have to get used to participating in events like this?

She groaned out loud at the way both sides of her brain were at war. *Stay. Go. Stay. Go.*

The crowd parted suddenly, and she looked right into Drew's eyes. Even though he was on the other side of the ballroom, she swore she could see heat in his expression. The same heat that had been there when he'd seen her wearing this dress for the first time, and then again on the bus this afternoon when he'd walked in on her touching herself.

She smiled at him, suddenly feeling incredibly happy that she'd stayed. Especially when he held out a hand and she knew it was for her.

All these beautiful women in the room and *she* was the one he wanted. It felt like a fairy tale. Like a dream come true. Even though she'd spent more of her life with her nose in a book or with a calculator in her hand than dreaming about Prince Charming, Ashley suddenly understood all those fairy tales her mother had liked to read to her when she was a little girl. Because when a man looked at you the way Drew was looking at—

Ashley stopped short as a positively stunning woman took Drew's hand, lifted it, and twirled around beneath it as if they'd choreographed the movement. And then, the next thing she knew, the woman was in Drew's arms, and he was holding her tightly against him.

Feeling as though she were standing in the middle of the train tracks able to hear the conductor's whistle, but not able to get her feet to move, she watched as the woman lifted her lips to Drew's for a kiss. Just then, someone moved in front of Ashley, but she'd already seen enough. And when she got another clear look at Drew a moment later, he was still holding on to the gorgeous stranger, even more tightly now, his lips close to the woman's ear as if he were whispering sweet nothings to her.

The music kept playing, people kept talking and laughing around her, but all Ashley could hear was the blood rushing in her ears.

Oh God, I am such an idiot!

She should have known better than to get all dressed up tonight. She must look like she was trying too hard. All her life, she'd done just the opposite—she hadn't tried at all. But after this morning and afternoon on the bus, she'd started to feel more sure about taking another risk like the one she'd taken on the beach in Los Angeles.

She'd assumed that when he said he wanted to talk with her tonight, he'd meant he wanted them to talk about taking things even further. But she must have been wrong, must have misunderstood...all because she wanted the fairy tale to come true so badly.

Ashley gulped air into lungs that felt like they were burning as she hightailed it through the hotel and back out to the bus, even though she knew it wasn't any sanctuary at all, because she was sharing it with Drew. She'd just have to pretend to be asleep when he got back.

But then it hit her—what if he came in with one of the models? Or *more* than one of the models?

Wait. No. She couldn't go back to the bus tonight. Not if there was even a hint of a chance that he was going to board it with someone else. She'd been saving for graduate school and had been really careful with her money so far on this trip, but it didn't matter how much a night in this fancy hotel cost.

"I need a room," she told the woman behind the reception desk. "Just for tonight."

The woman behind the counter shook her head. "I'm sorry, but we're fully booked."

"Can you recommend another hotel nearby?"

"All the other hotels I usually recommend are booked, as well. This tends to happen whenever a really big musician comes to town." The woman's eyes drifted to the newspaper on the counter, which had a picture of Drew on the front page. "Are you here for Drew Morrison's show tomorrow night?"

Knowing how the woman would react if she found out Ashley was *on tour* with Drew, she simply said, "I just really need a place to stay tonight. Are there any other options? Maybe a B&B or—"

She stopped when the woman gasped. "Those models were with him earlier. I think he must be about to come this way."

Ashley shoved away from the front desk so fast she nearly fell. She needed to get on the bus, grab her things, and then figure out where to go from there. Anything but trying to fake it with Drew and the models.

So much for the big night she'd been expecting. Looked like she was going to keep being the good girl her father expected her to be...and that everything made perfect sense after all.

Because the rock star wasn't going to end up with the normal girl.

CHAPTER NINETEEN

Drew hadn't wanted to tighten his grip around the stranger's waist, especially after she'd pressed her mouth to his in a sloppy approximation of a kiss he *really* didn't want. But she'd been so drunk it had been nearly impossible to keep her upright.

"Let's get you somewhere you can sit down."

"Don't wanna sit down." Her words slurred together. "Wanna be with you."

He helped the woman into a seat and texted James to let him know there was a problem he needed help with. A big one, considering that one moment Ashley had been smiling at him, and the next, when the model had draped herself around him like an octopus, she'd gone completely pale. And then had turned and left the party.

The next text he sent was to Ashley.

Can we talk now? I'll be on the bus in five minutes.

He stared at his phone, waiting for her response. But there was none. He knew he shouldn't have let the damned circus take over. The label had already gotten enough from him today.

And now he needed to find her right away. Needed to explain what had just happened. But most of all, he needed to talk with her about what they were doing. About where their attraction and friendship were taking them.

He'd never wanted anyone as badly as he wanted her—never liked anyone as much either—but having a fling while on tour with her still didn't feel right. Not just because of her father. Of course, he wanted to respect his former professor's wishes. But if there was one thing that Drew had learned from his mother, it was that the most important thing was to follow his own heart, no matter the sacrifice, regardless of how difficult.

And Drew's heart had been leading him toward Ashley since the moment he'd met her.

Ashley deserved more than a fling while they were on the road. They both did. Drew was ready to take the next step, not just into bed with each other, but toward having a real relationship. She'd be his girlfriend, he'd be her boyfriend, and the whole world would know they were together.

But would she want that, too? Or had she meant what she'd said to him out on the beach in Los Angeles? *"No one needs to know. Just you and me here on the tour bus having a good time for as long as we're both enjoying ourselves."*

If he'd seen the woman coming toward him, he might have been able to sidestep her lunge into his arms. But he'd taken one look at Ashley in that pretty pink dress and had been stunned stupid. Her dress wasn't anywhere near as revealing as the ones the models were wearing, but to Drew it was the sexiest damn thing he'd ever seen. The kind of dress that made a guy wonder about the secrets she had hidden beneath.

Secrets he'd only just begun to learn that afternoon.

Secrets he was *dying* to uncover completely tonight.

A night that he had been ready to begin hours ago, rather than being here at another party in what felt like a long string of them over the past few years. It was a stereotype that he'd played into for way too long.

He liked hanging out with his family, his friends, his crew. But he didn't need the big flashy parties. Didn't need to see his face and name plastered on walls as some sort of stroke to his ego. It was yet another thing that Ashley had helped him see.

Only, had he realized it too late?

James appeared at Drew's side and looked down at the girl, who was now holding her head and moaning. "Too much to drink?"

"At the very least," he told his bodyguard. "Can you take care of getting her some help? I've got to find Ashley. I'm afraid she has the wrong idea about what just happened here."

"Go find your girl, Drew. I'll make sure this one gets the help she needs to make it home in one piece."

Your girl. He was glad James realized just what Ashley meant to him, even without anything being spelled out publicly.

Drew headed through the crowd toward the exit. He kept his gaze on the door, but people from his label attached themselves to him anyway, all of them wanting a piece of him for something. To take pictures with more people at the party. To sign a hundred more photos for them to send out. To do "just a couple more quick interviews."

A hundred—maybe even a thousand times—before tonight, Drew had given his label whatever they wanted. But he'd finally found something—someone—more important than his music and career. And if he didn't get his act together fast, he was going to lose her.

Now, as the group tried to follow him out, he channeled his father—one of the most easygoing guys in the world, someone everyone liked. "Great party, guys. Great shoot today, too." He made himself smile as genuinely as possible, even though he had a bad feeling that the clock on fixing everything he kept screwing up with Ashley was running out. "Let's reconnect on those extra interviews tomorrow before I leave town. Thanks again."

Before they could try to convince him to stay, he made a fast beeline for the front desk. Ashley still hadn't responded to his text, so he asked the hotel employee, "Did you see a woman in a pink dress leave?"

The woman gaped at him for a few moments before finally saying, "You're Drew Morrison."

Drew went out of his way not to be rude to his fans. He got what it was like to meet someone whose songs you listened to on the radio. Every time he met one of his music idols, he had to fight through the same kind of speechlessness. But tonight he didn't have time to waste.

"I really need to find her. Her name is Ashley."

Finally, the woman snapped back to his question. "Does she have wavy, light brown hair? Really pretty, but not in a flashy kind of way?"

"That's her." Although as far as Drew was concerned, *pretty* didn't even begin to describe Ashley's beauty.

"I was just talking with her. She asked if I could rent her a room."

Drew bit back a curse. He'd tried to get the model off him at the party, but she'd been so drunk that if he hadn't put his arms around her when she'd tried to kiss him, she would have fallen. Clearly, Ashley had misinterpreted what had happened. And for good reason—it *had* looked like he'd been kissing someone else. That would have been bad enough after the past week they'd spent together on the road, but after what had happened between them this afternoon? Kissing someone else would make him the biggest douche bag in the world.

"Did you rent her one?"

"No. We're all booked up for the night."

"Did she tell you where she was going?"

The woman shook her head. "She said something about maybe trying to find a B&B, but we were cut off before she told me what her plans were for sure."

Drew ran through the hotel's foyer and out toward the back of the building, where his bus was parked. If Ashley planned to stay in a B&B for the night, she'd probably need to grab her computer first, wouldn't she?

He could barely type in the code next to the door correctly, he was in such a rush, and when it finally clicked open, he nearly tore it from his hinges in his haste to get inside. "Ashley?" he called as he hurried up the steps.

Thank God, she was standing right in the middle of the bus. But she had her hands on the bodice of her dress, and it looked like she was trying to rip the fabric apart.

"Ash?" He quickly moved to take her hands in his. "What are you doing?"

"This dress, I hate it. I want it off. *Now.*"

"No, it's beautiful. *You're* beautiful."

"Stop!" She shook off his hands and moved away from him. "You don't have to keep up the act. You can have them, any of those models and actresses. You didn't have to come here to try to convince me that I'm special, that I'm beautiful, when we both know I'm nothing compared to any of those models or their friends, or even the women in your audiences."

"You're usually right about everything, Ash. But right now, you're wrong. So damned wrong." He'd come to apologize, but he hated hearing her talk about herself as though she were less than anyone else, and he wasn't going to back down about this. "How can you not see that you outshine every single one of them?" He moved close again, put his hands around hers. "What you saw at the party, I swear it was innocent. She was drunk and could hardly stand. I only put my arms around her so that she wouldn't fall. If I could have stopped her from putting her mouth on me, I would have. I swear I didn't want her, Ash. I only want you."

He watched as Ashley's expression slowly changed from angry to surprised. But then, instead of looking happier, she simply looked resigned.

"I shouldn't have jumped to conclusions," she finally said, "but the two of you just looked so natural together. You don't understand how I'm not seeing things that seem obvious to you, but how can *you* not see that someone like her—like any of the women you've been with today—are a better fit for you?"

"Because she isn't. None of them are, Ash."

"But when your hands were on her hips..." She broke off with a shake of her head. "When I saw you touch her, I realized just how foolish I'm being. You and me—whatever we've been feeling is probably just because of our close proximity on the bus. Or because we each know the other is off-limits so that makes it seem more exciting. But out in the real world—"

His mouth was on hers before he even knew what he was doing. He just couldn't stand to listen to her tell them both lies. Not when everything they'd said to each other before tonight had been completely honest.

This was the real world.

The only world that mattered.

He was too wound up to be gentle. Too scared that he was going to lose her to do anything but thread his hands into her hair and deepen the kiss. He'd tried to show her with words just how much she meant to him, but she stubbornly refused to listen. Which left out every option but this—his mouth on hers, their bodies straining together, the aching need that had been building between them about to combust from nothing more than a kiss.

But then, he realized she was trembling, and sanity washed over him like a bucket of ice water dumped over his head.

"Ash." He slid his hands from her hair to stroke her cheeks, as gentle now as he'd been rough just seconds before. "The last thing I want to do is hurt you. Or scare you."

"You aren't hurting me. And you've never scared me." But when she inhaled deeply, he saw the way it shook through her. "I just...I've never felt this way. Never felt so *much*. I don't know how to process it. First, I was so happy after this afternoon. And then I was so jealous at the party. And now, after that kiss..." She shook her head. "It's like I'm completely full and yet empty all at the same time. Empty and *aching*."

"I've never felt like this either. Just with you. I know I'm going too fast, but the thought of losing you—" His chest squeezed tight at the thought of not seeing her every day. Of not being able to talk with her and laugh with her. Of never holding her in his arms again. "I don't want to lose you. Tell me what to do so that I don't keep screwing this up."

"If it were just us..."

She stopped and looked down at their entwined hands, and he finally realized just how small hers were inside his. She was so capable, so strong, that he'd never noticed before just how delicate she was—and it only made him angrier at himself that he'd just been so rough with her. All because he couldn't stand the thought of her leaving his bus tonight and never coming back.

"Honestly," she finally continued, "even *just us* is complicated, since you're a superstar and I'm just me."

"Just you?" Frustration bubbled up inside him again. "Why can't you see how amazing you are?"

"I know I'm good at numbers. And research. And being a good girl." She made a face. "But I don't know how to do the kinds of things normal, sexier girls do. My mother tried to teach me about clothes and makeup and boys, but I never felt like I measured up, so it was safer not to try to compete."

"I could tell you a million times over how special you are and how sexy," he said in a gentle voice, "but maybe that's where I'm getting it all wrong. Maybe I need to show you, instead. Can I show you, Ash? Can I love you the way you should be loved?"

At the word *love* her eyes widened and her gaze locked on his. "What about the promise you made to my father?"

"I put you on my bus to make sure that you left the tour the same way you came. But it's too late for that already, isn't it? Both of us have changed. From that very first conversation, nothing has been the same, has it?"

"No," she agreed, "it hasn't."

"I respect your father a great deal. And I'm a man who believes in keeping my promises. But this isn't about your father. You're right that you're not a little girl anymore. You're a woman who can make her own decisions about what she wants. You're a woman I've fallen head over heels for. You're a woman I can't stop thinking about. You're a woman I want to be with more than I've ever wanted to be with anyone in my life. More than I thought it was possible to want." He brought her hand to his chest and held it over his heart. "But you already know that, don't you? Deep in your heart, you can feel that mine is beating only for you, can't you?"

She didn't say anything for a few long moments. Long enough that renewed panic began to sprint up his spine. Ashley had made him happier in the past week than he'd been in a very long time.

Losing her right after he'd finally found her would be unbearable.

Finally, she nodded. "I can feel it, Drew. Everything. I feel *everything*."

Relief washed over him with such swift strength that he nearly had her mouth crushed beneath his before he realized she still hadn't given him the all-clear. And he'd never forgive himself if he took something from her that she wasn't ready to give, no matter how much pleasure he knew he could give her.

He could feel the unsteady beat of her heart crashing against his as he brushed the hair back from her forehead, looked into her eyes, and said again, "All I want is to love you. But what matters more than anything is what *you* want, Ash."

Thank God she wasn't shaking anymore as she met his gaze and whispered, "I want to love you, too."

CHAPTER TWENTY

Ashley's heart had been pounding so hard when Drew burst onto the bus that she'd barely been able to hear him say her name through the rush of blood in her ears. And then when he'd tried to get her to stop ripping off the dress, it had only pounded harder. Louder. So hard and loud that she'd felt as though her head were going to explode.

He'd kissed her before that could happen, before she could get any more wound up, before her insides could twist into any more knots. And though her heartbeat was still racing, it wasn't because she was upset. It wasn't because she was nervous either.

Amazingly, now that she'd made the decision to be with Drew, nearly all of her fears about her first time disappeared.

The two kisses they'd shared had been full of so many sexy promises that she couldn't wait one more second to be with him. Because if someone from his crew or the label knocked on their door tonight needing Drew, as had happened so many times before, her head really would explode. The past week had been nothing but one tempting moment after another.

"Give me your phone," he said.

She pulled her phone out of her bag, and he put it next to his on the kitchen counter. "I don't want any interruptions either," she said with a smile she couldn't contain. As he reached for her hand, she asked, "Does James know where you are?"

He lifted her hand to his lips and pressed a kiss to her knuckles. "He does."

"With me?"

He looked into her eyes. "With you."

Of course they couldn't keep this from James. Not when his job was to know exactly where Drew was at all times while on tour. "Your whole life is so open, so public." Her words were halting, and though she didn't want them to come out the wrong way, she still needed Drew to hear them. "Do you think we can keep this private?"

"I want to tell the whole damned world that you're mine, Ash." He paused for a moment. "But I'll do anything you want. Anything you need me to do."

She wouldn't let herself think about the future right now, wouldn't let herself get twisted up in worries. Not tonight. So she lifted her mouth to his and told him exactly what she needed. "Kiss me again."

His lips curved up into a sexy smile even as he lowered them to cover hers. Just minutes ago, his kiss had been rough, and oh so raw. Now his kiss was barely more than a whisper of breath and heat.

A low moan sounded from her throat at the stunningly sweet kiss. She'd never known there were so many ways to kiss or to be kissed.

The next thing she knew, he was saying, "Hold on to me, Ash," and then he was lifting her up as if she weighed nothing, with one arm under her knees and the other around her rib cage.

"Drew!" His name bubbled out along with her surprised laughter. "What are you doing?"

His eyes were so dark and full of heat that she nearly lost her breath when he looked down at her and said, "Taking you to my bed." With nothing but those five words, even though he was simply holding her in his arms, she nearly came apart right then and there. "Is that where you want to be?"

"Yes." Instinctively, she knew why he was asking her again—because he didn't want her to regret one single moment with him. But Ashley needed him to know that no matter what happened after tonight, she would never regret it. *Never.* "It's the *only* place I want to be tonight. And you're the only person I want to be with."

He lowered his mouth to hers as he walked toward the back of the bus and laid her down on his bed. Somehow, somewhere, she must have done something really right to get to be here tonight with the most incredible man on the planet.

He traced one of her eyebrows and then the other with the tip of one callused finger. "What are you thinking, Ash?"

She didn't want to hide anything from him, so she told him, "How lucky I am."

"I'm the lucky one." He crawled over her on the bed, then took her hands in his and lifted them so that he was holding them on either side of her head. "So damned lucky I can hardly believe it."

He was a master lyricist, knew exactly how to bend words to tug at people's heartstrings. But every word he spoke while she lay beneath him on his bed rang pure and sweet, straight to the center of her heart.

He lowered his head so that the tips of his hair tickled her skin, and he began to run more of those impossibly soft, heady kisses down from her lips and over her jaw. She arched her head back to give him better access to swipe his tongue into the hollow of her throat and lightly scrape his teeth over her collarbone.

Her breath came faster and faster, making her breasts swell up from the top of the pink sleeveless dress. She was dying for him to touch her there, but he didn't just touch. Didn't just kiss. Instead, he said, "I need to see you, Ash."

"I need it, too." So badly that she was trembling with anticipation.

He moved his hands from hers and slipped them under the thin straps holding up her dress and slowly slid the fabric down, kissing first one shoulder and then the next as he bared them to his hungry gaze. His hands were warm and strong as they slid behind her back to unstick her zipper and open it all the way. And then, *finally*, he was drawing the fabric down, and she was holding her breath waiting, waiting, waiting for—

Oh God, the way it felt when he put his lips, his tongue, on her. She'd never felt anything like the sensations currently rocking through her, never knew any part of her body could be so wonderfully sensitive. The dress had slid up her thighs when he'd laid her down on the bed and now she wrapped her legs around him to bring him closer.

He cupped her breasts in his big hands, and she marveled at how pale her naked flesh looked against his tanned skin. How *right* in a way she'd never been able to see her body before. Somehow, when Drew was touching her, the curves she'd never known what to do with finally made sense.

With every swipe of his tongue over her nipples, his groans vibrated through her. He'd told her that her voice was the prettiest melody he'd ever heard, and now the sounds of his pleasure, and his excitement at being with her, were easily the best song she'd ever heard. A song she wanted to play over and over and over again until she'd memorized every tone, every dimension, every subtly changing pitch.

"You're so pretty." His dark eyes were wild with need as he lifted his head from her chest, and she couldn't stop herself from falling even deeper as she reached out to run her fingers through his hair. "All I want is to make you feel good." He pressed another hot kiss to the pulse jumping at the side of her neck.

"You do. You are. Better than I knew it was even possible to feel. Especially when you..."

"Especially when I...?" he prompted her.

They'd already gone further than she had with any other guy, and it was difficult not to be shy. It would have been easier not to say the words aloud, but she refused to let herself hold anything back tonight, no matter how scary it was to put herself out there like this. "When you're kissing my breasts. Please, do it again."

"I could do it for hours and hours," he told her, but instead of going straight back to her breasts, his mouth captured hers.

Every time they kissed he poured even more passion into it, into *her,* and she wondered how she'd lived twenty-two years without ever feeling this way. By the time he finally pulled back from her lips to kiss his way back down her naked skin, she should have been ready to feel the wet heat of his mouth over her breasts again. But when he took one taut peak against his tongue and rolled the other between his thumb and forefinger—*oh God, the things he could do with his hands and mouth*—she cried out so loudly that anyone standing outside the bus surely would have been able to hear it.

"All of you." He moved his hands to the fabric pooled around her waist. "I need to see all of you."

The desperate need on his face stole her words, so she lifted her hips to show him that it was what she wanted, too. He wasn't moving slowly anymore, the way he had with her shoulder straps. Instead, the silky pink fabric came down in one hard yank.

He stilled as she lay before him in nothing but a pair of simple pink polka-dot panties. "Forever." He wrapped his hands around her hips as he said, "That's how long I'm going to remember seeing you like this."

The smile he gave her just then made her feel as good as his kisses and his caresses did. What was between them wasn't just physical—it was so much more than that. Because for every moment of sensual pleasure he gave her with his mouth and hands, his sweet words and smiles gave her just as many moments of joy.

And then he was bending forward to press more incredible kisses over her stomach and hip bones at the same time as he slid the final piece of fabric down, pressing his lips over each new tiny patch of skin that he revealed. She'd never been so open for anyone else, never been so naked, so exposed.

And she loved it. Loved knowing that Drew was her first.

Her *only.*

"Ash." Her name was an awestruck breath against the part of her that was so wet, so hot, so needy. For him. All for him.

"Please," she begged, the same word she'd been saying over and over since he'd brought her to his bed. "Touch me. *Kiss* me."

"God, yes."

Just those six little letters against her aroused flesh were nearly enough to send her spinning out over the edge. So when she felt the first sweet brush of his tongue over her sex, she couldn't contain her moan of pleasure or keep her hips from arching up even closer to his mouth. His hands slid beneath her hips to hold her steady as he continued to give her the naughtiest, most incredible open-mouthed kiss in the world.

His name spilled feverishly from her lips, and her hands tightened on his forearms as she exploded into a million beautiful pieces. And then, just when she didn't think she could take any more pleasure, he slowly slipped a finger into her, lighting up nerve endings that she'd yet to discover.

She'd been stunned breathless when he'd thrown her into that glorious climax. But now as he continued to play over her sex with his fingers at the same time as he ran damp kisses over the insides of her thighs, her belly, her breasts, she couldn't catch her breath. Couldn't stop begging him for *more.* Couldn't keep from lifting her hips to try to take more of him. Couldn't get enough of his mouth on her breasts, or the way he was pushing her way past her comfort zones.

Ashley had always been inclined to play it safe, but with Drew, she'd never been able to hide in the background or behind her computer. His music made her dance. His smiles made hers so much bigger. And his beautiful, passionate, heartfelt kisses made all the walls she thought she'd needed around her heart fall away.

So when he came face-to-face with her again and looked down into her eyes with such dark, deep intensity, everything went perfectly still. So still that she could not only feel his heart beating against hers, she swore she could hear it, too. *Ba-boom. Ba-boom. Ba-boom.* And then hers joining in, in perfect sync. *Ba-boom. Ba-boom. Ba-boom.*

Two hearts playing in unison until they sounded like one.

"You're so far beyond everything, everyone I've ever known," he whispered into the silence, each word dancing seamlessly over the rhythm section of their hearts. "The most beautiful woman I've ever seen. The most beautiful song I've ever heard."

The stillness shattered then, as the bliss he'd built up with his mouth, and then his hands, began radiating out from somewhere deep inside, growing bigger and bigger. So big that her bones, her skin—her very soul—couldn't possibly contain all the joy.

Couldn't do anything but let him play over her body until she truly felt as if she actually *was* the most beautiful song he'd ever heard.

CHAPTER TWENTY-ONE

Making love with Ashley was a revelation. She wasn't trying to impress him with how loudly she could moan or the tricks she could do. She wasn't here with him tonight because he was a rock star.

Every touch, every kiss, every breathless move she made beneath him as she came was so honest. So raw.

So damned good.

The hunger he felt for her was unlike anything he'd ever known as he put his hands on her hips, rolled onto his back, and pulled her up to straddle him.

She blinked down at him in adorable surprise at the new position. "Hi."

He reached up to stroke the backs of his knuckles over her cheek. "I swear," he said as he ran his thumb over her full lower lip, "I could just look at you all night."

"I'd rather you touched me all night."

He loved the way she was so easily telling him what she wanted now. "Where? Here?" He stroked her lip again, slower this time, groaning when she licked the pad of his thumb.

"Yes."

He moved his hand to caress her just beneath her earlobe. "Here?"

"Mmm..." She closed her eyes and leaned into his touch. "Yes."

He couldn't resist moving both hands to the undersides of her breasts. "Here?"

She gave him her answer by rocking her hips over the bulge in his jeans. Her nipples beaded up against his palms, and he pinched them lightly in time with her movements against him. Slowly, he ran his hands down from her breasts, over her waist, to her hips.

"Let me help take you all the way again, Ash. I can't get enough of watching you come."

When her eyes fluttered open again, they were foggy with renewed arousal, and he couldn't stop himself from sliding his hand over her hip bone and her gorgeously wet sex. A low moan fell from her lips, and she rocked once, twice, three times against his fingers, taking more of him each time. But suddenly, she stopped.

"Not without you." She was clearly determined as she reached for the zipper of his jeans and began pulling it down. "I don't want to come again without you inside of me."

The hot words falling from her lips were already enough to send him over—but combined with the light pressure of her fingertips as she worked his clothes down over his erection? Holy hell, he had no idea how he didn't lose it right then.

"Drew." She was staring at his shaft as though it held the answers to all the questions she'd never thought to ask. "You're beautiful." She reached out to touch, but then hesitated.

"Please," he begged. "Touch me."

The moment she wrapped her hand around him for the first time, and sighed with pleasure, was one he'd never forget.

"You don't have to be gentle, Ash."

She looked up at him, her hair falling over one eye, and gave him a small smile. "Show me."

He'd known being with Ashley would be good. But the way she made him feel with nothing but a smile and a simple request was so far beyond good that his mind and his body had already erased everyone who had come before her.

She was the only one who mattered.

The one he'd been *waiting* for.

His hand was shaking as he wrapped it around hers. Together, they stroked up, then down. Up, then down again.

"Your skin is so soft," she marveled, "but underneath..." Her eyes were wide with wonder as they met his. "You're so hard."

"A week, Ash." She tried to move her hand on him again, but he wouldn't let her. Not when he was *this close* to combusting. "I've been like this for a whole week. Before that, even."

Her voice was husky as she asked him, "Did you want me to do this?"

"Yes."

"What else do you want me to do?"

"Love me."

The answer was out before he could stop it. But he didn't want to take it back. Didn't want to do anything but thread his free hand into her hair to pull her closer for a kiss. Their mouths had barely touched when the vee between her legs naturally settled over his erection. Her heat seared him, her wetness beckoned him, her sweet sounds of bliss seduced him.

One slight shift of his hips and he could be inside her. And the truth was that he'd never been so tempted to break all the rules—every last one—and take her bare, with nothing between them at all. When she rolled her hips against his in just the right way to take him inside, he nearly gave in. But she meant too much to him to ever risk her in that way.

"Ash." He put his hands on her hips, both to still her movements and to lift her slightly. "Protection." He could barely think straight, which made words hard to come by. "I need to put on protection." He nodded at the small bedside table. "In there. Max, he stocks all his buses. But you're the only one for me, Ash."

She pulled out the new, unopened box and took one out. "I've never put one on before. Will you show me how?"

"Next time," he promised her. "Right now, I'm too close." With gritted teeth, he focused on the task at hand, trying not to notice just how avidly, how hungrily, she watched him roll down the latex over his hard flesh—and definitely trying not to think about how it would feel if she were the one doing it.

Finally, she was back where she belonged, straddling his hips. "Let me feel you, Ash, just moving over me."

She laid her hands flat on his chest, and her tongue flicked out to lick her lips as she focused on doing just what he'd asked her to do. She was at once sweet and oh so sexy as she rocked faster and faster over him, pushing her hips harder against his with every stroke. And then, with just the slightest tilt to her pelvis, she began to take him inside.

Her breath caught as she stilled over him.

"Ash?" Every sign told him she was a virgin. And the last thing he wanted to do was hurt her, or move too fast. "If you're not ready—"

"I *am.* So ready."

She'd never sounded so passionate about anything, and she backed up her words with another slow, sweet inch of slick heat over him.

He was nearly delirious by now with the need to consume her, body and soul, but he wanted her to know, "Only take what feels good. Only take as much of me as you can."

"All of you." She leaned forward to kiss him. "I want to take *all* of you."

Didn't she know? "You have all of me already."

"Not yet," she whispered as she took him into herself—slow, trembling, breathless, *perfect.* "But I will soon."

"Oh God, Ash, the heat of you over me. Surrounding me..." He groaned, trying to hold still, trying to keep from thrusting up, pushing as deep as he was desperate to go. "I've never felt anything so good. Never known anyone so beautiful."

He could feel how small she was, but she didn't stop, didn't pause to catch the breath that he could hear hitching in her throat. Instead, she continued to rock her hips over him, small, intense motions that took him inside of her little by little. He wanted more. So much more. But he couldn't stand to hurt her. Not even the slightest bit if he could help it.

"Ash—"

"I love it," she said now as she bent her arms to lower her face to his for a soothing kiss. "I love the feel of you inside me. You don't have to be careful with me. I won't break, I promise."

He knew how strong she was, but he didn't want her to look back on her first time and remember anything but pleasure. "I don't want to hurt you."

"There's only one way you could ever hurt me. By not being honest with me. By not being yourself. What do you want, Drew?"

"You."

Her lips curved up into the most beautiful smile he'd ever seen. "Then take me. All of me. Without holding any of yourself back."

Between the feel of her wet, hot body over his and the words falling from her beautiful mouth, he was so far out on the edge that he almost couldn't pull himself back. But he knew he needed to try.

"I've wanted you too much, for too long. If I don't at least try to keep control—"

"No." With that one word, she sank all the way down on him. Past any barriers that had been there before. Past the point of no return. "I don't want either of us to be in control tonight."

As if her words were the key to the final lock on his self-restraint, in the next split second, Drew had flipped them over so that she was on her back and he was looking down on such pure, sweet beauty that it was nearly impossible to take all of her in. But he already knew that he could look at Ashley for the rest of his life and never stop being stunned by what he saw. Such honesty. Such intelligence.

Such *heart.*

He rocked into her, and as he drew back, they both gasped as her inner walls clenched at him.

"Again." She grasped his shoulders so tightly he knew there'd be marks. Marks he would be proud to wear. "Do that again."

As he rolled his hips into hers again, sweat dripped from his body to hers. Even as she gasped with the pleasure of taking him into her, she licked out against his shoulder.

"So good." She closed her eyes and shifted her hips to increase the friction between their bodies. "I wouldn't have waited to sleep with you if I'd known it would be this good."

She'd made him smile from the very beginning, just the way he was smiling now. "If you had known, would you have seduced me that first night?"

"Yes." She tilted her hips again to take him even deeper, the most sensual creature ever put on this planet. *"Yes."*

"I knew," he told her as he threaded his hands through hers and put them on either side of her head. "I knew we would be this good."

"And you still made us wait when we could have been doing this since Los Angeles?"

He laughed into the crook of her neck as he nipped at her sweat-slickened skin, and she moaned at the way the small movement shifted his body inside hers. "A little anticipation never killed anyone."

"It almost did." Her words were borderline accusing, which made him laugh again...setting off another sequence of vibrations from his body to hers and then back again. "You have a lot to make up to me. All those hours without your body over mine. *Inside* of mine."

If her words hadn't already been enough to send him from still barely rational to pure insanity, the way she sank her teeth into the cords of his neck just then did it. And in that instant, he forgot that she had been a virgin just minutes ago. Forgot everything except how much he wanted her, how much he needed her—and how much she wanted and needed him, too. All that mattered was giving her the pleasure she craved. The pleasure she'd been *waiting* for.

He tightened his grip on her hands and, without warning, thrust hard. Deep. Her eyes went wide, and her breath came out in a whoosh. But he didn't give her time to recover before he did it again. Even harder this time. As deep as he could go. Her legs had been around his waist, but now she planted them on either side of his knees to give herself traction. Traction to take even *more* of him.

He wanted to memorize every incredible moment where she was giving herself to him. The way her eyes fluttered closed on a gasp of pleasure, then opened again as if she was determined to take in his pleasure, too. The way her skin shone with sweat. How the tips of her full breasts were tight with arousal that he needed to take against his tongue until her sex was clenching tight around him again with every pull of his lips. How she grew even hotter, even wetter, as he moved to lave her other breast with the same wild passion.

"*Drew.*"

For his entire life, he'd been putting emotions into words and music. But in this moment—one that felt like the most important of his life—there was only his mouth against hers so that he could drink in her sighs, her gasps, her moans while they made love.

And in that instant of beauty and wonder, Drew could suddenly see that for his whole life, he'd been holding back. Holding back a part of himself, even in his music.

But with Ash, he didn't want to hold back anymore. Couldn't hold back when she touched every last part of him, inside and out.

He whispered her name over and over against her lips as more heat, and more mind-blowing pleasure than he'd ever known was possible, built up between them. And then he heard a low cry vibrating from her throat, felt the tight, rhythmic pull of her body against him, and he fell with her. Way out over the edge. Way past control. Way past sanity.

Way past the man he'd been before she'd come into his life.

Straight toward something that felt exactly like *love.*

CHAPTER TWENTY-TWO

Ashley dreamed she was listening to the most beautiful song in the world. One that stirred her heart, moved her soul, and made her want to sing along.

As she slowly came awake to the now familiar feel of the bus's tires moving along the freeway, she realized she hadn't been listening to the song in her dreams. The music was coming from just beyond the bedroom door.

It didn't occur to her to put on clothes or to wrap a sheet around herself as she got out of bed, not when she didn't want to wait another second to see Drew again. She'd never heard him play this melody before.

Could it possibly be a new song?

As quietly as possible so that she wouldn't disturb his concentration, she opened the door and poked her head through. But of course Drew noticed her immediately. He stopped playing, put the guitar down at his side, then smiled and held out a hand for her.

"Sorry, I didn't mean to wake you."

She was surprised that she didn't feel shy at all about her nakedness as she moved toward him and took his hand. Then again, there wasn't really any room for *shy* when he was looking at her like this—with so much heat and desire that her hormones revved from zero to a thousand in the time it took him to pull her onto his lap.

"Don't apologize. I wish you had woken me earlier," she told him as she straddled his lap and lowered her mouth to his for a kiss.

He had put on a pair of jeans, but she could feel his erection pushing the zipper into the bare flesh between her thighs. It would be so easy to get lost in his kiss—and the way his big hands were moving down her back and then over her hips to cup her bare bottom and pull her closer—but she needed to know about his song first.

"The song you were playing...it's incredible."

"It's pretty rough still, but it's coming along."

He reached up to brush his thumb over her lower lip, a mesmerizing pattern that made it hard to think straight. However, the fact that he was writing again was such a big deal that even her newfound sensuality had to take a backseat to it.

"It didn't sound rough, Drew. I thought I was dreaming at first, dreaming of the most beautiful song I'd ever heard." She could see how pleased he was by her reaction to the song. "When did you write it?"

"Just now."

"Now?"

"You fell asleep in my arms, and I didn't want to get up out of bed. Didn't want to let go of you. Not ever, if I didn't have to. But then the music started playing in my head. In my hands, too. Like it was going to burst out of my bones and skin if I didn't grab my guitar that second." He looked amazed by it even as he spoke. "That's never happened to me before. I mean, I've been inspired, but not like this."

Ashley moved even closer and hugged him tightly with her entire body. "I'm so happy for you. So happy that your muse is back."

"It's you, Ash." He shifted them on the chair so that he could look into her eyes. "You're the reason it's back."

"Me?" Of all the things he could have said, nothing would have surprised her more. "How could I have anything to do with your song?"

"Because when we made love, the walls that had been building up, the blocks that had been settling into place..." He rubbed his cheek against hers, and it felt so lovely that she sighed at the sweet, simple pleasure of it. "All the pleasure, all the joy, all the mind-blowing bliss of being with you pushed the bad things out of the way."

Everything he was saying was so sweet, and incredibly flattering, too. But it was a lot for her to take in. Too much, honestly.

She'd never planned to be anyone's muse. And could barely believe that someone as normal as she could inspire great art.

But instead of fighting to unravel her strange feelings about it, she focused on Drew and his music. "Now that the inspiration is flowing again, you should keep writing. I can go back into the bedr—"

"Stay." He cradled her hips in his hands and scooted her even closer. "I want you again. I *need* you again."

Oh God, she needed him just as badly. But she'd never forgive herself if she got between him and his music, so she made herself say, "Promise me you won't forget the song you were writing."

"I promise I won't, but you've got to promise me something, too."

"What?"

"That you won't try to get up off my lap until I've made you come again."

Just like that, with nothing but his wonderfully dirty words, he took her right to the edge of release. "I promise."

He crushed her mouth beneath his as soon as the promise left her lips. And though the faint light creeping in through the blinds told her it had only been a handful of hours since they'd made love, she needed him again with the same desperate anticipation she'd felt right before he'd made her his for the very first time.

He swept her hair back from her shoulders with one hand, then gently tugged the strands so that her head tilted back, leaving her neck open for his lips and tongue and teeth. She didn't even realize she was rocking her pelvis into his until he used his other hand against her bottom to increase the pressure and the friction of the denim against her.

She'd told him last night that she was good at being the good girl, but she didn't feel like that good girl anymore. At least not when she was naked and straddling Drew in the middle of his tour bus, on the verge of coming apart on his lap while he urged her to do just that.

"Come for me, Ash. Just like this." He murmured the heated words against the upper swell of her breasts. "I love watching you come." He licked the tip of one breast, and she felt every muscle in her body clench. "I love feeling you come." He turned his focus to her other breast, drawing slow, wet circles around her nipple with his tongue. "I love hearing you come."

Barely a beat later, when he rocked her into his denim-covered erection at the exact moment that his teeth scraped over her incredibly aroused skin, she came for him, just the way he wanted her to. She rolled her hips into him, riding the wave of pleasure as long as she possibly could while it went on and on and on.

Just when she thought she'd never survive it, her system finally began to calm. But clearly Drew had other plans for her as he slid his fingers through the slick wetness between her legs.

"You're so hot right here, Ash." He lifted his fingers to his mouth and licked them, as if she were the most decadent, delicious treat ever made. "And you taste so damned good."

She didn't think, didn't second-guess, just followed her instincts and leaned forward to lick his fingers, too. She'd barely slid her tongue over the pad of his middle finger when his mouth stole in and captured hers.

He kissed her as though he'd never, ever get enough. And she couldn't stop herself from kissing him back the exact same way.

No matter what happened after this tour, she'd always have the sweet memories of feeling like the center of his world. She'd remember—and be grateful for—these stolen moments with Drew every day for the rest of her life.

But a split second later, when he slid his hand back down between her legs and thrust his fingers inside of her, she wasn't thinking about making memories anymore. She honestly couldn't think at all. Could only focus on how good everything felt as Drew whispered such incredibly sweet words against her sweat-dampened skin.

"Again, Ash. Let yourself go and I'll be here for you. Always."

No one had ever promised to always be there for her. Not her friends at school. And certainly not any of the guys she'd gone on dates with. Not even her parents, who had spent so much of their time at odds with each other.

Only Drew.

She looked into his eyes, wanting to ask how he could make her such a big promise. But when she saw the same vow in his gaze—and she felt it in his touch, as if heightening her pleasure would only serve to heighten his, too—any questions she might have asked were lost in the wonder of being with such an amazing man.

One who never just took what he wanted, but who gave. And gave. And gave.

Between one heartbeat and the next, another climax crashed over her, so strong that if Drew hadn't been holding her so tightly, she might have slid right off his lap onto the floor.

And then he was lifting her into his arms and carrying her into his bedroom. He sat with his back against the headboard and then brought her over him so that her legs were straddling his hips. Perhaps she should have been sated by now, but she was absolutely desperate to take him inside her body. Not just his fingers this time, not just his tongue. Every beautifully hard inch of him.

With shaky fingers, she reached down to undo the button and zipper on his jeans, but thankfully he was already working himself out of them and reaching for one of the condoms from the side table. He slid the protection into place, and then his hands were on her hips again, and he was lifting her up over him.

"I know we should be taking it slow, Ash. Last night was your first time, and I know you're not used to—"

She cut off the rest of his words by sinking down fast and hard onto him, taking all of him in one long, hot, perfect slide. Her breath whooshed from her lungs as he filled every last part of her, but she didn't wait to get it back before wrapping her arms around him and holding on tight as she rode him like the bad girl she'd never been until today.

"Can you hear it, Ash?" His words felt hot and damp against her earlobe as he groaned at the pleasure she was giving him. Giving them both. He bit down on the sensitive flesh, and she shuddered against him. "Can you hear the music playing?"

"Yes." Every moment she was with him was a symphony of pleasure. An opera of emotion. The perfect pop song that cut right to the heart of everything she was feeling. "Always."

The word *always* had barely fallen from her lips when Drew spun them around so that she was lying beneath him on the bed and his deliciously heavy weight was pressing her down into the mattress.

"Now, Ash." He gritted out the words as sweat dripped down from his chest to hers. "I need you to come again for me now. I can't hold back much longer."

"I don't want you to hold back, Drew. I'm desperate to feel *you* come inside of me."

His eyes dilated nearly to black right before he threw back his head and thrust into her so hard that she could barely hang on. He felt impossibly big inside of her as he took her again and again and again, and she loved every single second of it. Especially when every thrust brought her closer, took her higher, until the perfect moment when he gripped her hips and erased any distance that had remained between them, his climax setting off hers in a sequence of fireworks inside her body. The brightest, most brilliant and beautiful fireworks she'd ever experienced.

All because of Drew.

CHAPTER TWENTY-THREE

"Sooooo...." The disk jockey drew out the word, then paused for dramatic effect, clearly hoping to keep listeners in suspense over what she was going to ask Drew next.

But he knew exactly what was coming. The same question he'd been asked a million times during the past few years.

"Are you seeing anyone? Are millions of hearts around the world going to break if you tell us you've finally found that one special girl?"

The previous night, Drew had told Ashley that he wanted the whole world to know she was his. And this morning, after making love with her again and wishing he could just keep holding her instead of getting ready to do this interview, he wanted that more than ever. But she'd asked him to keep their new relationship private, at least for a little while, and he needed to respect that.

Still, he hated lying. Hated it even more when Ashley was watching and listening to the interview only a glass wall away. He caught her eye through the glass and hoped she could read his private message: *You're mine, Ash. I'm yours. And the second you give me the thumbs-up, I'm going to let the whole world know.*

Finally, he told the DJ, "This tour has been crazy busy. There's no way I could go on a date with anyone right now."

That, at least, was true. This tour was the most jam-packed he'd ever done—and he and Ash weren't actually dating. One day really soon, however, he wanted to be able to take her out to dinner or a movie like a normal couple.

But he was trying to see things from her point of view. She likely wasn't only worried about what her father would think, but also about the inevitable complications that came with dating a guy like him. Like the fact that her picture would be everywhere and people would want to know more about her...and then whatever they could find out would likely end up on the Internet, too.

The thing was, he'd met enough people like Smith Sullivan and his fiancée, Valentina Landon, and like Nicola Sullivan and her husband, Marcus, to see that relationships in the spotlight of fame weren't impossible as long as your partner was strong.

Drew had seen Ashley's strength from that very first night they'd met. She clearly hadn't felt like she fit in, but she hadn't let that stop her. Being scared was perfectly normal. But transcending those fears was extraordinary.

Just as extraordinary as the way she made him feel.

Because after all these months of wondering just what the hell he was doing, Ashley had helped him understand again why he wrote and played music. In the wake of his mother's death, he'd been making the mistake of using his music to shove his feelings, his emotions, down. Only, instead of working, it had made him feel more blocked by the day.

Finally, he understood that when he faced the pain and the fear—and when he allowed the joy to flow back in every second he was with Ashley—that was when the music started playing in his head. Playing so fast and clear that even now he was trying to memorize the melodies and lyrics rushing through him.

"In that case, Drew," the DJ said, "tell us what kind of girl you're looking for. What qualities will the perfect girl need to steal your heart?"

Again, Drew couldn't stop his gaze from moving to where Ashley was sitting behind the glass wall. He was pretty sure she was blushing, even though she'd lowered her head to look at the tablet on her lap. James was sitting next to her grinning like a fool. He and Drew hadn't talked about Ashley—even if his bodyguard had asked, he'd never kiss and tell—but his friend had clearly figured out that everything had worked out all right last night after Drew had left the party to look for her.

"My perfect woman is smart. Fun. Caring. Insightful. And so beautiful that every time I look at her I'm stunned by her all over again."

"Wow." The DJ fanned herself. "Do you think you'll ever be able to find a woman like that?"

He grinned and finally told the truth to the whole damned world the way he'd wanted to all along. "Yes. The answer is definitely *yes*."

* * *

At nine that evening, Ashley's phone buzzed. Just seeing Drew's name on her screen was enough to make her heart race, even before she read the message.

Can you come by my dressing room before the show starts?

James was standing beside her in the wings backstage. The opener had come off ten minutes ago, and the crowd was getting antsy waiting for Drew to appear. She was antsy, too, mostly because she hadn't seen him since earlier that day when he'd been doing the radio interviews downtown. He'd been deep in writing and recording mode the rest of the day, and she'd been just as busy working on her own brainstorming about the indie label. That is, when she wasn't daydreaming and getting all hot and bothered about the incredible things they had done together in, and out, of his bed.

She hadn't thought of herself as a creative person before, but ever since they'd made love, the world looked entirely different. Brighter. Exploding with color—and endless possibility.

Before joining Drew's tour, she'd been desperately worried about what would happen if she applied to Stanford Business School again and didn't get in. But now?

She smiled, thinking about all she'd accomplished today. Not just putting together a business plan for starting a record label. But a record label that was artist owned and operated. One that changed all the rules the music business had ever played by. Ashley couldn't wait to show her fleshed-out plans to Drew. She already knew his feedback would be hugely helpful and important in working out the kinks.

But as she went to say a quick hello to Drew in his dressing room before he went on stage, the way her body was heating up more and more with every step had nothing whatsoever to do with the business plans on her computer.

And everything to do with needing to kiss him again more than she needed to take her next breath.

The security guard stationed outside Drew's dressing room knew her on sight and smiled. "Go on in. He's expecting you."

This world of backstage bodyguards that had once seemed so foreign to her was now practically normal. When she'd joined Drew's tour, she'd had no idea just how far and wide her education would go—on *all* fronts, both business and personal.

She'd barely opened the dressing room door when she was yanked inside. Her breath went as Drew simultaneously pulled her into his arms and locked the door behind her. His mouth crashed into hers a beat later, his kiss ravenous. Desperate.

Perfect.

His hands roving greedily over her body aroused her just as much as his lips did. God, she loved stroking her tongue across his. Loved, too, the rough, raw, seriously *yummy* sound of his groan as she kissed him back just as greedily.

"There were too many hours without you today, Ash." His hands gripped her hips tightly, holding her flush against him as if he didn't want any space there at all. "I missed you."

"I missed you, too." She wanted to kiss him again, but first she needed to know, "How was your recording session?"

"Really good. But it would have been better if you were there. Everything is better when you're there."

The next thing she knew, he was lifting her up, then placing her on the table in front of the mirror. He was so much bigger than she was, and so strong, that he was able to pick her up as if she weighed nothing at all. He slid off her jean jacket so that he could run hot kisses over every inch of the bare skin of her shoulders and arms that he'd just revealed.

She only had two dresses—the simple white one she'd been wearing when she fell into the pool and the fancier pink one Valentina had given her. When he began to run his hands slowly up from her bare calves, she was *really* glad she'd decided to wear the white dress tonight. There truly was nothing as good as Drew's hands on her skin. Only his mouth could trump it.

"You taste so good," he murmured against her lips as he slid his hands up to her thighs. "I need to taste more of you. *Now.*"

There was nothing she wanted more than for Drew to do just that. But the good girl still hovering inside of her couldn't help but remind him, "You're on in five minutes."

"I know," he said as he knelt on the ground in front of her and slipped his fingers beneath the sides of her panties, "but I won't be able to make it through my show tonight if I don't get to at least taste you now."

She helped him lift her hips so that he could draw the fabric down her legs and off over her feet.

Yes, the clock was ticking, but so was her body—a sensual bomb that was on the verge of detonation. Just as soon as Drew—

Oh God.

His mouth.

His tongue.

His hands.

Her head fell back against the mirror behind her as she tried to remember that there were people outside the dressing room who would hear her if she moaned too loudly. But as Drew's tongue and fingers played over her sex like the maestro that he was, it was nearly impossible to keep her pleasure to herself.

"Gorgeous." He whispered the word against her overheated skin. *"Mine."*

That final word—along with the perfect flick of his tongue—was all it took for her to start breaking apart. She threaded her hands into his hair and, through her lashes, stared in wonder at the beautiful man kneeling between her legs.

"Yours," she gasped as he drew her orgasm out with both his mouth and fingers.

After the last blissful aftershock had finally rumbled through her, Drew looked up at her with eyes so dark with heat and full of intense desire that she lost her breath all over again. She searched her pleasure-drenched brain for something to say that would let him know just how good he made her feel.

But just then, a loud knock sounded on the door. "It's James. They're ready for you out there, Drew."

Drew didn't rush to head to the stage. Instead, he threaded his hands into her hair and kissed her again. His kiss was still hungry, but alongside desire was so much emotion it overwhelmed her. Or maybe it was tasting herself on his lips, his tongue, that pushed her into overload territory.

All she knew was that, for a moment, she felt as though she were drowning. She simply didn't have enough experience with things like this to know what to think or how to feel about everything that was happening. Especially not when it was all happening so darn fast.

Drew helped her down from the table and gently smoothed her skirt over her bare skin. When she walked out of the dressing room, would people be able to guess what had happened just from looking at her? Or would she still look like the good girl she'd been up until approximately twenty-four hours ago?

"Do you have any idea how happy you make me, Ash?"

Louder knocks sounded. "Drew," James called, "you've got sixty seconds to get your ass out there before the audience starts to lose it."

He gave her one last kiss, and the last thing she saw was his huge grin before he headed out the door to go and be a rock star.

Without his arms around her, her legs felt wobbly. The truth was, her insides did, too. Not because Drew had made her feel anything other than special and precious...but exactly for that reason. He seemed to care about her so much on all fronts—not only when they were making love, but when they were talking about business or family, too. And she'd never felt this good, or this happy, before.

But she remembered hearing her mother saying to her father once how happy she was. That happiness had quickly spun toward hatred because her parents were so different.

Standing in the dressing room, Ashley knew she should be heeding those memories. She shouldn't be forgetting the hard-learned lessons of her childhood and giving herself so wholly, so completely to someone so very different from herself. But letting down her guard for a couple of days—or weeks—wouldn't destroy her, would it? Their connection was intense and wonderful, and of course she hoped they'd remain friends even after the tour was over. And at least she wasn't foolish enough to think that what was between them now would last forever.

With a *now* that was this utterly, blissfully, mind-blowingly incredible, couldn't she let herself enjoy every second of it without letting her worries and concerns get the best of her? Especially since it had been only twenty-four hours since making love with Drew for the first time.

She heard the screams of the crowd amp up and knew he must have just taken the stage. Not wanting to miss a second of his show, she looked for her underwear so that she could put it back on and head out of the room. But she couldn't find them anywhere. Had Drew taken her panties with him when he left to go play his show?

Between knowing she was bare beneath her skirt as she headed toward the stage with the security guard silently accompanying her—and wondering if Drew actually *was* on stage with her panties in his pocket—her arousal immediately ramped back up.

Throughout the show, one that was so spellbinding she felt as if she were watching him perform for the very first time, Drew's gaze kept returning to her again and again, just the way it had during his interviews that morning. She blushed even more tonight than she had then. Blushed and fantasized about all the ways *she* wanted to give Drew pleasure, just as he'd given her so much pleasure again and again.

She'd known she was pretty darn innocent before she and Drew had made love, but every time they'd come together had only proven it more. Every delicious moment in Drew's arms was an epiphany.

"He's on fire tonight, isn't he?" James asked in the space between songs.

His question broke through her naughty thoughts, and her cheeks flamed at the way she was standing backstage mentally stripping off Drew's clothes. Just because she knew every other woman in the audience was doing the same thing didn't make her any less cool-headed about it.

"He really is." Drew's show tonight was truly spectacular, as if he had unearthed a new and even bigger well of creativity on stage in the same way that he seemed to have found his writing mojo.

"Like I said before, you're good for him, Ashley. He hasn't been happy in a long time. Not until you showed up."

Ashley wasn't egotistical—or delusional— enough to think that Drew's huge breakthrough had come about entirely because of her. But she was beyond happy that she might have played at least a small part in helping him feel better about everything. "He deserves to be happy."

"So do you," James said as the next song started up.

CHAPTER TWENTY-FOUR

Two hours later, she was about to head back toward the meet-and-greet rooms when James told her, "They're a little behind on setting up for the fans tonight. Can you let Drew know he's got fifteen minutes before he needs to head back?"

Drew's guitar was still slung around his neck when he walked over to Ashley, the hunger in his eyes barely banked. She wanted to reach for him, wanted to kiss him, but she couldn't do any of that and still keep what they were doing a secret.

"You have fifteen minutes before they'll be ready for you to meet your fans." She'd never been the aggressor before, but just as he'd said he'd never make it through the show if he didn't get at least a taste of her, she suddenly knew she'd never make it through the meet and greet if she didn't get a taste of him.

Thank God they seemed to be of one mind as they headed toward his dressing room. Ashley could barely keep herself from sprinting.

Before the show, as soon as she'd walked through his dressing room door, he'd pulled her into his arms and kissed her. Now it was her turn to pull his mouth down to hers. *"Drew."* His name fell from her lips again and again between passionate kisses. But even though she loved kissing him, it wasn't enough. Not tonight when fifteen minutes with him felt like such a huge gift.

The cautious good girl that she'd been up until last night would have been shocked by everything she'd already done with Drew tonight. And she would have been utterly astonished by everything she wanted to do with him now. But her desire for Drew was stronger than her worries and feelings of emotional overload, at least for one more night.

She put just enough space between them to reach for his guitar strap and lift it over his head. She couldn't resist pulling off his shirt while she was at it— nor could she stop herself from lowering her mouth to his sweat-dampened skin. He groaned as she licked his chest.

Though she'd never done anything like this before, it somehow seemed perfectly natural to drop to her knees on the cement floor in front of Drew.

"Ash..." He threaded his hands into her hair as she looked up at him. "You're so damned beautiful."

She pressed a kiss over his stomach, and his muscles rippled beneath her tongue as it snaked over to lick his salty skin. "So are you. I want to see more of you." She reached for his belt. "I need to see more of you."

But instead of letting her undo his buckle, he moved one hand from her hair to hold both of hers still. "You don't have to do this."

Everything she'd done with him beyond kissing had been new. New and wonderful. Just as she instinctively knew this would be.

"Before the show, you said you wouldn't make it through without getting a taste of me first. That's how I feel right now. If I don't get to taste you before the meet and greet, I'll combust."

She moved her hands back to his buckle, and this time he let her undo it. Last night on the bus she'd gotten to see his naked body for the first time, but not like this. Not up close, with the dressing room lights on to illuminate every hard inch of him. Ashley held her breath as she pulled his zipper down, breathless with anticipation instead of the nerves she'd always assumed she would feel if she ever got into this position with a guy. He helped her tug his jeans down and, finally, he was hard and hot and *gorgeous,* right where she wanted him.

She couldn't wait to wrap her fingers around his thick length, and his rough groan reverberated through the room as she immediately pressed her lips to him, too.

"Ash..."

She licked him from base to tip once, then twice, then again, and her excitement grew with every stroke of her tongue. She'd never before known the pleasures of being naughty. Never before imagined all the ways there were to feel good and to make a man feel good.

Not until Drew grabbed her hand—and her heart—and took her into this amazing new world.

She was smiling as she looked up at him. "How many times do you think this has happened in here? A hundred? A thousand?" Maybe the thought shouldn't have excited a good girl like her, but it did.

Probably because she wasn't quite so *good* anymore...

"Never like this." His words rasped from his throat. "Never with anyone as beautiful as you, Ash. Never with anyone as sweet." She licked another line of heat up his hard flesh a beat after he'd called her *sweet*. "Never with anyone as sexy." His hands threaded into her hair. "Never with anyone who makes me feel so good in every way."

And it was true...all she wanted was to make him feel good. As good as he'd made her feel right before the show. As good as he was making her feel right now while he stared down at her with dark, hungry, awe-filled eyes.

She opened her mouth to take him deep, as deep as she possibly could, but the next thing she knew, he was lifting her up from the floor. "I need to have you. *All* of you."

She felt the cold wooden door against her back a moment later, and then the deliciously hard weight of his body pressing into her as he kissed her as though it had been years since he'd last kissed her instead of mere minutes.

Even though they'd only first made love yesterday, wrapping her legs around his waist and moving her hips into his felt like the most natural, perfect thing in the world now. As natural as breathing. And when he tugged the skirt of her dress up around her waist with one hand, then positioned himself at her core—still bare without her panties—she lowered her mouth to scrape her teeth over the muscles flexing at his shoulder.

Oh God, it felt so good to have him slide his rock-hard length against her, and she was already mindless with pleasure even before he took her.

But then, he suddenly stopped with a rough curse. "I haven't been with anyone in months, Ash. I swear. Not since..."

"Shhh." She pressed her lips against his so he wouldn't have to go back to that dark place. Not tonight. "I believe you." And she really did. Because even though she knew he'd had plenty of sexual experience in his life, she could also feel just how special their connection was.

"Are you on birth control?"

"No. But I—"

Now he was the one saying, "Shhh," and kissing her. "I'll always protect you. Always."

It was their word, she realized. *Always.* A word that thrilled her just as much as it frightened her. Because while there was nothing she wanted more...it was also the one thing she had the hardest time believing in.

Could there really be an *always* for her and Drew?

But almost more frightening was that when she was with him, she got so wrapped up in her desire—and in the emotion that swamped her every time he looked into her eyes and told her how much she meant to him—that she forgot to be safe. Forgot all about condoms and birth control. Forgot that he was a hugely famous star. Forgot everything but how much she wanted him. How much she *needed* him.

But after he put on protection, he didn't just take her. Instead, he looked into her eyes and simply held both of them in place for several long moments in which her breath caught and her heart raced. Last night he'd asked her again and again if she was okay, if he was pushing her too fast or too hard, and it was obvious to her that he needed to know the same thing now. And while she couldn't predict the future, there was no question at all that this one precious moment with Drew was better than anything she could ever have imagined.

And she would never forgive herself if she didn't appreciate every single second of bliss.

Her mouth curved up at the exact moment that she shifted her hips and took him into her body in one glorious plunge. His eyes first widened, then closed as he moved his hands to her hips and dragged her even closer. Her head fell back against the door, and he pressed his lips to the open arch of her neck to run nipping kisses across her skin as they thrust into each other.

She could feel the beginnings of a climax so good, and so strong, that she wasn't sure she'd be able to keep holding on without his help. "Please," she begged as she rocked and rubbed against him, "I need—"

But it turned out he already knew. Because before she could even get the rest of her sentence out, he drove into her at just the perfect angle to send her rocketing into an explosive orgasm. He was barely a heartbeat behind her, holding her hips so tightly that there was no way she could possibly fall and groaning her name against her neck as he buried his face there and sucked on her sensitive skin, making her release feel as if it were going on forever.

She didn't know how long they held on to each other, both of them breathing hard. All she knew was that she never wanted to let go. Never wanted to come back to reality.

And definitely didn't want to hear the knock on the door that came just then. The knock that meant her way-too-brief idyll with Drew was over because he had a job to do. A job that meant everything to him. A job that made such a huge difference to all of his fans' lives.

"They must be waiting for you in the meet-and-greet rooms."

He didn't move for a few moments, just kept holding her. Finally, he pulled back and said, "You'll come with me?"

She nodded, but waited until they'd both put their clothes to rights and he was just about to open the door before saying, "I know we talked about keeping things private yesterday. We're still on the same page with that, right?"

God, she hated needing to confirm this right after they'd been so intimate—but the only time she could think straight was when he wasn't touching her, wasn't kissing her. She'd just been so caught up in him that she'd almost made love without protection. Just as she should have been more careful with her body, now she needed to make sure she was being vigilant with her heart.

He didn't answer right away, simply looked at her with an expression she couldn't quite read. Well, that wasn't exactly true. She knew he wasn't happy that she wanted to keep their relationship a secret from everyone. Yesterday he'd told her he'd do it if that's what she wanted. Had he changed his mind?

"I don't like it," he said with a frown, "but I'm trying to respect your wishes, Ash. Although, when my family comes out to meet me in New Orleans tomorrow for my birthday—"

"We can't tell them." The words flew from her mouth before she could pull them back.

His frown deepened. "Because it will get back to your father?"

"Partly. But also because they love you and they'll think I'm just some scheming groupie who planned this whole research project to get into your pants."

His frown fell away as he laughed. "There's no way they would think that."

"Even if they wouldn't..."

She suddenly felt like she couldn't breathe right. When she was in the moment with Drew, when she was in his arms, when she was listening to him play his music, everything was so exciting, so exhilarating. But then, whenever she tried to come back down to earth, she couldn't stop the spinning, and it felt like everything was spiraling out of control.

Not just because her physical need for him was so overpowering, but because her *emotional* need for him was becoming just as strong, if not stronger. Even after he'd just made love to her, she wanted to be with him just to see him smile, just to hear him laugh, just to see him look at her again as though she was the most important person in the world to him.

"Ash." She felt his hands on her cheeks as he cupped her jaw, and she focused her panicked gaze on him. "I didn't mean to push you too fast. It's just that I already know what I want—*you*—and I'm not used to waiting. But I'll wait. As long as it takes, okay?"

Even though his words were meant to soothe, she could still hear the impatience behind them. Impatience for her to own up to being with him, not only in dark rooms in a concert hall or a tour bus, but with their families...and millions of strangers. All of whom would surely wonder the same things: *Why her?* And *how long can it possibly last?*

The knocking came again, louder this time, along with James's voice. "We really need to get to the meet and greet, Drew."

She made herself smile at him. "I can't wait to meet your family tomorrow, and to celebrate your birthday with you." He'd given her the best week of her life. No matter what, she would make sure that he had the best birthday ever. Which meant freaking out like this was not an option. She pressed her lips to his, then said, "Go make your fans' dreams come true. I'll be just a step behind you, okay?"

She opened the door before he could answer and gave James her biggest smile. "Sorry, I didn't mean to steal Drew away from his fans. If they're mad, it's my fault, not his."

"No one's mad," James said.

But she didn't chance a look at Drew's face, in case it turned out that he was indeed mad at her for not happily claiming the place he wanted her take at his side—as his girlfriend.

CHAPTER TWENTY-FIVE

New Orleans, Louisiana

The next morning, Ashley tried to slide carefully from beneath Drew's arm without waking him, but she'd barely moved when his arm tightened around her.

"Don't go." His voice was heavy with sleep, but intense nonetheless. As if he truly never wanted to let her go.

"I just want to get your birthday present."

With his eyes still closed, he smiled, but didn't loosen his hold on her. "I already have the best birthday present in the world. You, here with me in bed."

It would have been so easy just to snuggle back into him, but she knew how quickly Drew's world moved, especially while on tour. If she didn't give him his present now, who knew when she would get another private moment? Especially because she wasn't sure he would want to share it with anyone else. Actually, both of his birthday gifts—the one she wanted to give him now and the one she would give him tonight when they came back to the bus after his show—were private.

She pressed a kiss to his incredibly sexy mouth, loving the way his morning stubble scratched her cheeks before she pulled away. "I'll be right back. I promise." She slid off the bed and out of reach before he could stop her.

All week she'd been hoping that the gift she'd had made for Drew would be delivered in time, and thankfully, Max had taken receipt of it yesterday afternoon. He'd texted her right away to let her know that it had arrived at the venue's business office and he'd put it in her bunk. She didn't have any wrapping paper with her, but at least it was still in the box, so Drew would have the pleasure of opening that.

Taking the small package out of her suitcase, her heart started thudding hard in her chest. She so hoped Drew would like it and that her gift would make him happy. She'd taken a risk by making it for him, but it was one she'd been compelled to take.

He was sitting up with the sheets loosely pooled around his waist when she returned to the bedroom. Even though she'd seen him naked more than once, the sight of his six-pack abs, muscular chest and arms, and smiling face was enough to make her stumble as she came through the door.

"I feel the same way, Ash. Every time I look at you." His grin shifted from slightly wicked to *very* wicked as he added, "Especially when you're walking around the bus without any clothes on."

She felt her skin flush all over, but even though she wasn't used to being naked in front of anyone else, the way Drew looked at her when she wasn't wearing any clothes made that little bit of lingering shyness *more* than worth it.

She moved to the side of the bed and held out the gift. "Happy birthday."

He took the present, but instead of opening the box right away, he put it down beside him and pulled her onto his lap to capture her mouth with his. He was grinning when he let her up for air, resting his hands gently, but possessively, on the curves of her hips. "Have I mentioned yet today how happy you make me?"

"I'm pretty sure that's what you just did," she said, her smile so big it almost hurt her cheeks. Not only was she flushed, but he'd just melted her insides, too. "You make me happy too, Drew. And I really hope you like your present."

"I know I will. Because it came from you."

She wiggled back enough for him to pick up the gift. She laughed when he shook it, just like a little kid trying to guess what might be inside. In the same way that he liked to build up their anticipation when they were making love, he took his time undoing the tape on the small box. She always shredded packages as she tore them apart to get to what was inside. It was exactly the way she felt with Drew—utterly desperate to have him. And powerless to control her urges.

Finally, he reached into the box and pulled out a tiny handmade wood, steel, and porcelain guitar hanging from a silver chain.

"It's my first guitar." His words sounded choked, as if he could barely get them out. "The one my mom gave me." He looked up from the necklace. "How did you know what it looked like?"

"After you told me about it, I scoured the Internet until I found a picture of it." She was unsure from his expression whether she'd done well...or horribly. "I just thought it was so lovely that your mother bought you your first guitar and that you ended up being so inspired by—"

His arms came around her, hugging her so tightly against him that the oxygen she needed to finish her sentence whooshed out of her lungs.

"Ash." She could feel how hard his heart was pounding against her own chest. "This is the best birthday gift anyone has ever given me."

She smiled and hugged him back as relief hit her. But at the same time, tears threatened to come, too. Her parents meant just as much to her, and she couldn't imagine losing them. And yet, when was the last time she'd seen her mother? At least a year ago, on her mother's last trip out to California.

Drew's phone buzzed from the corner with James's ring tone, and she knew their private time for the morning was up.

"I'm really glad you like it," she said when he finally loosened his hold on her.

"I *love* it."

For a moment, he looked as though he was going to say something more, and her heart nearly stopped beating at the thought that he might be about to say he loved her, too. Nothing in her life had ever moved as fast as her relationship with Drew. It had all been amazing so far, but in the light of a new day, all those worries she'd made herself stuff down last night wanted to come popping back up like the Whac-A-Mole arcade game.

In the end, though, all he said was, "That's my half-hour warning bell from James. How about we see if we can both squeeze into my shower before he comes pounding on the door?"

Silently bopping her worries over the head with a mallet so that, at the very least, they would go away for the rest of Drew's birthday, she smiled at her amazing rock-star lover. He was the only man who had ever made her entire body heat up like this, with nothing but a few naughty words.

"Is your shower bigger than the one I've been using?"

He already had her in his arms, had grabbed a condom from the bedside table, and was carrying her toward the shower. "A little bigger, but not by much." He grinned down at her. "We're going to have to get real creative in there."

Creative. Oh my, just the thought of getting creative with Drew was enough to nearly send her over the edge.

"I have a minor in math," she told him when he put her down to reach into the shower to turn on the tap. "I was particularly good with space-filling models. I could always make things fit that no one else could."

"Jesus, Ash." He dragged her under the water. "Show me." His hands roved in dangerous and wonderful ways over her naked, wet skin. "Show me how we fit together better than any two people ever have."

The water was hot, but she still shivered at the passion beneath his words. All she wanted was to be close to him—there was nothing as good as that moment when he pushed inside her—but the shower wasn't big enough for her to wrap her hands and legs around him the way she wanted to.

The kisses he was running down over her neck and shoulders and then the swell of her breasts didn't help her brain work any faster. For several long moments, all she was capable of was soaking up the dual sensations of his mouth and hands on her.

He slid one hand down over her stomach and between her legs, then groaned as he slipped and slid over her aroused skin. The sound was low and raw and breathtakingly sexy in the small space.

"How long have you been this ready for me?"

Her response came before she could even think to edit it. "I always am."

He crushed his mouth to hers, and his unleashed desire matched hers perfectly. Even if she'd wanted to hold something back, there was no way that she could. Not today. Not when his mouth tasted like heaven, and his hard, rippling muscles against her naked skin were as close to nirvana as anyone could possibly get.

Well, almost as close. Because she knew that having *all* of him would be even better...

She tore her mouth from his as inspiration hit. "I've figured it out." She was too lost to desire to second-guess herself. Besides, while she didn't have anywhere near the sexual experience that he did, she had always been a fast learner.

As she began to turn around, the warm water—and the unfettered need coursing through her veins—made her movements slower than they would otherwise have been. Finally, when she was facing the shower wall, she placed her hands palm-down against the wall next to her head and looked over her shoulder at Drew.

"Like this. Take me like this."

He didn't move right away, simply stared at her with eyes so dark and intense that she shivered again even as hot water sprayed over her. Finally, he ripped open the condom wrapper and slid it on.

"I always want to be gentle with you," he said as he slowly ran his large hands from her shoulders, over her back, then placed them at her hips. She felt his fingertips grip down on her wet, naked skin as he shifted her hips up slightly so that her back arched and she could feel his hard length pressing between her legs. "I swear I'll try harder not to lose control this time."

"I love it when you lose control." She rolled her hips so that he was poised at her entrance. "Take me. Please, I need you so badly."

"I need you, too."

Between the span of one heartbeat and the next, he drove into her. So hard, and so deep, that she cried out. Not in pain, but with perfect, ecstatic pleasure. Her nails were scraping down the tiled wall in an effort to hold on to something, and her cheek was pressed against the tile as she whispered, "More."

Her name became a rhythmic chant from his lips—*AshAshAshAsh*—as he gripped her hips even tighter and thrust into her again and again with absolutely no control.

There was nothing gentle about the way he took her, but she wouldn't have wanted there to be. Not when every moment, and every experience, was so precious. All her life, she'd remember these amazing moments with him on tour. Moments when nothing mattered but each other—not their pasts, not their futures. Only how happy they made each other right *now*.

As her climax began to slowly shudder through her, Drew slid his hands from her hips to play with her breasts. A split second later, she was shattering so completely, so helplessly, that her hands began to slide down the tile wall. With one arm around her waist to hold her up and his hand splayed out over her pelvis, he thrust once, twice, three more times...and then he buried his face in the exposed crook of her neck and groaned her name one last time.

When the water began to turn a little bit colder, she felt a bar of soap slide over her skin, but she was too loose from their incredible lovemaking to do anything but let him wash her skin and hair clean. After everything they'd already done, it was surprisingly intimate. And oh so lovely to be taken care of like this.

A short while later, he turned off the tap and reached for a warm, fluffy towel. And as he wrapped it around her, he stared into her eyes and said, "It's already the best birthday ever. But *best* doesn't even come close anymore."

CHAPTER TWENTY-SIX

Drew was aware of the necklace beneath his T-shirt all day long...and all day long he'd wanted to grab Ashley in front of his crew and kiss her breathless. He was beyond touched that she'd had it made for him, a perfect little replica of the guitar his mother had given him.

Yet again, he thought about how much his mom would have loved Ashley. Just as much as he knew his siblings and his father were going to love her.

As if he'd conjured them into being, when he stepped out of his last interview for the day, his youngest sister, Maddie, came running toward him.

"Drew!"

He opened his arms and caught her. "What did you do with my baby sister?" Maddie was one of his favorite people on the planet, but he wasn't sure he liked the short length of her skirt or the makeup she was wearing.

She rolled her eyes. "I'm going to look like a nun tonight compared to the rest of your fans."

He wasn't sure about that, but scowling at her when he hadn't seen her for way too long was out of the question. "You're a sight for sore eyes, Mads. You excited about starting college soon?"

She nodded, but the light he'd hoped to see in her eyes wasn't completely there. "I've been emailing with my new roommate, and she seems really nice."

"That's great," he said in a gentle voice, "but you could have applied to one of the cooking schools you really wanted to go to. You don't have to go to Stanford, you know."

She shook her head. "Dad would have freaked if I'd gone to the Cordon Bleu, even if I could have gotten in. He likes knowing I'm going to be safe and sound at Stanford, just down the road from our house, with his fellow professors watching over me."

"I'll talk to him," Drew promised her. "I'll make him understand."

But her frown only deepened as their father walked in. "It's okay, Drew," she said in a low voice. "It's only four years. I'm sure I'll have fun at Stanford like the rest of you did, and then he won't have to be any more stressed-out than he already is."

While Drew was growing up, their father had been easygoing about things that other parents freaked out about, like grades or staying out late. Even when their mom got sick, he'd still held it together pretty well. But then at the end, he'd lost it on all fronts. Work. Sleep. Fun. None of those things happened anymore for Michael Morrison. All of them tried to pick up the slack as much as they could, but the truth was that you couldn't make a person laugh if they didn't feel like it. You couldn't order a person to fall asleep if all they did was have nightmares whenever they closed their eyes. And there was no point in their dad staring blankly at a computer screen all day either.

Drew wished he could help his father—they all did—and it killed him that he hadn't figured out how to do that yet.

"Happy birthday, son."

As his father hugged him close, Drew was upset to feel his ribs protruding slightly. His father was a great cook, and so was Maddie, who was still living in the house with him. But his appetite clearly hadn't yet returned.

"Thanks for coming all the way to New Orleans, Dad. It means a lot to me that you travel to wherever I am on my birthday." Except for last year, when their mom hadn't been well enough to fly or drive long distance.

"We don't see you nearly enough. It looks like the road is agreeing with you on this tour, Drew. I'm glad to see it."

It's Ashley. She's the reason everything is better.

"Everyone else should be here shortly," his father continued. "We've all been looking forward to tonight."

Drew couldn't wait to see the rest of his siblings. But this time, his happiness came from more than simply knowing he was going to spend time with his family. He really wanted all of them to meet Ashley, too. And though he wasn't yet able to tell them what she meant to him, he wouldn't be surprised if they all saw it as clear as day, even without him saying, *She's my girlfriend.*

"There's someone I really want you guys to meet." He craned his neck to see where Ashley was and found her chatting with one of the radio station staff members. She obviously intended to give him time to greet his family alone. Unlike pretty much everyone else in his world, she never wanted to invade his space. Didn't she know she was the number one person he wanted by his side? He told his sister and father, "I'll be right back."

When he moved beside Ashley, it was nearly impossible not to put his arm around her or even take her hand. Just hours ago, they'd been as close as two people could be. Now, it felt unnatural not to be able to touch her. To kiss her.

"Ash, I'd like to introduce you to my family. Come over and join us."

"I'd love to. But I know your time with them is limited, so maybe I shouldn't—"

He moved another step closer, close enough to inhale her fresh, clean scent. "You definitely should."

"Okay." She made an adorable face. "I don't know why I'm being so weird about this. Especially since your sister and father look so nice."

"You don't have any reason to be nervous. They're going to love you."

He put his hand in the small of her back and led her over to where his father and sister were standing. "Maddie, Dad, this is Ashley Emmit. She joined the tour last week as part of a research project she's doing on the music industry for her Stanford Business School application."

"It's very nice to meet you, Ashley," his father said as he shook her hand.

"It's so nice to meet you, too, Mr. Morrison."

Maddie's smile was huge. "Wow, you're really pretty. Are you having fun on tour? Isn't Drew great? All of my friends are in love with him. I swear at least a dozen of them begged me to bring them with me today. I can't believe you've been in Palo Alto all these years and we've never met before. Have you met Olivia or Sean or Justin or Grant at Stanford?"

Drew laughed out loud as he watched Ashley try to process everything Maddie was throwing at her. Luckily for her, before she had to figure out which question to answer first, his brother Sean walked in hand in hand with Serena, his supermodel girlfriend. Ex-supermodel, actually, since she'd recently given it up to study English at Stanford.

"This is Ashley, guys," Maddie said before Drew could introduce her. "Her dad is Drew's former professor, and she's on tour with him to learn about the music business. Ashley, Sean is one of my older brothers. His twin, Justin, will be here soon. And Serena is Sean's girlfriend. They met at Stanford, and she's not modeling anymore because she's super into books."

Drew loved his little sister, but she was a handful. Someday she was going to make some guy really happy...and drive him crazy all at the same time. Just as crazy as she drove all of them.

Fortunately, Sean, Serena, and Ashley were all laughing as they shook hands. "I've heard so much about all of you," Ashley said. "It's really nice to meet you in person."

"It's great to meet you, too," Sean said, before turning to give Drew a look that he easily read. *If she's heard all about us, then why haven't we heard about her?*

Drew sent back a silent message: *It's complicated, but hopefully it won't be for long, because she's special. Really, really special.*

If anyone knew about things being complicated, it was Sean and Serena. They'd had a heck of a time when they'd first started dating. Being a new couple wasn't easy for anyone, but due to Serena's fame, they'd had to deal with paparazzi—and a crazy, lecherous professor, too. Thankfully, the two of them had come out on the right side of it all, and he could see that they were more in love than ever.

Sean's twin, Justin, was laughing with someone Drew couldn't see as he walked in, but Drew would bet his savings account that it was Taylor, his brother's closest friend. A moment later, when his father shifted to one side, Drew confirmed it.

Justin and Taylor had been friends ever since their first day at Stanford. And yet, for some reason none of them could understand, given that Taylor was cute, fun, and as brilliant as Justin, they'd never dated. Drew had hardly been able to wait a week to kiss Ashley. How the hell his brother had already waited three years was beyond him.

Drew pulled his brother in for a big bear hug, but he was much gentler with Taylor. Before Maddie could beat him to it with Justin's and Taylor's full histories, Drew said, "Ashley, this is my brother Justin and his friend Taylor."

"Are you having a good time on tour?" Taylor asked.

"The best. The most I had hoped for was to be on the fringes of the crew and observe from a distance. But Drew includes me in absolutely everything."

When she turned to smile at Drew, he was *this close* to chucking his promise to keep their relationship private. He wanted to hold her hand the way Sean was holding Serena's. But even more than that, he'd never held back something so important from his family before.

As if she could read his thoughts—and felt guilty about withholding this final piece of herself from him—her smile fell slightly.

Life, he'd learned the hard way, could be far too short for holding back. But at the same time, pushing her right now would be akin to trying to bend her to his will. Ashley was one of the strongest people he'd ever met. And the smartest, too. Surely it wouldn't be long before she took in all the data she needed and made the same decision he had: That they belonged together for the whole world to see.

"I'm really lucky," she told his whole family.

But he needed everyone to know, "I'm the lucky one."

His two other siblings, Grant and Olivia, arrived just then. After they hugged and he introduced Ashley, Grant said, "Drew emailed me a couple of days ago with an idea that you gave him about a radically new way to approach a record label. It struck me as really smart, and I'd like to chat with you about it in more detail, if you can spare a few minutes over dinner."

"I'd love to," Ashley said, flushing with obvious pleasure at the compliment. "I actually have my laptop with me, so I can show you the business plan I've been putting together if you're interested in seeing it."

"The restaurant we're headed to is just down the street," Drew said. "It's supposed to have the best gumbo in New Orleans. So why don't we all head over, and then the two of you can geek out once we're sitting down?"

Olivia was quiet as the group headed out to the restaurant, walking beside their father. Maddie, of course, was talking Ashley's ear off. Sean and Serena were lost in each other. Justin and Taylor were too busy trying to ignore the sparks between themselves to pay much attention to anything else. And Grant brought up the rear with Drew.

James, who already knew them all, was keeping an eagle eye on everyone and everything. Drew appreciated the way he paid especially close attention to Ashley's safety. Though Drew knew she could take care of herself, she wasn't familiar with any of the big cities they were touring through. Plus, he knew his fans could get a little overexcited sometimes, and he couldn't stand the thought of Ashley ever getting hurt because of him.

"So," Grant said, "that's Ashley."

Drew grinned at his oldest brother. "Beautiful, isn't she?"

"Damned smart, too, and you only gave me a hint of her ideas, didn't you?" When Drew nodded, Grant shot him a serious look. "You really are thinking about going indie, aren't you?"

Until now, the only person Drew had talked to about this was Ashley. Despite all the rules she'd obviously tried to follow in her life to please her father, she was a fiercely independent thinker. Day by day, he found himself depending on her more and more. Especially when he couldn't just drop into his brother's office on a whim to talk things through.

Even more thankful that his family had shifted their busy lives around to clear this day in New Orleans for him, Drew told Grant, "The label is pushing hard for my next album. But I know what they want, what any label would want given the sales we've had—more of what I've done before. My manager keeps calling and emailing about the new contract on the table. But I just don't think I can do it, Grant. And even if I could, things have changed too much for me to want to repeat the past."

"Whatever you decide," Grant said, "keep me in the loop and let me know how I can help."

"I will." But Drew needed to talk more than business with his brother. He needed the inside scoop on his family, since he couldn't be there to see them day to day. "How's everyone doing lately?"

"The good news is that Dad seems to be surfacing a bit more. Olivia, on the other hand, doesn't say much, which worries me. But you know how she is—the harder you push, the more she closes down. Justin spends most of his time trying to pretend he isn't in love with Taylor. Maddie is still playing cheerleader for Dad way too much, so I've been making sure she gets out with her girlfriends this summer before they all head off to college. Only Sean seems truly happy now that he and Serena have found each other. He's always got his camera with him, which is good to see."

Grant had always been one hell of a listener. It was one of the many reasons why he'd earned his first billion before he was thirty. Grant also wasn't one to talk about himself. He didn't need to build up his ego like so many guys in his circle did. But tonight, Drew wasn't going to let his brother get away with skipping his own update.

"What about you?" Drew asked. "How are you holding up?"

"All right." But his brother was frowning as he said it. "We're in the thick of a couple of pretty intense acquisitions right now, so the hours are even longer than usual. I don't mind the work, though."

Drew understood why Grant was perfectly willing to work from sunup to sundown and most of the hours before and after, too. Working helped a lot of people block out painful memories. But it had never really been the solution for Drew. Not when the songs had stopped coming and the music playing in his head had become barely recognizable.

"I don't think Ashley has been able to get a word in edgewise," Grant commented as he nodded up the sidewalk to where Maddie had looped her arm through Ashley's and was still chattering a million miles a minute.

Drew let his brother change the subject. Even when they were kids, Grant had always mulled things over for a really long time. Clearly, he needed to work through his emotions awhile longer. And the truth was that Drew would have been right there with him were it not for Ashley.

"She's a good listener," Drew told his brother.

"Is there anything she isn't good at?"

"Nope. Everything about her blows my mind."

Finally, Grant smiled.

* * *

After their meal, one that thankfully was full of more laughter than Drew had seen out of anyone in his family for months, they hopped onto his bus, which Max had pulled around to the curb, and headed to the venue. Maddie made all of them laugh some more as she played with the knobs and switches on the high-tech vehicle, before turning to Ashley and asking, "How has sleeping on a bus been?"

Ashley's eyes were huge as she looked at Drew. He knew she hadn't intended to do so, but in that moment she gave them completely away.

Fortunately, Sean stepped in. "I could never get much sleep on the bus when we traveled for games. But Drew has always been able to sleep like a rock, anytime, anywhere."

"I've actually slept really well," Ashley finally answered his sister. "Drew's schedule is super busy. He's up early for radio, has interviews or recording sessions all day, and then his shows and meet and greets don't end until late. By the time my head hits the pillow, I'm pretty much out."

Except, Drew thought, *when I'm keeping you up by making love to you.*

"You're recording again?" Olivia asked him. "Does that mean you're writing again, too?"

Olivia hadn't said much all night, but she'd obviously picked up on the most important points. First, that Drew couldn't keep his eyes off Ashley. And second, that he'd finally busted through his musical block.

"I am."

"His new songs are incredible." Thankfully, Ashley seemed to have forgotten the awkwardness from a few minutes ago as she smiled at him and said, "I can't wait until the whole world gets to hear your new music."

"I'm really inspired, Ash." *Because of you.*

"Who *has* gotten to hear the new songs so far?" Maddie wanted to know as the bus pulled into the lot behind the venue, and James checked in with security to make sure everyone was in place for their arrival.

"Just the engineers I've been working with in the studios we've dropped into on the road...and Ashley." If his family hadn't figured things out by now, that was the final piece of the puzzle they'd need to slide into place.

They were all inside the venue a few minutes later. Drew and his father stood off to one side while Ashley chatted easily with everyone. He was glad to see that her earlier nerves seemed to have all disappeared.

"Ashley is great, Drew." His father was smiling as he said it, the first real smile Drew had seen on his face in a very long time. "She's exactly the kind of woman I was hoping you'd find one day."

Michael Morrison had always known what his kids were thinking and feeling. Even better, he'd *understood* them. Just as he understood Drew now, regardless of all the things Drew couldn't say yet about the woman he'd fallen head over heels for.

"I'm lucky to have found her. *Really* lucky. But—" Damn it, he hated having to say, "We're trying to keep things private for now. Even though I want to tell the whole world she's mine."

"I'd be nervous about being with a big star, too," his father said with a nod, as if Ashley's request made perfect sense to him. "Heck, your mother wasn't even famous, and I was still terrified about asking her out. And then when she said she'd go out with me? I completely panicked and almost told her to forget it."

Drew had never heard this story before. What's more, he hadn't heard his father talk about his mother at all since she'd passed away, as if it hurt too much even to share memories. "If Mom said she wanted to be with you, why'd you panic?"

"Because she was the most beautiful, vibrant, incredible woman in the world. And I was just me. I honestly couldn't see how it could work."

"It worked great. You had the best marriage of anyone I knew growing up."

"We did." His father inhaled a shaky breath. "We sure did." He shook his head as if to clear it before adding, "I know you would never want to overshadow anyone, Drew—"

"No one could overshadow Ashley."

His father met his gaze and held it. "Because she's the most beautiful, vibrant, incredible woman in the world to you?"

"Damn straight she is."

His father pulled him in for a hug, and they both held on tight. But Drew could see that Olivia's brain was on overdrive as she watched Ashley talking about the music business with Grant.

Ever since their mother had gotten sick, Olivia had tried so hard to step into Lisa Morrison's shoes and keep the family together. She'd done a great job, but Drew didn't want her to think she had to worry about him anymore. Not now that he had Ashley.

James gave him a hand signal to let him know he had ten minutes before he needed to hit the stage. "I'm going to see if I can grab Olivia before the show starts. Thanks, Dad. For everything."

He gave his father another hug, then headed toward his sister. "Can you hang with me in my dressing room for a few minutes?"

"Sure, I've been wanting to grab you for a private chat."

Olivia didn't say anything as they headed for his dressing room, but as soon as the door closed, she said, "I thought you weren't going to go near your professor's daughter." She parroted his words from a family barbecue a while back: '*I wouldn't touch her in a million years.*' Isn't that what you said to all of us? Does her father know about you two?"

"Not yet."

She raised an eyebrow. "You say that like you're actually planning on telling him."

"I am."

"I haven't had Professor Emmit for any classes, but I know plenty of people who have, so I think I have a pretty good sense of what he's about. He likes rules. Likes everything to line up neat and straight. Especially his daughter, I'm going to guess."

His sister was too damned smart to miss a thing. "Right."

"Which means you're the very last guy he'd ever want to see her with." She held up her hand before he could respond. "You're my brother and I love you and I think you're great. The greatest. But the fact is, you're still a rock star. And life with you is the exact opposite of straitlaced and neat and tidy." Just then, screams from his fans pierced the door, and she shook her head. "Plus, it's gotten even crazier than it was before. You're really, really famous now."

He couldn't deny any of that either. But that didn't mean he was willing to give Ashley up. "We can make it work."

"How? Long distance, with her in school and you on the road?"

"If that's what it takes. I'm not willing to give her up, Olivia." Just the thought of it made every part of him tense up. "Anything but her."

His sister's expression softened. "You're different with Ashley, Drew. Happier. And so much lighter, too. I know how hard losing Mom has been for you."

"For all of us."

"Yes. All of us." She closed her eyes, and in that moment, he watched her fall apart, then put herself back together. "Sean is lucky. He found Serena, and she's helped change everything for the better for him. And Justin always has Taylor to lean on, even if they're both too dumb to realize that they're actually in love and not just best friends."

"Things are going to hit a breaking point soon for them," Drew predicted.

"God, I hope so, because it's just gotten downright painful to watch the two of them circle each other." She pinned him with her laser-focus gaze. "Do you think that maybe what you're feeling for Ashley seems so strong because she's helped heal you?"

"She has helped heal me," he told his sister. "But that's only one of the reasons why I love her."

His sister's eyes went big. "Love?"

He'd been circling it himself for a while now. Since the very beginning, if he was being totally honest with himself. "I'm in love with Ashley." It was the biggest thing he'd ever known. And the best. If he could have shouted it from the rooftops, he would have.

"Does she know?"

Just then, a knock came at the door. "Two minutes, Drew," James called.

"Not yet," he told his sister as they both got up to head out of the room.

And he'd be counting every second until it was just the two of them alone on the bus so that he could tell Ashley she was absolutely everything to him.

"Thanks, sis," he said to Olivia. "I miss you, miss hanging out with all of you."

"I miss you, too," she said, her voice as thick with emotion as his. "But we'll always be there whenever you're ready to come home. Just like Mom always said, we want you to live your dream."

CHAPTER TWENTY-SEVEN

Ashley was blown away by the Morrisons.

Not just because they were all so beautiful that it almost made her eyes hurt to look at them standing together in the VIP section of Drew's show. And not just because they were all so smart and successful.

It was the way they loved one another. She'd never seen anything like it. They watched out for one another. They helped one another. They were simply *there* for one another.

Madison was adorable and hilarious. Ashley loved the way Drew doted on his youngest sister. Madison had clearly thrived as a result of the endless affection and encouragement that she'd been given by her family.

Drew had said that Olivia was someone Ashley could be friends with, probably because they were both the quiet, studious type. Ashley was a little surprised that the two of them had never met before on the

Stanford campus. If they had, she definitely would have been drawn instantly to someone as bright and utterly unaware of her shockingly good looks as Olivia.

Grant was the lone Morrison in a suit, but it looked exactly right on him. He didn't look like other high-tech CEOs in their sweatshirts and jeans, but Ashley had read enough case studies of *Collide* to know that Drew's oldest brother had always marched brilliantly to the beat of his own drummer. They'd had a fascinating conversation about the music business during dinner, and he'd asked her if she would email her indie label proposal to him to look over. In fact, the part he'd seemed to be the most interested in was her conviction that there should be women in the executive level positions at the new label. Women who understood other women. Women who had once been the girls in the audience at shows like Drew's. Women who weren't afraid to support music that touched you deeply.

Ashley was almost more nervous about showing her indie label proposal to him than she was about whether or not she'd get into Stanford Business School next year. But she was excited, too. Just being able to get personal feedback from someone as brilliant as Grant was a dream come true.

As for the Morrison twins, Justin and Sean might look alike, but Ashley could see how different they were. Both of them were great, but Justin was more the precise scientist, whereas Sean came across as laid-back. Drew had been right about the way Justin and his friend Taylor looked at each other when they thought the other wasn't looking. And Sean and Serena were almost too gorgeous together—and so sweet, too, considering they hadn't let go of each other's hands all night long. She also appreciated that neither Serena nor Sean seemed to notice that they outshone every other human on the planet. All but Drew, of course. Because Ashley was positive that no one could possibly shine more brightly than Drew.

And then there was Drew's father, Michael. Throughout the concert, she'd noticed him lowering his head to wipe his eyes. He was clearly so proud of Drew, and Ashley kept choking up herself as she watched him marvel over his talented son.

She hadn't meant to listen in on any of their conversations, but since it was necessary to yell to be heard over the noise of the crowd between songs, she'd ended up catching snippets for the past couple of hours.

Sean to Justin: "How do you think Dad's doing?"

Grant to their father: "Drew is even better now than he used to be, isn't he? I'm pretty sure I know why."

And Maddie to Olivia: "Wouldn't it be great if Justin and Taylor started kissing out of the blue?"

That one had made Ashley laugh.

They were all so welcoming to Ashley, too, each of them going out of their way to include her in their conversations. It was so lovely to feel like a part of such a close family, even if it was just for a little while. With the way her parents had fought her whole life, the three of them had never been a particularly tight unit. Tonight gave her the tiniest taste of what Drew's childhood must have been like. Yes, it was noisy. Sure, it was a little chaotic. But what fun he must have had with his brothers and sisters. The kind of fun Ashley had only ever wished for. Her mother, she knew, had wanted more kids. But that had never happened for her parents. If it had, would that have changed anything? Or would her parents have fought even more?

"Everything okay?"

Ashley surfaced from her thoughts as Olivia put a hand on her arm and looked at her with concern.

More than a dozen times throughout dinner with Drew's family, Ashley had begun to reach for him, or to lean into his broad chest, or say something to him that only two lovers could possibly understand. All night it had been really, really hard to be in the same room with him without wanting to leap into his arms and kiss him. But each time she'd caught herself just in time.

And each time, she'd had to ask herself yet again why she was so darn scared to go public with their relationship. Sure, he was a huge star and she'd be subject to millions of people on the Internet asking one another how on earth he could have picked her. But Ashley had never much cared what other people thought of her, and even though she suspected it would hurt the first few thousand times a stranger commented online that Drew was way out of her league, she could figure out how to deal with that.

The answer she kept circling back to was the same one that had been there from the start—that she and Drew were too different to make it work. At least, beyond the bedroom, where they *clearly* worked in the most amazing way possible.

Only...were they really too different to see eye to eye in the long run?

Or was it just that watching her parents fight so long and hard all those years had colored her view of *any* relationship she might have been a part of and made her scared to risk her heart?

"I'm so glad you could come here tonight for Drew's birthday," she said in lieu of directly answering Olivia's question. "He was so excited about seeing you, and I know how much he loves all of you."

"We love him, too," Olivia said. "It's a big deal that he's writing new songs again. Do you have any idea what the big change was that helped him finally break through his block?"

Drew's sister had been perfectly nice, but was more aloof than the other Morrisons. Ashley understood aloof, having been called that more than once, but it was less that Olivia was shy...and more that she seemed to want to make absolutely sure Ashley didn't take advantage of her brother in any way.

"I'm sure he'll sit down with you soon to tell you all about his reasons," Ashley said carefully.

Was Olivia looking at her approvingly for not giving away any of Drew's secrets? Again, Ashley wasn't sure quite what his sister was thinking as Olivia said, "But you know the reasons, don't you?"

Ashley felt like a deer caught in headlights. Yes, she knew what Drew had told her—that she'd helped him see that it was okay to risk pursuing a new musical direction rather than continuing to tread the same hugely successful paths he had before. But she still wasn't sure she believed that *she* could possibly have had such a big impact on him.

"I've always been a fan of his music, and it's been really nice getting to know him better as a person. We've had a lot of time to talk on the bus."

"You've been staying on his bus? Just the two of you?"

Too late, Ashley realized this was news to his sister. She knew what Olivia must be assuming—that they were sleeping together. The problem was, his sister was spot-on. And Ashley had never been any good at lying. "My father was really worried about me joining Drew's tour. Your brother promised him that nothing would happen to me. That's why Drew wanted me to be on his bus."

Olivia nodded, but Ashley still had the sense she wasn't completely convinced that things between Drew and Ashley were quite so cut-and-dried. Of course, knowing Olivia was right made Ashley feel more than a little guilty for not just 'fessing up to the complete truth about her relationship with Drew.

But what *was* the truth? Of course Ashley was head over heels for Drew. Who wouldn't be? But was it just a crush? Was it just inescapable and incredible heat between friends?

Or was it more?

So much more that even thinking about one particular four-letter word made her lose her breath.

"The two of you look like you've gotten pretty close."

A part of Ashley wished Olivia would just come right out and ask if they were a couple. That way she wouldn't have to keep fighting her own internal battles over whether to keep them a secret or not.

"Drew and I, we've become friends. Really good friends. And..." Ashley felt completely out of her depth in this conversation, but she still needed Olivia to know one thing. "His happiness means everything to me. That's why tonight has been so amazing. Because he loves all of you so much, and he misses you terribly when he's on tour. I know he'll be on a high from seeing you for a long time."

"He already looked happy when we got here." Finally, Olivia smiled. "I'm glad you're with him, Ashley. We all are."

Just then, the house lights went dark and the drummer started playing a riff that made the crowd go crazy again in the hopes that Drew was coming back out for the first of, hopefully, many encores. When he did, he headed for their side of the stage and began singing straight to her.

She'd been worried about people guessing about whether she and Drew were an item. But every time she got lost in his eyes, in his songs, in the sweet emotions on his face...she forgot everything except for how happy he made her feel.

So happy that for a little while, she even forgot to be scared of a certain four-letter word. A word that perfectly described everything she was feeling for the rock star singing his heart out to her in front of tens of thousands of his fans, and his family, too.

CHAPTER TWENTY-EIGHT

It was later than usual by the time Drew and Ashley got back on the bus and headed out of town. "It was so amazing that your family came out for your birthday," Ashley said. "They're all so great."

"They loved you, too, Ash." He pulled her close, never wanting to let her go. "I knew they would. Best birthday ever."

"Actually..." She bit her lip. "I know it's past midnight, but I have one more little birthday gift I'd like to give you. We should probably go back into the bedroom for it, though."

He already knew that look, the one where she clearly wanted to say or do something sexy, but was still a little shy about her newfound sensuality. "Great, let's go." He grabbed her hand and practically dragged her into his bedroom. "Where do you want me?"

"Everywhere." Her eyes went big. "I just said that out loud, didn't I?"

He grinned, as happy tonight as he'd ever been. Ashley Emmit was simply perfect. Beyond perfect—he'd never thought he'd be able to find a woman this beautiful *and* this brilliant.

She quickly amended her answer to, "On the bed would probably be best."

"Clothes on or off?"

Her cheeks grew even rosier as she said, "How about shirt off, pants on?"

He whipped his T-shirt off and threw it across the room. "Ready whenever you are." But she didn't move, didn't say anything, just stood there looking a little uncertain. "Ash, you don't have to do anything you're uncomfortable with."

"I know. I want to do this." She licked her lips again, and then the next thing he knew, she was reaching for the buttons on the front of the shirt she was wearing and opening them one at a time.

By the time the first button was undone, Drew was already on the verge of dragging her onto his lap to devour her. The only thing that stopped him was the fact that he didn't want to mess up Ashley's final birthday gift for him.

The first hint of what her gift might be was revealed by the opening of the third button—very sheer black lace bra cups that just barely covered her nipples.

"You were wearing black lace all night?"

She nodded, looking shy again as she undid the final two buttons and let her shirt fall to the floor. "I felt different in it. Sexier."

"You're always sexy," he said, "no matter what you're wearing. But if I'd known—"

The rest of his words dried up in his mouth as she undid the button on her jeans and drew the zipper down to reveal more sheer black lace. She shimmied out of her jeans, then stepped out of them, leaving her skin barely covered by a bra and thong.

"*Ash...*" He couldn't keep his hands off her for another second as he reached out to drag her onto his lap, his hands caressing the bare skin at her hips, his mouth playing over the sweet swell of flesh above her bra. "If I'd known about this," he finally managed to say, "I wouldn't have been able to remember a single word to any of my songs."

"I'm glad you like it."

"Like it?" He kissed her hard. Long. Deep. "This is another of the best damned birthday presents anyone has ever given me."

She looked pleased. "There's more."

"More?"

She nodded again, her skin flushing as she said, "I thought maybe we could put on some music and I could..." She put her hands over her face. "I can't believe I'm still shy with you."

"I love it, when you're shy and when you're not. All sides of you, Ash, they're all beautiful. Tell me what you're going to do once you put on some music."

"Well...you're always saying that you love seeing me dance in the audience at your shows, so I thought maybe I could dance for you in private tonight. First with the lingerie on. And then—"

"—with it off," he finished for her.

It took every ounce of control not to take her right then and there, just to rip off the lace and silk and give them both what they were dying for.

"I really do love watching you dance, Ash, and I'm dying for you to do it now in black lace. But you have to know, I'm not going to be able to wait too much longer to have you tonight."

"I can't wait too much longer either," she whispered.

When her tongue flicked out to lick his lower lip, he nearly fast-forwarded past her striptease, but she had already slid off his lap and was scrolling through her phone for a song to play.

She settled on an instrumental with a sensuously driving drumbeat, one that matched the pounding in his chest. He'd have to remember to ask her later who this was they were listening to, but for now, all he cared about was the way she was moving her hips, swaying from side to side. Her back was still to him as she let the music rumble through her, anticipation ratcheting up and up and up as she slowly began to turn toward him at the same time that she inched the straps of her bra down over her shoulders.

He held his breath as the lace slipped lower and lower, and by the time she was facing him completely, the bra cups were barely staying in place over her nipples. "Take it off, Ash." Each word was raw. Hungry. *Desperate.*

Still moving her hips in time to the tribal beat, she brought her hands to the hook at the center of her chest and met his eyes at the exact moment that she snapped it open.

"Beautiful." He exhaled the word in one long breath.

Her lips turned up at the corners as she slid her hands down over her bare breasts and over her rib cage and stomach. Once she reached her hips, she slid her fingers beneath the thin strip of lace holding up her thong. Not once did she look away from him as she slowly slid the fabric down, then let it fall to the floor.

The next thing Drew knew, she was lying beneath him on the bed. He couldn't remember reaching for her, just that he couldn't wait another second to have her.

Drew put his hands on her hips and gripped her tightly, her skin soft beneath his fingertips. He wanted to touch her everywhere, wanted to memorize every inch of her skin, first with his hands and then his mouth.

Her eyes were dilated nearly to black as she looked up at him, her breath coming fast, her skin flushed a gorgeous rose. *"Drew."*

God, he loved it when she said his name like that. With so much need. With so much *emotion.* She tried so hard to stay rational all the time, to keep from letting her passions spill over. But when they were together this way, she could never hold anything back from him.

Everything she felt, everything she seemed to think she needed to cage up, poured into him in her kisses. In the way she looked so deeply into his eyes. In the way she whispered his name.

The first time he'd ever set eyes on her, he'd thought she was the most beautiful woman in the world. And he knew he'd always feel that way, that he could catch a glimpse of her from across the room a million times—or be looking at her just like this when she was soft and warm and perfect beneath him—and never get used to the way her beauty pierced right through him.

Every day, he was running a million miles an hour for his career. These moments alone with Ashley were precious. So precious that he wanted to draw this one out as long as he could with more kisses over the rapidly beating pulse at the curve of her neck and then by taking her sweet mouth again and again and again.

Until there was no way to hold back any longer...

He kicked off his pants and had on protection a second later. Levering himself up on his forearms so that he could watch her expression as he took her, he slid into her tight, wet heat. She gasped as he filled her, arching up into him to take even more of him, one glorious inch at a time.

"Tell me." His words were rough and ragged from the pleasure taking him over. "I need to know."

"Anything." The one word from her lips was coated in bliss, breathless with ecstasy to come. "I'll tell you anything."

"How does this make you feel?" He gripped her hips harder and pushed deeper. Her eyes closed as her head fell back. He licked at her sweat-slicked skin before saying, "How do I make you feel?"

"Good." Her eyes opened, and when she looked into his, his chest clenched tight. "So good."

"More." He put his hands on her thighs and lifted her legs to wrap around his waist. "Give me more. Trust me with more, Ash." It wasn't just a request anymore, wasn't just a question. It was a plea. A plea for her to reveal the secret parts of herself. He put his hands on either side of her face and gently caressed her. "Please, Ash. Tell me what's in your head right this second."

"I think about you all the time." Her words came out in a rush—*Ithinkaboutyouallthetime.*

When she realized what she'd said and flushed with renewed embarrassment, he wouldn't let her look away. "I think about you all the time, too, Ash."

"And this. I think about *this* all the time." This time, thankfully, she didn't look away. Instead, she wrapped her legs even tighter around his hips as she lowered her voice to a whisper. "I want you inside of me every second of every day."

Of all the things Drew had thought she might say, he'd never dreamed of her echoing the same thing he wanted himself. He repeated her words on a hoarse groan of need.

"Every second"—he came nearly all the way out of her, then thrust even deeper, and she gasped with pleasure—"of every day."

"Yes." She lifted her mouth to his, and he captured her *"Please"* in a kiss more raw than any he'd ever experienced before.

"No more space," she gasped as she gripped his shoulders so tightly he knew there would be marks. "There's too much space between us."

"Not anymore," he promised her. "All you need to do is let me in." Her inner muscles clenched over him then, and the pleasure was so intense that he could barely get out the words, "Let me all the way in, Ash."

And when she put her mouth to his while their bodies moved in perfect unison, Drew's passion for Ashley was wild.

Unraveled.

Unleashed.

These past months, he'd been numb and then hurting. He'd been running as fast as he could and then alternately trying to find that still place. But with

Ashley, he didn't need to fight past anything or to pretend.

He just needed *her*.

CHAPTER TWENTY-NINE

"I know I promised to give you time," he said a short while later, "but I really think we should tell him." Drew had shifted his weight slightly to the side so that Ashley could breathe, but his need to touch her all the time was so strong that he kept one leg across hers.

Her eyes were still hazy from her climax when she opened them to look up at him. "Mmm?"

He loved her like this, when she was so sated with pleasure that her awe-inspiring brain momentarily shut off. He leaned down and licked over her lips, slowly and thoroughly, until her breath was coming faster.

But even though he was ready for her again and he could tell that she was just as ready, they needed to talk about her father—and the fact that they weren't going to be able to keep their relationship a secret forever. Especially given how much he'd hated keeping it a secret from his family today. He wanted to proudly tell the whole freaking world, *She's mine. And I'm hers.*

Still, he couldn't resist running his thumb over her damp lips. And when she licked out against the pad, he groaned at how good it felt. "Do you have any idea what you do to me?"

"If it's anything like what you do to me..." She bit her lower lip, and desire nearly won out over the talk he knew they needed to have. "Now that I said what I said..." Her skin flushed again. "Well, now you know exactly what I'm thinking. What I'm feeling."

It was huge that she'd told him just how much she loved making love to him—the words *I want you inside of me every second of every day* were better than the best lyric ever written—but he still wanted more. "I love you."

Her eyes went huge, and her lips parted in shock. "What?"

"I'm in love with you, Ash."

She licked her lips, shook her head, tried to slide out from beneath him. "How can you..."

He threaded his fingers through hers to keep her from moving away. "How can I not? I want everyone to know. My family already guessed. And I know my crew and band aren't stupid either. I promised your father I'd keep you safe, and I want him to know that I have." He stroked her cheek. "Safe with me."

She shook her head, the force of her panic strong enough for her to wriggle out from beneath him, the sheets bouncing over her naked skin as the bus hit a rough patch of freeway. "He won't think I'm safe."

Drew had never told a woman he loved her. He hadn't honestly thought he'd do it anytime soon. But then Ashley had appeared in his life and made him feel whole again.

So now, even though it hurt not to hear her say the words back to him, he tried to tell himself that with enough patience, they could work through her fears together. He understood how deeply the pain of losing a parent—even to divorce rather than cancer—could run. Knew, too, that he'd do anything to avoid that kind of pain again.

Anything, except giving Ashley up.

"Your father knows me. From before all of this." He was sitting across from her on the bed now. "He knows the family I come from. He wouldn't have trusted you with me if he didn't."

"But if we tell him about us, everything will change. I know I'm an adult. I know my choices are my own. It's just that I'm all he's ever had. I know what he wants from my life. And I know what he thinks of this one. How much it scares him to think of me anywhere in it. I had to fight to get him to accept that I wanted to be a part of this tour. And now...I just don't want it to end too soon."

Even as a kid, Drew could hear between the lines to what people were *really* saying—but never more so than now. Ashley kept saying that she didn't want things to change, that she didn't want the summer to end too soon, and that it all tied into her father.

But Drew was afraid her reasons for trying to keep space between them didn't have nearly as much to do with her father as she thought. What if the real reason she didn't want her father to know was because all she thought they were doing was sleeping together? After they'd broken past trying not to touch each other, he'd assumed they were on the same page with everything. But what if they weren't?

What if he was gunning for something that looked like forever...and she wasn't?

"Are you really sure your father is the one who won't think you're safe with me?"

In a split second, he saw her eyes shutter. From as open as they'd been before, when she was whispering *every second, every day* to him...to completely closed.

"You've got early radio tomorrow, and it's been a really busy day and night for you." She moved to slide off the bed. "I should let you get some sleep."

Drew didn't think, didn't pause, before reaching out and wrapping his arm around her waist. "Don't run, Ash. Please don't freeze me out."

He could practically hear the thoughts racing through her head, not in straight lines the way they normally did, but in jagged zigzags. He appreciated that she was a woman who didn't like being confused by anything or anyone—it was one of the reasons she looked so deeply into everything. And he would have done anything he could to clear up her confusion about the two of them, if only he could figure out exactly the right thing to say.

She'd told him he was a good listener, and for now, something told him it would be better to listen...but first he prayed she would trust him enough to at least keep talking.

"I know I shouldn't run," she finally said as she slowly began to relax her tense muscles, "not after I watched my parents run and freeze each other out for fifteen years, and it only ever made things worse. All night it was so hard to try to keep our relationship a secret from your family. I kept asking myself why I was. Especially when Olivia all but asked me if we were together. Not because she's nosy, but because she loves you and doesn't want you to get hurt by anyone." She shifted slightly so that she could look into his eyes while still remaining in the circle of his arms. "I swear I'm trying to wrap my head around everything that's happened, Drew. Trying to wrap my head around us. I know you must be so frustrated with me."

"I am frustrated, Ash. But only because I want you to love me back just as much as I love you."

"Drew."

"We don't have to tell your father yet. But taking more time to get comfortable with telling him doesn't mean my feelings are going to change." He shifted her so that she was straddling him on the bed. "I'm still going to be in love with you. And I'm still going to hope that you'll let yourself fall in love with me, too."

After watching his father and mother together over the years, he knew when it made sense to back off. Ashley was a very strong woman. One who would never let anyone tell her what to feel, who would never let anyone bully her into saying or doing anything she didn't want to.

So he wouldn't push her more tonight. Not with words, anyway.

* * *

Moments after telling her just how much he loved her—*again!*—Drew's delicious mouth was on hers, and his big hands were holding Ashley captive on his lap.

But that was a lie, and she knew it. *She* was the one holding herself captive. Utterly ensnared by a man whose life—whose entire world—was so big, and so fast-rising, that it was taking every last bit of energy she had just to keep her head above water.

She couldn't think straight when he was kissing her, when her hands were instinctively reaching for him, when he was saying her name in that raw voice, when she was opening herself up to him again and taking him deeper than she'd ever known it was possible to be with anyone else.

She closed her eyes as she held on tight and pleasure stormed her system again. She couldn't breathe anymore. And yet, for a few precious moments, nothing else mattered but the way Drew was saying her name over and over and over against her lips as she rose in a blaze of light and color, then fell fast and hard. And then she shattered into so many pieces against him that when the lights finally faded, she didn't have the strength to do anything but burrow into his strong, warm arms around her as both physical and mental exhaustion finally pulled her all the way in.

CHAPTER THIRTY

Miami, Florida

The next day was by far the craziest of any on the tour so far. Ashley had never been to Miami before—her mother had always come to California to visit her rather than the other way around—but as soon as they got off the bus that morning and stepped out onto the beach, she could see exactly how well the sun-and-energy-filled city fit her mother.

Camila had been born and raised in Miami, but when her parents passed away and she'd met Ashley's father in her early twenties, she'd left her tropical home behind and settled in Palo Alto with him. Ashley knew her mother had always craved the hottest days and constantly wanted to take day trips to the ocean. Only, it turned out that the cool and cliffy northern California coastline was nothing like Miami's endless stretches of hot white sand and blue water.

What's more, the crowds of Drew's fans were not only bigger and louder here—they were extremely passionate, too. More than one group of girls started to cry when they caught glimpses of him as the TV cameras moved around him and his interviewers on the beach.

Ashley hadn't inherited her mother's dark skin or hair—her father's pale genes had won, hands down—and when she felt as though she was both overheating and burning, she told James, "I'm going to see if the owners of that slushie stand will let me hide out in their building for a while."

James nodded, but he didn't take his eyes off Drew or the fans who were pushing really hard against the barriers that the local police had set up a short while ago to deal with the rapidly growing crowd.

She'd nearly reached the small building when she suddenly heard something crash and break. Turning, she watched as hundreds of girls and women began to stampede toward Drew and the cameras. While the local security crew and police moved as quickly as possible to block their progress, James sprinted toward Drew, doing something that looked like sign language. Drew started running, but still couldn't escape a few overzealous fans who grabbed him and nearly tackled him to the sand before the security guards could pull them away.

She was still standing frozen on the sand when Drew ran up to her. "James wants us to wait it out in here." He pulled her inside the pink building filled with slushie machines. All of the employees were out front by then to see what the commotion was on the beach, so no one saw them slip into the back storeroom.

"Are you okay?" she said, stunned by how fast things had fallen apart.

"I'm fine. I just hope everyone else is all right. I wouldn't have agreed to do the interviews on the beach if I'd known this was going to happen."

"Is Miami always like this?"

"The fans are always excited, but this is the sort of thing we've only ever had to watch out for in New York and Chicago."

"You're more popular than ever. I wonder if it's going to be like this everywhere soon?"

Of course she was thrilled that Drew had so many ardent fans, but at the same time, she could see how easily things could spin even more out of control than they already were, considering it was already difficult for him to walk down the street without being mobbed.

But she wasn't sure he was listening anymore, not with the way he was pressing his cheek to hers while he ran his hands down her arms. When he reached her hands, he pulled them around his waist.

"I don't like you being out here in this, Ash. I can't stand the thought of anything happening to you. If you had been in the middle of that crowd..."

"Don't you think I feel exactly the same way?" That was when she saw the cuts on his arms from where his fans' nails had cut into his skin. Her stomach hurt as she gently brushed her fingertips over the marks. "Don't you think I'm scared for you when everyone is being so crazy?"

"I can handle it," he told her, just as he'd said after his fans had ambushed them at the airport that first night.

She knew that he really was strong enough and resilient enough to handle anything that came his way. She only wished she could say the same about herself. But the truth was that she didn't know if she actually could handle it. Not just her fears that something might happen to him one day because of his fame and popularity around the world...but all of it.

Everything that came with being *his*.

Ashley hadn't realized she was going to come on this tour and fall in love. But she'd ended up falling for Drew so fast that her head, and her heart, were both still spinning from the whirlwind of it all. And ever since he'd told her that he loved her—and that he wanted her father and the rest of the world to know how he felt about her—she'd been outright panicking.

He'd momentarily soothed her with words and caresses that aroused her past the point where she could think at all, but she'd still woken up with that seed of panic in her stomach growing bigger by the second.

It was just all so much. So fast. A half-dozen worries spiraled around and around inside her head at once.

I don't know how to stop worrying about everything. That we're too different. That what we have now could never last outside of this fairy tale. That all I'm doing is repeating my parents' mistakes and that one day you'll resent me the way my mother resented my father, for clipping your wings with all my spreadsheets and business plans.

Drew had been so open and honest with her, and Ashley had tried to be just as honest with him...at least until last night, when she hadn't confessed her love for him. She hated the feeling that she'd not only lied to his family about them, but that she was also now lying to Drew by not telling him exactly how she felt about him.

Somehow, she needed to get up the nerve to tell him everything—all her fears, all her worries. Right here, right now, in the slushie shack on the beach. But Drew's phone dinged before she could stop spinning and panicking long enough to speak.

"It's got to be James." Drew pulled out his phone and looked at the message. "He needs us to come to the front of the building right away. He's got a car waiting to get us out of here safely." He took her hand, and thirty seconds later, they were in the backseat of a black town car with James.

"Sorry about that, boss," James said, looking none too pleased with the situation. "I should have been more on top of things before it all went to hell. The area wasn't nearly secure enough from the start."

"We all should have been better prepared, and we'll make sure we are next time," Drew said. "Everyone okay out there?"

"Everyone's fine, thank God."

"We need to move the rest of the interview inside," Drew said.

"Already on it," James confirmed.

Drew was still holding her hand, but James didn't make a big deal out of it, didn't stare at them or raise his eyebrows. She knew it had to be because their relationship wasn't a surprise to him in any way. Drew had said his family had guessed last night, as well. Which meant that she was the only one fooling herself about keeping things "private." Pretty soon, the entire world was bound to know.

Was she ready for that?

"After your interviews," James said, "you've got lunch with the mayor in support of the Music for Miami foundation, and then your recording session will take you through to your show tonight."

"Sounds good. Thanks, James." Drew turned to her. "You look like you got a little too much sun. Your skin is flushed."

"It doesn't take much for me to burn," she said, but that wasn't the entire reason she was so flushed. It was all the conflicted questions burning inside of her, too. Questions she desperately wished she could already have figured out the answers to.

They pulled up outside a high-rise, and when James got out to open the door, Drew pressed a kiss to her lips and whispered, "I love you," before slowly letting go of her hand and heading out of the car to do his very demanding job.

He'd said *I love you* again and again last night, but hearing the three little words in the light of a new day was at once the most beautiful thing Ashley had ever heard...and the most terrifying.

She wasn't at all afraid about her physical safety while on tour, not when Drew and his team went out of their way to make sure no harm came to her. She wasn't sure her *heart* would survive the tour. Because she loved him so much she actually felt like it was going to burst all the way out of her chest.

She'd always gone to her dad for help when she was confused about something at school. But this wasn't a math problem. Wasn't an English paper she needed help outlining. This was love and sex—the two things she was absolutely certain her father couldn't handle talking about. Especially with Drew Morrison associated with both of them.

But she would burst if she didn't talk to someone soon. Not just anyone, but someone who knew her really well. And someone who understood exactly what it was like to be in a relationship with someone so different from them.

So when Drew headed into the studio to record for a few hours before his show, Ashley told James she was going to run some errands. Though she hated to miss hearing Drew work on his new songs, there was something she needed to do—and someone she needed to see—before she lost it completely.

Her mom.

CHAPTER THIRTY-ONE

"Mom."

Ashley was taken completely by surprise by the tears that began to fall when she got out of the taxi and ran into her mother's arms. Tears she couldn't keep from falling. Partly because she was so confused about her relationship with Drew...and partly because it had been so long since her mother had held her like this.

"Oh honey, it's so good to see you. I've missed you so much."

"I've missed you, too." Ashley tried to get a grip as she wiped her eyes with her fingertips. "I don't know why I waited this long to come see you."

"You needed time."

Her mother had always been like that, she suddenly realized. So forgiving. So accepting. Ashley was the one who had been unwilling to accept or forgive. She'd been so angry with her mother for leaving her and her father that she had never really appreciated just how hard her mother had tried to stay in the marriage for fifteen years.

"Miami is such a great fit for you," she said as her mother led her inside the bright, colorful home near the water. "It was the first thing I thought this morning when we got to the beach. How much you belong here."

"I do love it here. But not more than I love you, Ashley. I know you've said in the past that you didn't need me to come back to California, but if you've change your mind—"

"No!" Ashley's mother's eyes widened at the force of her response, and she realized she needed to be more clear. "Of course I want you close by, but Palo Alto never worked for you. I see that now. You need to live where you're happy." She took a good look at her mother and felt as though she was really seeing her for the first time. "You're glowing. Not just your skin, but all of you. I'm glad you're happy here, Mom."

"But are you happy, honey?"

"Sometimes it's like I've never been happier in my whole life. But then, other times, I'm just scared."

Her mother squeezed her hands. "Oh honey, are you in love?"

In that moment, it was as though a dam burst. "He's a rock star. A really famous one. I don't know what I was thinking, but I couldn't resist him. I've been in love with his music forever. So maybe that's where it all started, but when I finally met him, our connection was—" She made a crackling sound and waggled her fingers in the air to mime static electricity. "Instant. Amazing. We ended up sharing so many things with each other, all the things we haven't been able to tell anyone else, like how much it hurt him when his mom passed away and how difficult it was for me when you and Dad split up. We connect so deeply over music, too. And then he kissed me, and it was amazing so I told him I wanted to be with him. But he had promised Dad that he'd *keep me safe*." She put the words in air quotes. "So he thought he needed to do the right thing by keeping his distance from me. Only, neither of us could do it, and we couldn't keep from sleeping with each other. And even though I had no experience, he made it so wonderful. More wonderful than I ever thought it could be. But now he wants to tell everyone about us, especially Dad, and I just don't think—"

She had been pacing in front of her mother's picture window, but she suddenly stopped short as her words ricocheted back through her ears. "Oh my God, I just told you that Drew and I have been having sex."

Though her mother did look worried, she smiled and said, "I'm glad you feel comfortable enough to talk to me, Ashley. About anything at all. You know I'll never judge you."

And it was true—even when her mother had offered to take her shopping or to the makeup counter as a teenager, as soon as Ashley had made it clear that she wasn't interested, her mother had let her be herself.

Ashley suddenly realized that was why she'd been drawn to her mother's house—because she must have known her mom would listen the way she used to when she was a little girl and she needed to talk to someone about the playground drama at school. But it had been a long time since Ashley had given her mother a chance to listen, or to help. Ever since things had gotten really bad in her parents' marriage, it had seemed easier to just shut down and try to block it all out with work. And studying. And, most of all, Drew's songs.

"Now," her mother said, "if we could back up for just a second—his name is Drew?"

"Morrison."

Her mother's eyes widened. "I just saw an interview with him on the news this morning. He's a very handsome young man."

"I know. Which is one of the reasons it's crazy that he thinks he's in love with me."

"Oh honey." Her mother pulled her into her arms again. "That's so wonderful. The two of you are in love."

"He told me he loved me last night, but I didn't say it back. I couldn't, not when I should know better."

"Know better?" Her mother pulled back and frowned at her. "Is this something your father said to you?"

"No. Like I said, he doesn't know about me and Drew. Before he was a big rock star, Drew was one of his students at Stanford, and when Dad connected us so that I could go on tour to learn more about the music business, Dad basically told Drew to make sure I came home as pure as I was when I left. But I'm not. Not anymore."

"Of course you are, Ashley. Just because you're having sex doesn't mean your heart isn't as pure as it has always been. I know your father wants you to stay his little girl forever, but he's just going to have to accept that you're a woman now. A beautiful, incredible woman who has her own life to live. Even if that life may not be right there beside him at Stanford the way he's always wanted it to be. You're allowed to spread your wings, honey. And I'm not just saying these things because your father and I rarely saw eye to eye. I'm saying them because they're *true*."

"But even if they are," Ashley said, "things with Drew are still impossible. We're oil and water. Free and constrained. I'm a good girl and he's a wild boy. Maybe being with me is fun and different for now, but I'm sure he'll get tired of our differences soon."

"How can you even think any of that, Ashley?"

"Because it was just the way you and Dad got tired of each other. Don't you remember? Those were all the things you used to yell at each other."

"Oh God." Her mother sank into the nearest chair, her olive skin pale now. "All of this is my fault. I never meant for you to internalize all the horrible things I said to your father over the years. I know you can probably never forgive me—"

"You loved Dad. And he loved you. I know you did. But you still couldn't make it work. And that's why I should never have let myself fall for Drew. Because there's no way that our ending is going to be any different from yours."

"Ending? Why are you so sure there has to be one?"

"Because this is just a crazy break from reality. Of course it will end."

"I know I haven't always been able to say the right things," her mother said, "and I've also made so many mistakes that I'm not sure I'll ever be able to forgive myself for them. But I've always loved you beyond everything else. And all I want is for you to be happy with yourself and your place in the world. And to trust in yourself and your strength."

"I'm not strong, Mom."

"Yes, you are. You are so much stronger than I am, worlds stronger than your father. You have always been the rock, the one who kept us from breaking apart for so long. That's why I finally had to make myself leave. Because it wasn't fair for you to always have to mediate between parents who couldn't figure out how to make their love work in practical terms."

"Drew and I don't work either."

"Are you sure about that? Because from everything you've said about him, it sounds like the two of you fit together beautifully. So what if he's on a stage and you're behind the scenes? It doesn't matter which side of the curtain the two of you are on for a couple of hours every night—it's where you are the *rest* of the time that matters. Standing together no matter what, through good times and bad."

Ashley was stunned by how much sense her mother was making. Because the truth was that she and Drew had always been incredibly compatible, even from that first night, when they'd caused a commotion at the airport while picking up her bags. They made each other laugh. They shared a deep love for music. And whenever they touched? There was no greater pleasure to be found in the world.

Just as her mom had said, though all the signs were pointing to them being a perfect fit, Ashley had been working overtime to focus on the reasons they *weren't*.

Because she was scared. Not only scared to give her heart to someone who was different from the person she'd always assumed she'd fall for. But also because she was scared to embrace the part of her she'd kept stuffed down for so long. The secretly passionate and sensual and *wild* part she'd kept hidden away out of fear that it would destroy her.

"Can I be both those people? Can I be rational and wild? Analytical and creative?" Drew had told her he loved all sides of her, but she hadn't wanted to let herself believe him.

"Just be yourself, Ashley. Because if you're honest and loving and *real,* then everything will work out perfectly. I know it will."

"Thank you." She threw herself back into her mother's arms. "Thank you for being such a great mom. I'm sorry I didn't appreciate you more growing up."

"It wasn't your job to appreciate me or your father. It still isn't, even if I love hearing you say it. You don't have to make me any promises. You don't have to make your father any promises. Only to yourself—a promise to live every day to the fullest despite your fears. There's always something to be frightened of, honey. Just like there's always something to be excited and happy about. I know you're worried about things going wrong in the future, but if you ask me, the happiness and love you're feeling far outweigh that."

"You're right." Ashley blinked up at her mother, feeling as though she was seeing things clearly for the very first time. "I am happy. Happier than I even knew it was possible to be." She stood up. "I need to tell Drew. I need to tell him that I love him."

"Go." Her mother stood and hugged her again. "Go be young and in love. It's one of the most wonderful feelings in the world."

"Come with me. Come meet him."

"I'd love to, honey. But I think tonight needs to be about the two of you."

"He's playing two nights in Miami. I really want you to meet him before we leave, so can we plan on tomorrow?"

"I can't wait to meet Drew. He sounds like a wonderful man. Just the kind of man I've always wanted for you—one who sees just how special and precious you are. Now," her mother said as she wiped away her own tears, "we should probably call you a taxi."

But Drew wasn't the only one who needed to know how Ashley felt. "I love you, Mom."

And this time when her mother hugged Ashley and her tears fell, they were happy ones. Because Drew had helped her find more than happiness and love with him—he'd helped bring her closer to her mother.

CHAPTER THIRTY-TWO

The new song came to Drew so fast—between being on the beach with Ashley and the end of his interviews—that he had to record it immediately. Some songs he worked on for weeks or months. But this one, he didn't need to mess around with. He didn't need to rewrite it a million times.

All he had to do was let his feelings out in melody and lyric.

The song was called "Inside." And every word, every note, was a love song for Ashley.

You're inside of me.
Every second of every day.
Every look.
Every touch.
Every kiss.
I was lost until you found me.
I was hurt until you healed me.

Until you took me all the way
Inside.

Drew had hoped Ashley would be there to hear the song while he recorded it. But when he looked up from the sound booth and saw that she wasn't with James, he'd decided it would actually be better if he could play it when they were alone on the bus. Just for her, so that he could watch her face as he sang about how much he loved her—and how she'd changed his life in the best possible ways.

Six hours later, they'd finished recording and mastering the song. He'd overlaid all of the parts on his guitar, the studio's piano, and a bass guitar he'd borrowed from his bassist. He didn't usually play all of the parts himself, but he'd wanted every note to be from him to Ashley, with no one else in between.

"She's going to love it, Drew." James didn't normally comment on his songwriting, but he clearly couldn't help himself this time. "The whole world is going to love it, but I know Ashley is the one you care about most."

Max had brought the bus around to the back of the studio, but when Drew stepped inside, Ashley wasn't there. "Did she say where she was going?"

"To run some errands." James frowned as he looked at his watch. "But she said it was only going to be for a couple of hours."

Fear immediately pricked up Drew's spine. A part of him knew he was overreacting, but after the situation on the beach that morning, he couldn't help but worry that something had happened to her. He'd not only promised her father he'd keep her safe, he'd also promised *her* that he'd never let anything happen to her.

He texted Ashley.

Just got out of the studio. Are you close by or still running errands?

He stared at his phone, waiting for her response. But when nothing came back, instead of texting again, he pressed the call button. By the time his call went to voice mail, he started to lose it.

"James, she's not texting back or picking up her phone."

Max knocked, then came through the door a beat later. "Traffic is way backed up. We've got to head to the venue."

Drew's gut was twisting. "We need to wait here for Ashley to come back."

"I know you're worried about her," James said in a measured voice, "but she's an intelligent, capable woman who knows where you're playing tonight. I promise you that I will do everything I can to find her as soon as possible. But if you don't show up to play tonight, there's a good chance that twenty thousand people will riot."

Drew's curse echoed off the walls of the bus.

"She looked a little overwhelmed earlier today," his bodyguard and friend added, knowing him well enough not to pull any punches. "Maybe she just needed some time to herself to clear her head. You're a great guy, Drew, but you've got to see that it's a pretty big deal to date someone like you."

If he had been able to think straight, he would have seen this for himself. After all, hadn't he said he loved her last night—and then immediately insisted they tell her father about their relationship? He was just so crazy happy about being with her that he didn't want to admit he was pushing her way too hard and too fast into a relationship. Hell, she'd been a virgin, but he hadn't even stopped to think about how hard just that life transition must be for her. Instead, he'd been too focused on taking her again and again and again.

"You're right. I've been such an idiot. I'm just so in love with her that all I'm doing is pushing her away."

Was her father right? Was he not a safe guy for her? Everything in Drew fought against believing that...but just because he didn't want it to be true didn't mean it wasn't.

"Like James said," Max chimed in, "Ashley's as smart as they come. And tough enough not to let anyone push her around. Not even you, Drew. We all see the way she looks at you. And the way you've always looked at her. Needing a little breathing room is normal. At least," he added with a grin, "that's what my wife always tells me."

Drew appreciated the way his friends were trying to help him see things more clearly. But at the same time, he hated the decision he had to make. In the end, however, it was the knowledge that James and Max were both right about how smart and capable Ashley was—and how upset she'd be if she found out he'd canceled his show over her—that had him saying, "Let's head out for the venue. But if she needs me..."

"If she ever needs you, I'll pull you off stage in a heartbeat," James promised as Max left to take the wheel. "Riots or not."

* * *

The traffic on Interstate 95 was the worst Ashley had ever seen. Her taxi had literally been sitting in the same spot for the past fifteen minutes. To make matters even worse, her phone was dead and the driver said he didn't have a cell phone that she could borrow.

She'd told James that she would be back at the studio before they left for the venue, but there was no way she was going to make that now. Heck, at this point, she wasn't even sure she'd make it by the time the show ended. And after what Drew had said to her in the slushie shack on the beach—*I can't stand the thought of anything happening to you*—she could easily guess that he'd be worried.

She felt like she'd been heaping lies on top of lies, and she hated it. All she wanted was to be back in Drew's arms so that she could tell him how much she loved him. She still needed a game plan in place to approach her father with the news so that he wouldn't totally freak out, but at least Drew would know exactly how she felt.

The minutes ticked by so slowly in the boiling-hot taxi that she grew more agitated by the second, and stickier, too. By the time it finally pulled up at the venue—right when Drew usually took the stage—she paid the driver, then got out and begged the nearest stranger to let her use her phone to make a call.

She could tell by the way the girl raised her eyebrows that she must look like a crazy person. Her wavy hair had poofed way out in the humidity, her skin was flushed from the heat, her clothes were horribly wrinkled, and her eyes were probably still red from crying in her mother's arms. Thankfully, the girl agreed to let her make the call anyway.

Drew picked up on the first ring, and the sound of his voice was so sweet that all of her nerves that had been turned up to eleven that morning immediately settled down.

"It's Ashley."

"Where are you?"

"Outside the venue."

The call went dead, and when she called him back, he didn't pick up. Then she heard it...the gasps and screams that Drew's fans always made when they spotted him. But when she looked up and saw him coming toward her, it didn't look as though he noticed any of his fans freaking out as they clamored for him.

He only had eyes for her.

She'd been apart from him for only one afternoon, but it felt like a lifetime. She leapt into his arms, and when his mouth covered hers, it was like coming home. A sweeter, more exciting—and *way* sexier—home than she'd ever dreamed of having.

"Ash." He put his hands on her cheeks. "Thank God you're okay."

"I got stuck in traffic on the way back, and my phone died." But that wasn't the full truth, and she wouldn't let herself be afraid to tell Drew the truth again. "I didn't go to run errands. I went to see my mom. I should have told you, but..."

"I get it. I'm pushing you too hard, too fast."

"No. You're not. You're great. You're *amazing.*" Somewhere in the back of her mind, she registered the dozens of cell phones capturing their conversation, but she didn't care. She couldn't wait another second for Drew to know exactly how she felt. "I love you."

His mouth curved up in the biggest smile in the world, and then he was twirling her around and kissing her again. Around them, the crowd cheered...which was when Drew obviously realized everything they were doing in front of the venue was for public consumption.

"Let's head inside."

She nodded, slipping her hand into his. Saying *I love you* to Drew had just made her so happy, but given that at least one of the videos his fans had just shot of the two of them was bound to make it on the Internet within the next few minutes, she was going to have to tell her father about them really, really soon.

"Ashley."

Wait...she hadn't just conjured up her father's voice out of thin air, had she?

She was still holding Drew's hand when she turned to see her father standing in the middle of the crowd.

CHAPTER THIRTY-THREE

"Daddy, what are you doing here?"

Instead of answering her, Charlie Emmit scowled at Ashley's and Drew's linked hands, then turned his fury on Drew. "What the hell is going on here? What have you done to my daughter?"

Before she or Drew could answer, James and his local security team descended, blocking the three of them from Drew's fans. "We need to get Ashley and Drew inside immediately, sir," James said when her father started to protest at being led away.

She wanted to try to fix things with her dad before he got any angrier, but Drew didn't let go of her hand.

"It's going to be okay," he said to her in a low voice. "Let me handle your father."

But she couldn't do that, couldn't expect anyone to take the reins of her life but herself. Going to see her mother today and talking everything through had opened her eyes to so many things—most of all to the knowledge that she *was* a strong person. In fact, it was in large part because she tended toward the quiet side and always took her time to think things through that she realized she could trust herself to make the right decisions. Even for the really hard questions, like whether she was willing to risk all of her heart with Drew.

"You need to get on stage as soon as possible, Drew," James said.

His fans were hollering for him to get on stage, and his band was waiting in the wings, clearly wondering just what in the hell was going on, but he was completely focused on her. "You're more important than the show. A million times more important."

It meant the world to her that he thought so. And it was amazing to actually be able to shelve her doubts that he could truly mean it. But she still needed to have this conversation with her father alone.

"I love you, Drew. So much it's crazy. And I definitely want you and my dad to patch things up. But first, I need to talk with him. Not just about you and me...but about everything."

Her declaration of independence had been a very long time in coming.

Drew's eyes roved her face as if he were trying to make absolutely sure that she meant what she said and wasn't just trying to let him off the hook. "If you need me, even if it's in the middle of a song, tell James and he'll grab me."

She had to kiss him again then, even though her father still looked as furious as she'd ever seen him.

"Everyone here in Miami loves you, Drew. Promise me you won't be distracted by this while you're out there."

"You never distract me, Ash. You inspire me. *Every second of every day.*"

He stroked her hair back from her face and gave her the gentlest, sweetest kiss in the world, before finally signaling to his band that he was ready to take the stage. And even though Ashley knew the conversation she was about to have with her dad wasn't going to be an easy one, she was smiling as Drew stepped out of the curtains and twenty thousand people went wild.

When she finally turned to head over to her father, he looked stunned. She didn't know if it was because of how much Drew's fans obviously loved him...or if he still couldn't quite wrap his head around his little girl having fallen in love.

"Dad, this is James," she said, realizing that in the heat of the moment she'd forgotten to introduce her father to anyone.

"It's nice to meet you, Mr. Emmit. Your daughter is a treasure, and you've obviously done a great job raising her."

"Thank you," her father said, clearly taken more than a little off guard by the heavily tattooed bodyguard being so respectful and complimentary.

"James, is there an open room back here where my father and I can talk?"

"Absolutely." James led them down the hall to an empty dressing room that had a couple of couches and a table with a few chairs around it. But neither Ashley nor her father sat. Instead, they stood facing each other as the door closed quietly.

There were a thousand things Ashley needed to say to her father, but the most important was, "I love you just as much as I always have. Just because I've also fallen in love with Drew doesn't mean that has changed."

"You love him." Her father ruminated on that information for several long moments, before he finally asked, "Does he love you, too?"

"He does. And I understand that all of this must seem really crazy and unexpected to you, because that's how it seemed to me, up until today…when I went to see Mom."

She hadn't thought her father could look more stunned than he had earlier, but his eyebrows went up nearly to his hairline. "Has she known about this the whole time?"

"No. No one has. But I needed to see her today." She shook her head. "I should have come to see her in Miami before now. But I was too scared that if I came here, I might want to stay. And I couldn't leave you, Dad."

"Ashley." Her father reached for her hand, and even now his touch was as warm and comforting as ever. "I thought you stayed in California because that was where you wanted to be."

"I love where we live, but now that I've been to Miami, I can see why Mom loves it so much. And I can see that there's a part of me that would have loved it, too. Everyone just seems so free. So relaxed. Like they know the rules, but don't treat them like a prison."

"I didn't mean to make you feel like you've lived in a prison all these years."

"Oh Dad, you didn't. Not at all. But it's always been easier for me to hide out in a library or behind a computer. Coming on this tour was the first really scary thing I've ever done."

"You were scared? You didn't say anything about being scared."

"Because I didn't want you to worry about letting me go any more than you already did. And it turned out that coming on tour with Drew was the best thing I could have done, for so many reasons. Not only because I met him and fell in love...but also because I had to learn to trust myself. My own decisions. And I've been learning how strong I can be. Strong enough to take risks that are worth taking."

"You've always made good decisions. And you've always been strong. How could you ever doubt either of those things?"

"That's just what Mom said." Ashley stared at her hand in her father's and decided it was long past time to delve even deeper into the hard stuff. "She also said that she left because of me."

"No." Her father shook his head so hard that his hand pulled free of hers. "She left because I could never be what she needed. What she wanted. Not because she wanted to be apart from you. She hates not being close to you."

"I know that wasn't how she meant it, Dad. She just didn't want me to be stuck in the middle of you two anymore, always trying to mediate or to feel like I needed to go hide."

He looked stunned. "You were the only thing either of us could ever agree on. How much we loved you. That we wanted to protect you. Always. If we'd known we were putting you in that spot—"

"You would still have tried to stay together, just like you did for fifteen years. Because you loved each other, Dad. I could see that, even when you were fighting. I could see the love that was still holding you together. And that's what scared me the most—that even when you love someone, it doesn't mean things are guaranteed to work out. Which is why I thought it would be better not to let myself love at all."

Looking shell-shocked, her father said, "I did love your mother. You and she are the two great loves of my life. I lost her, but I don't want to lose you, Ashley."

"You haven't lost me, Dad. And you won't, even if I grow up and move away and fall in love."

He put his arms around her, and his hug felt so good. But even though they'd talked about so much already, there was one more thing she needed to discuss with him. She pulled back slightly and said, "There's one more thing, Dad." Before she lost her nerve, she said, "Drew told me what you said to him before I joined his tour. That you were trusting him to keep me safe." Neither of them had really ever been angry with the other before, but evidently there was a first time for everything. "It's like we were living in medieval times and you wanted to send me out in a chastity belt."

At the words *chastity belt,* her father's face turned a ruddy red. "That's not fair, Ashley. I just wanted to protect you the way I always have."

"I know you did, but I'm twenty-two. I'm not a little girl anymore, like that picture you insist on keeping in your office that was taken almost ten years ago. You had to know that I was going to grow up and fall in love one day."

"I did know that," he said in a resigned voice, "but I hoped it would be with someone normal. Someone steady. Someone safe."

"Drew *is* normal and steady and safe. He's also exciting and brilliant and the most fun person I've ever been around." Despite his enormous fame, she'd seen that right from the start. "You know how great his family is and how great *he* is, too. So why would you think that would change just because he's a big star?"

"It's less that he's a big star," her father said slowly, "than that he's always had big dreams and plans. I can't see him being happy buying a house in Palo Alto and settling down."

"But you're assuming I would be happy doing that."

Her father started at the unintended sharpness in her tone. "Well...I suppose I have always assumed that."

It wasn't fair to be angry with her father for that. Not when she'd always assumed the same thing. "Like I said, I was really nervous when I first joined his tour, and I thought I would be totally out of my element and that I belonged in an office somewhere. But I *love* being on the road. I love how every day is a new adventure. I love coming up with new ideas and trying new things. And, most of all, I love being with someone who has never for one second thought about making his big dreams smaller."

"You really are happy, aren't you?"

She reached for her father's hand again. "I really am. I mean, I'm still scared, too. But I'm starting to think that some fear is good...because it means I'm risking. Risking for what really matters. Risking for love."

Her father's eyes grew watery then. "I love you, honey. But you have to understand that it's going to take a while for me to learn to deal with all of this. And not just because it's Drew. It could have been any guy and I would have had just as hard a time letting you go."

"I'm not asking you to let me go, Dad. Just to let him in."

Finally, her father nodded and gave her a small smile. The first one she'd seen from him so far. "I'll try, honey."

That was all she could ask him to do, just to try to give her boyfriend—*oh, what a lovely word that was*—a chance. "Do you want to go watch his show?"

Her father began to shake his head, then stopped himself. "Sure."

She put her arm around him, and he did the same. Together, they walked out of the room and headed to the side of the stage, where James was keeping an eagle eye on Drew. She gave him a smile to let him know everything was going to be okay, then let Drew's music take away her worries and fears, just the way it always had.

* * *

Two and a half hours later, Drew strode off stage and immediately pulled Ashley into his arms to kiss her. For the entire show, she'd been at the forefront of his mind. Thankfully, part of the way through she'd appeared side stage with her father, their arms around each other. Now it was his turn to make sure his former professor knew just how much he loved and respected his daughter.

"Professor Emmit, I'd like to speak with you once I'm done with my after-show duties—in about an hour, if that's not too late for you."

Her father's expression wasn't exactly open and friendly as he looked at Drew, but he nodded. "Certainly."

Ashley looked a little nervous as she glanced between the two of them, but she simply said, "Can we both come to your meet and greets?"

"Of course." He slid his hand through Ashley's. "I was hoping you'd be there."

When she smiled at him and he saw the love she felt for him shining from her eyes without shadows anymore, even the major upcoming confrontation with her dad couldn't dim Drew's joy.

* * *

An hour later, Ashley headed back to the bus with Max, while James took Drew and the professor to a small, late-night coffee shop a short way from the Miami strip.

Making sure he was facing the corner rather than the door, after they ordered two cups of coffee, Drew took off his baseball cap and said point-blank, "I'm in love with Ashley. She's brilliant and funny and beautiful and has the biggest heart of anyone I've ever known."

"She is all of those things," her father agreed.

It felt like he was talking to an impenetrable brick wall, but Drew couldn't let that stop him from trying to break through it. "I know I'm the last person in the world you want her to be with. She knows it, too, which is why we both tried so hard to fight what we were feeling for each other. But I couldn't stop falling more in love with her by the second."

The waitress brought their coffees, but instead of picking up the cup, her father closed his eyes and took a deep breath through his nose. After quite a long while, he opened them and looked straight at Drew. "I promised Ashley I would try. But I have to tell you just how hard it is, after you promised me you would keep her safe."

"She is safe with me, sir."

"If it were just the two of you in Palo Alto, then maybe I could find that easier to swallow. But your life—I honestly can't even begin to understand how crazy, how unpredictable, how unsteady it is. All I've ever wanted is for my daughter to feel secure. She should have everything she wants."

"And if she wants me? If she wants this life?"

Professor Emmit shook his head. "I don't understand it."

"I see a lot of you in Ashley," Drew said after a few moments. "How methodical she is, how she keeps asking questions and doing research until she feels that she truly understands something."

"She and I have always been a lot alike."

"Doesn't she also share a lot of qualities with her mother?"

"Well... I..." Her father frowned into his untouched coffee. "They have the same eyes. And their laughter sounds the same." His frown deepened. "And I suppose Ashley always loved riding roller coasters and diving into the ocean in a way I never have."

"Just like her mom."

The professor's gaze met his again. "Yes. Just like Camila."

Drew could hear all the longing, the frustration, in the other man's voice as he spoke of his ex-wife.

"What if," he said slowly, "Ashley is living the life she wants? What if being in a relationship with me is just the perfect mix of steady and unpredictable?"

Her father pressed his lips together. "It's not easy for me to see things that way, but for my daughter, I'll try. Although there is one thing I will never bend on, Drew. You'd better go out of your way to make her happy every single day or—"

"Or I wouldn't deserve her." He smiled at his girlfriend's father. "She's everything to me. Just like she is to you. Absolutely *everything*."

Her father still didn't smile. He didn't reach out to shake Drew's hand. But he wasn't scowling or frowning anymore. And when he asked the waitress to bring him a fresh cup of coffee, then said, "You put on quite a show tonight," Drew hoped he'd succeeded at taking the first important step toward Ashley's father accepting him as her boyfriend.

CHAPTER THIRTY-FOUR

An hour later, Drew and Ashley were alone on the bus. He would be playing in Miami again tomorrow night, and there was a hotel room they could have gone to for the night. But both of them wanted to be here on the bus where they'd first made each other laugh. Where they'd first fallen in love. And where they'd first slept in each other's arms.

Her entire face was lit up with the biggest, brightest smile he'd ever seen as she took his hands in hers. "I love you. And I don't want to hide our relationship from anyone anymore. I want the whole world to know that you're mine."

"I love you, too, Ash." He'd never grow tired of hearing her say *I love you* to him, or saying it to her. Just as he'd never get enough of kissing her gorgeous mouth the way he was right now. "And I'm going to love telling everyone on the entire planet that you're my girlfriend," he whispered against her lips.

"I still might be a little nervous about it," she admitted, "but that doesn't mean I don't want it. It just means I'm still getting my feet wet with all of this. I've never been in love before."

"I haven't either, Ash."

"Aren't you even the slightest bit nervous?"

"Only with your father."

She bit her lip, clearly worried as she asked, "How'd your talk go?"

He didn't want to upset her, but he couldn't lie to her. "It was pretty rough going there for a while. For most of our talk, actually. But I have a good feeling that he's going to come around." He smiled and added, "Eventually."

He was really glad to hear her laugh out loud. "I think it's all hard for him to take in. Both that I'm officially grown up now and that I won't be right there at home all the time anymore."

"Because you'll be..."

"With you."

"There's nowhere I want you more. But my dreams aren't the only ones that count. Yours do, too. So when Stanford Business School begs you to attend, you can't turn them down to be on the road with me."

"Honestly, I've finally accepted that getting into the best graduate program in the country is a pretty big *if.* And if they do accept me next year, we can figure things out then. But even if they don't, I'm going to be okay with it—especially after the email Grant sent me while you were doing your meet and greet tonight."

"He wants you to come work for him, doesn't he?"

"Kind of. He said he'd like to hire me as a consultant to do some research into the nuts and bolts of actually starting an artist-run indie label from the ground up." She was glowing as she told Drew the great news. "Thank you for telling him about my idea."

"This is all you, Ash. Your brains. Your ideas. Your enthusiasm. I can't wait for everyone else to meet you and see what I see." He brought her closer and leaned in to kiss her. "But you should know I'm going to keep all of your beauty, and your gorgeous sensuality, for myself."

"They're all yours."

Her lips were soft and sweet, and so damned seductive beneath his that he lost the thread of everything but her for several heady moments. But he didn't want to wait any longer to tell her his news either.

"There's actually another reason that I'm glad you're going to be working with Grant on figuring out how to put together a new record label. I've decided not to sign the second Chief Records contract."

"Wow. That's huge." She studied his face for a few moments before smiling and saying, "You're really happy about it, aren't you?"

"I didn't realize just how handcuffed I felt working for someone else. Or maybe it was that I didn't want to see it, because it was easier to follow the plans that have worked for their other artists. At least at first." He looked down at their linked hands and told her the rest of the truth he'd only begun to understand. "At first, my songs couldn't come because I was shutting down my feelings to block out my grief over losing my mom. But then when I thought I needed to stop falling in love with you, that's when everything broke completely apart. Because I couldn't stop falling, Ash, and it tore me up to even try. Just destroyed me. Once I knew I loved you no matter what, and that I wasn't going to let anything keep us apart—that was when everything finally started to make sense again. You're the person I've been looking for. The woman I've been waiting for. The only one who can help me see the things I've been hiding from. And the only one who can pull me from the darkness with nothing but a look, a touch, a smile, a kiss."

But instead of giving him one of those smiles, she whispered, "I'm so sorry."

"Sorry? For what?"

"You once said I would never hurt anyone, but I hurt you when I wasn't brave enough to tell you that I loved you, too. I do, so much. I just thought we could never make things work because we're so different. And it was easier to tell myself I was holding back because of my dad and his relationship with my mom than it was to face the truth. You're the brightest light I've ever known—one of the brightest lights on the planet. And I thought I wasn't exciting enough or strong enough to be, well, *enough* for you."

"You aren't just enough, you're my heart. My soul. I love you, Ash. The brainy side of you. The wild side of you. I love all of you, exactly the way you are. And even though I'll always miss my mom, every day of my life, it feels now like the wounds are finally starting to heal."

Just as she'd held him in the desert, she simply pulled him close now and laid her cheek against his chest. He didn't know how long they stood holding each other, just that music played inside of him the entire time. Music he needed her to hear.

"I know you just listened to me play for over two hours, but there's a song I'd really like to play for you."

Without saying a word, she slid her hands from around his back, picked up his acoustic guitar, and handed it to him. As soon as she was on the bed in front of him, sitting cross-legged so their knees were touching, he began to play and sing.

* * *

Drew had never looked so serious, or quite so shy, as he did just then. He should have been a world away from the larger-than-life star she watched perform on stage every night. And yet, with just his guitar and his voice, he was even *more* powerful.

Especially when she realized where his lyrics had come from.

> *You're inside of me.*
> *Every second of every day.*
> *Every look.*
> *Every touch.*
> *Every kiss.*
> *I was lost until you found me.*
> *I was hurt until you healed me.*
> *Until you took me all the way*
> *Inside.*

She'd said the words while they were making love—*I want you inside of me every second of every day*—and though it might have sounded like nothing more than desire, Drew had known the truth all along.

That she was saying she loved him the only way she could.

Tears streamed down her face as he played, but they were happy tears this time. Tears of wonder. No, she and Drew weren't exactly the same, but where they didn't overlap, they filled each other's gaps and made each other whole.

When he was done playing, he put his guitar down, then took her face in his hands and kissed her. So sweetly that her heart flipped over in her chest at the same time that her body ached for him to take the kiss deeper. Neither of them spoke as he slowly, silently stripped away her clothes—every caress awestruck, every kiss he pressed to her soft skin reverent—and she did the same for him and then slid on protection.

And then there was no more patience for either of them as they fell onto the bed in each other's arms. Their hungry mouths wrote the melody, their desperate hands played the rhythm, and their breathless gasps of pleasure sang the lyrics for the beautiful new song they were writing together.

EPILOGUE

"I can't believe we have front-row tickets to this show." Taylor turned to look behind her at the thirty thousand screaming fans who had come to hear Nicola Sullivan and Drew Morrison do the kickoff show for their fully acoustic combined tour. "I heard it sold out in seconds."

"Perks of being related to one of the people on stage," Justin Morrison said as he grinned back at one of his favorite people.

Justin and Taylor had been friends from their first class at Stanford, a bio lab where they'd been partnered up. He'd never met anyone as smart. Or as beautiful. But she'd had a boyfriend from high school, and even though he was all the way back in Rochester, New York—and sounded like he didn't come anywhere close to being worthy of her—Taylor had remained faithful. From everything she'd told him, though, it sounded like her parents had set the whole thing up as some sort of modern-day arranged marriage. The guy never called, and Justin had wondered more than once if Taylor's boyfriend was as faithful to her as she was to him.

They'd been platonic friends for more than three years. Three years in which Justin had tried like hell not to step over the line with her. But damned if it wasn't getting harder by the second. Especially when she was wearing a tank top and jean shorts due to the heat at the outdoor summer concert. Her clothes were downright demure compared to some of Drew's fans, but he still thought she was the sexiest woman he'd ever set eyes on.

"And I'm so glad that everything worked out for Drew and Ashley," Taylor said as she tucked a lock of her hair behind her ear. A lock that Justin was dying to feel flowing through his fingers. "I thought they were sneaking romantic glances at each other that night in New Orleans for his birthday."

And yet, somehow, she'd never noticed all the glances Justin was constantly sneaking at her. "They're a perfect fit." *Just like we could be,* he found himself thinking before he could shut it down the way he always had before. "And I know Grant is really happy to be working with both of them on the new label. He said it's a perfect combination of his expertise with social networks and theirs with the music business."

He was glad that his family was slowly starting to heal from losing their mom, especially Drew and Sean, who had both fallen in love. Justin had been lucky to have Taylor there for him from the start. But even though he couldn't ask for a better friend, more and more lately, he'd gone to bed eaten up by frustration.

The stage lights were still down when Drew and Nicola started to play "Fire and Rain" with Drew on guitar and Nicola on piano. Slowly, the stage lights began to rise as their mesmerizing music floated out over the packed amphitheater...

And as Taylor grabbed Justin's hand and sang along softly in an adorably off-key voice, he had to work harder than he ever had before to fight the craving that only grew bigger with every second that he tried to hide his feelings from his best friend.

* * * * *

For news on upcoming books, sign up for Bella Andre's New Release Newsletter:

http://www.BellaAndre.link/Newsletter

Watch for Justin Morrison's story, LOVE ME LIKE THIS, coming soon! And be sure not to miss KISS ME LIKE THIS, the first book in the Morrison family series, about Sean Morrison.

ABOUT THE AUTHOR

Having sold more than 4 million books, Bella Andre's novels have been #1 bestsellers around the world and have appeared on the New York Times and USA Today bestseller lists 27 times. She has been the #1 Ranked Author (on a top 10 list that included Nora Roberts, JK Rowling, James Patterson and Steven King), and Publishers Weekly named Oak Press (the publishing company she created to publish her own books) the Fastest-Growing Independent Publisher in the US. After signing a groundbreaking 7-figure print-only deal with Harlequin MIRA, Bella's "The Sullivans" series has been released in paperback in the US, Canada, and Australia.

Known for "sensual, empowered stories enveloped in heady romance" (Publishers Weekly), her books have been Cosmopolitan Magazine "Red Hot Reads" twice and have been translated into ten languages. Winner of the Award of Excellence, The Washington Post called her "One of the top writers in America" and she has been featured by Entertainment Weekly, NPR, USA Today, Forbes, The Wall Street

Journal, and TIME Magazine. A graduate of Stanford University, she has given keynote speeches at publishing conferences from Copenhagen to Berlin to San Francisco, including a standing-room-only keynote at Book Expo America in New York City.

Bella also writes the New York Times bestselling Four Weddings and a Fiasco series as Lucy Kevin. Her "sweet" contemporary romances also include the USA Today bestselling Walker Island series written as Lucy Kevin.

If not behind her computer, you can find her reading her favorite authors, hiking, swimming or laughing. Married with two children, Bella splits her time between the Northern California wine country and a 100 year old log cabin in the Adirondacks.

For a complete listing of books, as well as excerpts and contests, and to connect with Bella:

Sign up for Bella's newsletter:
http://www.BellaAndre.link/Newsletter
Visit Bella's website at: www.BellaAndre.com
Follow Bella on twitter at:
http://www.twitter.com/bellaandre
Join Bella on facebook at:
http://www.facebook.com/bellaandrefans